RED HILL BLUES

Erica Harth

With illustrations by Karen W. Klein

March 2014

*For Marjorie
With love,
Erica*

DISCLAIMER

Although the physical setting and historical events of this novel are real, all characters other than the historical ones are fictional. Any resemblance between the fictional characters and people from real life is purely coincidental.

In memory of my parents and their world

CHAPTER ONE

Perfect day for an execution. A nice spring day guaranteed to bring out the crowds. And the bigger the crowd, the stronger the protest. Around Christabel Gooding the press of people thickened. But then, she thought, no day was a good day for an execution, was it? Especially not for the execution of Julius and Ethel Rosenberg.

Just after five o'clock, Chris, her best friend Rosie Novac, and Rosie's mother arrived from Croton-on-Hudson at the site of the rally on New York's 17th Street, just off Union Square. The hope that Julius and Ethel Rosenberg would be reprieved had been dashed, and the couple's stay of execution had been dissolved, clemency denied. The vigil had begun for the husband and wife convicted of passing atomic secrets to the Soviet Union. So they would be executed in several hours. Today, June 19, 1953, was to be their last day on earth.

"Hey, Richie," a young male voice called out. "Over here!"

A woman with a large tote bag complained, "They could at least have let us onto Union Square."

Next to her, a middle-aged man nudged the bag away from his right hip. "Sure, but then the press would have gotten a better view of us. We don't look as impressive here as we would on the Square."

"Union Square, that's where all the big rallies always are," the woman persisted.

"Place is crawling with G-men—see 'em?" someone else said.

"Fry the spies!" a heckler shouted.

And another, "Death to the traitors!"

For two years, ever since she was twelve, Chris had been following the case of Julius and Ethel Rosenberg. Her heart constricted whenever she saw photos of the Rosenbergs' two little boys, Michael and Robbie. They were six and ten now, and in one of the recent press photos they were shown with their parents' lawyer. With their plaid jackets, the brothers looked like ordinary little boys, except that they had just been visiting their parents in the death house at Sing-Sing. The evidence in their parents' trial consisted of things like a Jello box top—supposedly an ID for one spy to show to another—and a drawing of a bomb that Chris figured might have amused a first-grader but could hardly be considered a blueprint.

Rosie's mother lurched forward and clutched her ankle. "Aïe!"

"What is she saying?" Chris asked Rosie.

Rosie, head bent over a book, mumbled, "French for 'ouch!'"

Mrs. Novac hopped around on one foot, moaning in pain.

A portly man in a pearl grey, three-piece pinstripe suit and matching felt hat seemed to materialize from nowhere. Corey Sylvester, owner and publisher of Croton's weekly newspaper, looked as if he were enveloped in an invisible cocoon of air conditioning. "My beautiful Lili," he said, "whatever is wrong? Did you hurt your foot? Here, take my arm."

He offered her an arm folded over his chest.

Rosie looked up from the music score she was studying and raised her eyebrows at Chris. Chris tried to smother a giggle

"I must have twisted my ankle," Mrs. Novac said. "With so many people, it's hard to see where you're going. Don't worry about me, though, Corey. As long as my lithograph survives." She was holding a sign aloft.

"Let me escort you to a place where you can sit down for a minute," Mr. Sylvester said.

Mrs. Novac was hanging onto his shoulder now, and limping. "I really hate to bother you."

Mr. Sylvester didn't look in the least bothered.

Like a caravan caught in a sandstorm, the four of them struggled through the crowd toward Madison Avenue. Mr. Sylvester deposited Mrs. Novac on the nearest street bench and sat down beside her.

Mrs. Novac rubbed her ankle and then stretched out her legs.

"Any better?"

"Thank you, Corey. Sitting down was just what I needed to do."

Mr. Sylvester set the lithograph he had been carrying for her across his knees and inspected it.

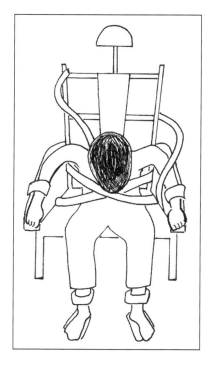

"Worthy of Liliane Carrière," he said, using Mrs. Novac's maiden name, which was how she was known as an artist. It was fun to hear people use Mrs. Novac's professional name. It was as if she had a dual identity. With her silvering blonde hair, Rosie's mother was the most glamorous woman Chris knew. Plus she was always ready to talk serious politics with Chris. Not like her own mother, who seemed to dismiss everything Chris said.

Chris and Rosie stood facing the bench.   Rosie pinched Chris's arm. She liked to call Corey Sylvester a fat Maurice Chevalier. He was always making eyes at the ladies, she said. Chris pinched back and the two girls linked arms. Mr. Sylvester fingered his watch fob—he always did that.

A woman in a broad-brimmed hat tapped Chris on the shoulder. "Your little sister should be wearing a hat—she's so fair."

Chris never understood why people thought she and Rosie were sisters. They didn't look the least bit alike—Rosie with her curly chestnut hair, Chris with her long, black ponytail. Even though they were the same age, it was easy to see why people thought Rosie was a few years younger. She was very slight, and she still wore undershirts. Chris almost envied her; her own curves embarrassed her no end.

Mrs. Novac said to him, "I'm surprised to find you here, Corey."

"Thought I might write up the demonstration."

Oh no. Chris had planned to do a story on the event for her high school newspaper. Mr. Sylvester just better not write her story, about reasons why people had come to the rally. It would be hard to compete with *him*.

"And what," asked Rosie's mother, "will be your point of view?"

Mr. Sylvester leaned back and tipped his hat to her, wagging a forefinger. "Objectivity, my dear. Objectivity! It's our trademark. An editorial is one thing, but in a news story objectivity reigns."

Ha! Mr. Sylvester had been bashing Rosie's father's architectural work in print for a while now.   He was a fine one to talk about objectivity. He didn't like Mr. Novac's politics, so he didn't like anything else about him either. How could Mrs. Novac even speak to him?

"Look," Mr. Sylvester said to Rosie's mother, "why don't you let me go get you a cup of coffee?"

"No, thank you, Corey . . . ."

He cut her off. "You just stay there and let the girls take care of you until I come back."

After about fifteen minutes, Chris began to get fidgety. Finally she spotted Mr. Sylvester, across Madison Avenue, talking to a man in a brown suit. The man in the brown suit had funny ears that protruded from his head like the handles of a jug. Behind them a very old man with a white beard was holding a sign that said, "Judgment Day is here." What a great photo that would make! Chris pulled her Kodak Brownie camera from her book bag. She had just clicked the button when a small man with spiky, black hair darted in front of Mr. Sylvester and his companion. Mr. Sylvester moved on in their direction and set the coffee cup on the bench next to Mrs. Novac, who sipped it with a faint expression of distaste. She didn't like American coffee, and anyway by now it was probably lukewarm.

A movement in the crowd around them stirred a ripple of murmurs. A group of police reinforcements headed toward the barriers.

"You see," Mr. Sylvester said, "how efficient the city police are? They aren't taking any chances. You do know, don't you, that Commissioner Monaghan has the city on special alert in case of a Communist attack? They're guarding power stations. The little demonstration at Sing-Sing must be a lot tamer."

Why did the mention of communism give everyone the heebie-jeebies? Chris wondered. The demonstrators, like the Communists Chris knew in Croton, believed in the rights of the people and in a fair break for everyone. They weren't about to blow up bridges. But people needed someone to blame, scapegoats. The Cold War was heating up, and witch-hunters were sniffing around for Communist traitors. The Rosenbergs were the biggest scapegoats of all. Rosie's mother said it was easy to make Jews the scapegoats. It was going to be like the Dreyfus affair, or like a continuation of what happened in Europe during the war.

"Oh, there's Mrs. Sedgwick!" cried Chris. "I have to interview her. C'mon, Rosie, let's go." But Rosie was deep into her music book, and she shook her head no. All she thought about these days was her upcoming violin recital. Why did she even bother to come?

Dragging her sign, Chris elbowed her way toward her favorite former teacher. She caught up with her just as the teacher was turning on to 17th Street. With her were two girls from Chris's high school in Croton. Mrs. Sedgwick embraced Chris, but she didn't look happy to see her. "What a world to grow up in!" she said.

"It's just a question of time," a burly man with a salt-and-pepper beard was saying to a small group of people clustered around Mrs. Sedgwick. "They have to do it before sundown, before the Jewish Sabbath."

"Do what?" Chris asked, although the pit in her stomach told her the answer.

"Execute them."

Chris noticed that Mrs. Sedgwick's light brown hair had a new, long gray streak in front.

"Let me introduce you to some of my New York colleagues," Mrs. Sedgwick said, as if Chris were a fellow teacher. "They've helped out a lot in planning this event." Chris figured that they were Quakers, too, like Mrs. Sedgwick. They clamored to offer Chris lemonade from a keg they had with them. If she stuck around, she'd probably get good material for her story.

Chris fished in her green book bag for her notebook and pen. "Is it all right if I take notes? I want to do a story on the demonstration for our high school paper. And could I take a picture of you too?" She clutched the Brownie camera in one hand and wedged her notebook under her arm, while balancing her sign between her knees.

"Are you sure, dear, that the 'Tiger Rag' will run such a story?" Mrs. Sedgwick asked. "I wouldn't want you to get into trouble."

No one objected to her taking notes or pictures.

"Well, we've attracted considerable interest, I see," said the burly, bearded man. Chris followed his glance to the small man she had seen dart out in front of Mr. Sylvester and the man in the brown suit. His crew cut looked like the boar bristles on her hairbrush. He was stuffing a little camera into his breast pocket.

The small man returned their looks with a scowl and approached the group. "Shouldn't you teachers be grading exams?" His voice was surprisingly high and thin.

Mrs. Sedgwick and her friends stood still in their tracks. The burly, bearded man took a step or two closer to Bristle-Head, until he towered directly over him. "What are you going to do? Report us to the truant officer? You think we don't know your game?" He reached down and pulled back the man's lapel, to reveal an F.B.I. badge.

One of the women snickered.

"It's no laughing matter," the agent squeaked. His voice dropped a tone. "Where you folks from?"

A brief silence. The woman who had snickered spoke up first. "The city."

"I'm from Croton-on-Hudson," said Mrs. Sedgwick.

"And you, miss?"

"Croton. Why are you so interested in where we're from?"

"Let me see that camera of yours," he said, pointing to her Brownie. He looked back at Mrs. Sedgwick. "She your daughter?"

Chris dropped her camera, notebook, and pen back into her book bag. "No. She was my teacher in fifth grade. I'm in ninth grade now."

The two other Croton girls drifted away.

The agent kept his eyes on Mrs. Sedgwick. "So you're giving her a civics lesson?"

Chris swung her book bag to her other shoulder, the one further away from the agent. "Look, I just ran into her here. She's not my teacher now, anyhow. I came with someone else."

"Who," asked the agent, "did you come with?"

"A neighbor. How do you plan to use your information?"

"Your neighbor's name?"

Burly Beard growled at the agent. "Leave the girl alone, will you?"

"I'm not talking to you, buddy, so I'd mind my own business if I were you."

The agent turned back to Chris. "Your name?"

"Anne Shirley," she said. It was a good bet that Bristle-Head hadn't read *Anne of Green Gables.*

"Hm-m-m," said the agent. "What have you got there, in the notebook, Anne—homework?"

Burly Beard, who had stepped back, moved forward again. "Aw, quit harassing the girl. She's only a kid."

"Now look . . ." the agent began. Then he returned to Chris. "Let me see that notebook and camera of yours."

She looked over to Mrs. Sedgwick and the other adults for guidance, but she was met only with set jaws and worried eyes.

Somewhere people were singing and chanting. Someone had spilled a bottle of coke near her feet, which mixed with the smoggy heat to ooze a sickly sweetness. Shards of glass littered the curbside. Chris started as a passing man jostled her. He was bearing a large placard with "We are innocent!" and a photo of the Rosenbergs on it. A young mother was trying to push her baby stroller eastward.

Chris held on tightly to her possessions. "It's just a school notebook."

"From a Croton-on-Hudson school?"

"Yes."

"Let me take a look at it," the agent demanded. "And the camera too."

Chris scanned the little circle of teachers. Their faces were like tautly stretched rubber.

People were trying to clear a space for the stroller, and that's when Chris bolted. She charged past the mother and child, heading in the only direction available to her. She bumped up against walls, doorways, shoes, hips, and elbows. Missing a curb, she landed on the street knees first, and the sign that she had carefully lettered in bold blue ink ("Spare the Rosenbergs!") splayed out above her head. Her right knee, where her dungarees were now torn, was burning.

Embarrassed, she accepted a helping hand stretched toward her. The guy in the brown suit! Jughead! Before she could even thank him he was gone. When she got up and dusted herself off, she looked around for her bookbag. It was lying in the gutter, empty. Next to it was her now illegible sign.

♦   ♦   ♦

In the fracas, Chris realized that she had left Rosie and Mrs. Novac far behind. She elbowed her way to within yards of the speakers' platform, near Broadway. From her vantage point, she had a fairly good view. It was almost six o'clock—when the prayer meeting was supposed to begin—and the sound truck still not arrived.

"Hey, Monaghan!" someone yelled, "You can't silence us!"

"Get a bullhorn!" someone else yelled.

"Go home to the Soviet Union!" came a shout from an open window.

Policemen began to mass on the Broadway side of Union Square, and barriers were shifted around in order to make room for the truck. Chris pushed forward.

Tests from the sound truck crackled above the noise of the crowd. Finally the speaker could be heard saying that the Rosenbergs were braving their accusers. They were facing death with courage and fortitude. They were destined for execution because they dared to stand up for peace and justice in a nation "whose sons are being killed in Korea, while Korean children are being massacred." The Rosenbergs were "little people who had become giants because they refused to crawl."

With thousands of eyes as anxious as hers, Chris followed the hands of the clock on the Con Edison tower as they crept toward the couple's appointment with the executioner. To the west, behind the crowd, flamed the rays of the setting sun.

When the clock's hands pointed to 7:58, someone announced from the sound truck that the couple was now in the death chamber. Chris stiffened. All around her people were weeping. From the loudspeaker rose the strong voice of a young woman. "In memory of the Rosenbergs. . . ." she began, but could get no further. The sobbing and screaming of the crowd overpowered her. Soon the voice reemerged, singing "Go Down, Moses."

Abruptly the loudspeaker was cut off.

And then a few people around Chris, their voices thin at first, began to take up the refrain, "Go Down, Moses . . ." More voices joined in, with greater strength, and Chris sang along. "Way down in Egypt's la-a-and." And yet more voices, the street vibrating with song. "Tell ol' Pha-a-ro-oh. . ." It was the entire crowd now, thousands and thousands of voices in unison: "LET MY PEOPLE GO!"

Chris, standing tall, felt goose bumps all over her arms.

A brief vacuum of silence before horns began honking like angry geese.

The crowd quieted down, their spirit and energy draining away. The Rosenbergs were dead.

Demonstrators were beginning to straggle off, but Chris saw no one from the Croton crowd. She felt chilled and alone. She hurried to the bench on Madison, but Rosie and her mother were no longer there. With a start she realized that they would be worried about her. There was nothing to do but to go back to Grand Central for the 8:56 express and hope to meet them at the train. She started uptown on Madison. Her saddle shoes felt like dead weights.

Madison was deserted and dark, except for the greenish glow of puddles cast onto the curbsides by sparse street lights. A bus was crawling to the next stop, and she was tempted. But, along with her train ticket, she had only a dollar with her, and she wanted to save it for a possible emergency. Soon she reached the stately mansion that housed Rodgers and Meacham, the publishing company where her father worked as a book illustrator. Since taking over the position of Croton's Village Manager, he had reduced his hours at the publisher's. She turned to look at a notice on the mansion's gate. Out of the corner of her eye she glimpsed a familiar-looking shape about a block behind her. Either her imagination was working overtime or it was the man in the brown suit again. There was no mistaking that jug head.

♦   ♦   ♦

Chris trotted up to the train just as the conductor began to fold up the steps to the first coach. In front of the second, the designated meeting place for the Croton demonstrators, Rosie and her mother were waiting on the platform, craning their necks. As Chris approached, Rosie shouted and ran to her.

"Oh, Chris, Mama and I were so worried about you! We weren't going to get on the train if you didn't come. We asked policemen to look for you at the rally, but no one could find you."

Mrs. Novac was walking with a bit of difficulty, but at least she wasn't hanging on to anyone or wincing in pain.

By the time they climbed aboard there was only one pair of seats left in the Crotonites' coach. Chris, filled with guilt, insisted that Rosie and her mother take them. She would try the car behind theirs.

"All right," Mrs. Novac said. "At least my nicotine-addict husband will be in that car. He never made it to the rally, you know—big meeting at the office. I think he's having a word with Corey Sylvester. So stay close to Sandor. We don't want you to disappear again!"

The smoker coach she entered was much stuffier than the non-smoker in front of it, where she left Rosie and her mother. Chris found a seat on the

Hudson River side, right behind Rosie's father, who was sitting across the aisle from Corey Sylvester. She picked out faces of a few other Crotonites she knew. And then there were faces that looked familiar, but she couldn't attach names to them. In the window seat next to Mr. Novac sat Mrs. Sedgwick.

Mrs. Sedgwick turned around to Chris as the train began to rumble out of the tunnel. "We were all so worried about you, dear," she said. "That F.B.I. man bullied you terribly."

Chris hung her head and muttered that because she lost her notebook she wouldn't be able to write her story. And her pictures were gone too.

"Well, I'm sorry you lost your material," Mrs. Sedgwick said. "But don't worry too much about it. There will be plenty more stories for you in these terrible times." She turned back to her reading.

Chris let herself be lulled by the gentle lilt of the train and the string of lights at Spuyten Duyvil, blurrily visible through the grimy windows. She drifted in and out of a doze. At one point her watch said 9:45. They must be about to pull into the Harmon Station. She leaned forward to try to catch what Mr. Novac and Mr. Sylvester were saying.

" . . . Just don't take it personally," Mr. Sylvester said.

"Not take it personally? You write in your paper that my building is 'Stalinism in glass and steel,' and I shouldn't take it personally?"

"Look, it's not *your* building. Your firm is responsible for that building."

"Come on, Corey. You know damn well that the design was mine. And since when are you an architecture critic anyhow? Aline Loucheim interviews you for *The Times* about my Tarrytown Arts Center design, and you call my dove of peace a monster glass bat. You'll use any opportunity to take a swipe at my politics, won't you?"

Mrs. Sedgwick turned back towards Chris again. Rats! Chris would miss out on the conversation just when things were getting interesting. "You know, I saw your classmate, Connie Waldo, in the library the other day. Do you see much of her?"

Chris murmured a reply and tried to catch more of the two men's conversation.

"All right, I've had just about enough of your hostility," Corey Sylvester was saying. With that, he got up and headed toward the front of the coach.

Chris thought she saw him open the door to the lavatory, but at that moment the train lurched to a halt, and the lights in the coach flickered and went out. She could barely make out the shape of a man who seemed to be walking right behind Mr. Sylvester. The train had just crossed the railroad bridge, so they must be pulling into the Harmon Station, the express stop where the Crotonites would get off. There were a few grumblings among the passengers, but since they were largely commuters they were used to such delays. Chris yawned. She was definitely ready for bed.

Here and there cigarette lighters clicked, and little glowing clusters of ash punctuated the darkness.

Another rough jolt of the train startled her to attention. The lights came back on and the car jerked forward. Mr. Novac turned toward her and smiled, "Well, we've all had a long day, haven't we? It will be good to get home." Mr. Sylvester's seat was vacant.

"Ha-a-a-r-mon Station," bellowed the conductor.

People got up and started to gather their things.

The car jerked once more and came to a halt. The lights dimmed and went out again.

"What the hell . . . ?" hissed a man from somewhere behind her.

All around her was the rustling and creaking of people rearranging their belongings and sitting back down.

After a few moments a woman's voice rang out, "It would be helpful if the conductor gave us some information."

A bright light punctured the darkness and shone in Chris's eyes. People on the other side of the aisle got up and leaned over passengers on the river side in order to look out the windows. A large man brushed Chris's shoulder. Outside, lanterns and flashlights were swirling around the railroad tracks. Sirens screeched, stopped, and then sounded again. Passengers shuttled back and forth from either side of the aisle to report on what they could see.

"Two fire engines!"

"There's an ambulance, too!"

"See the state police car?"

In a blinding flash a giant floodlight beamed on the tracks, and Chris let out a cry of shock. An arm severed at the elbow! It seemed to be clothed in the sleeve of a suit jacket.

Abruptly the floodlight went off, and the vision disappeared. Was she having hallucinations? Did anyone else see the arm? Butterflies fluttered wildly in her stomach, but she forced herself to twist sideways for another look out the window. Flashlights were still panning the area, but all she could see was a group of men huddled in a semicircle.

Still no sign of the conductor. The only light in the coach was an occasional flicker of a cigarette lighter or a flash from outside.

Slowly people returned to their seats. Comments subsided to murmurs, and finally the coach was quiet.

Mr. Novac said nothing to her. Did he see that arm? Was he worried about Rosie and her mother? Chris tried to see the time on her watch. Almost 11? Was it possible? The 8:56 was due to arrive at 9:50. What would her parents be thinking?

The door to their coach creaked open, and a flashlight shone in. The conductor belted out, "There's been an accident, folks. We'll be delayed here a while. The police will be coming through. Please stay seated, and cooperate with the authorities."

More flashlights as two state troopers followed the conductor. They were stopping at every pair of seats. Before they got to her, Chris realized that they were identifying the passengers and keeping track of the ticket receipts that the conductor always wedged into the slot at the back of each seat.

When they got to the row ahead of her, the policemen asked who had occupied the empty seat there.

"Mr. Corey Sylvester," Mr. Novac replied.

"Where is he now?" one of the policemen asked.

No one in the row could say, although Mr. Novac reported that Corey Sylvester had gotten up when the lights first went out.

There were no stops between New York City and Harmon on this express train. So Mr. Sylvester couldn't have left the train. After Chris saw him get up, did he ever return to his seat?

CHAPTER TWO

In the middle of her breakfast the next morning Chris remembered her dream from the night before.   A severed arm was hanging in the sky, like a grotesque distortion of a crescent moon. The ring of the telephone made her choke on her English muffin. Forget breakfast.   She coughed and picked up.

The male voice was unfamiliar. "Cristabel Gooding?"

She struggled to regain her voice. "Yes, that's me."

"My name is Chuck Riley. I'm a patrolman at the Croton municipal police station. Is your father there?"

"No, but my mother is. Do you want to speak to her?"

Her mother snatched the phone from her. Tapping her foot, she listened for a minute or two, and said into the receiver, "Well, it's all right with me, but you'll have to ask my daughter. Gil should be in his office by now." She handed the phone to Chris.

"Christabel? With your parents' permission, we'd like you to come over today for questioning. Your father will be here too." Chris's father was already in his Village Manager's office in the Municipal Building, upstairs from the police station.

"What did I do?" she asked.

The patrolman chuckled. He sounded young. "Nothing—at least not so far as we know. But we understand that you were seated in the same coach as Mr. Corey Sylvester on the 8:56 p.m. train from New York last evening." He wanted her there at 2 o'clock.

Uh-oh.

As soon as her mother went upstairs, Chris picked up the phone. "Rosie, the police just called. I'm going over there later today. Have you heard anything about what happened last night?"

Rosie's voice was almost inaudible. "Oh, Chris, my father's already at the police station." She stifled a sob.

"Why?" Chris asked, not really wanting to hear the answer.

Rosie was sobbing now. "Chris. That was Mr. Sylvester on the railroad tracks last night."

So sometime during the darkness, when Chris was dozing on the train, an arm was severed and something terrible happened to Mr. Sylvester. But why didn't she hear any sounds? How could it be?

Between her sobs, Rosie continued to speak. "And my father was sitting right next to him on the train."

"Across the aisle," Chris corrected her.

♦ ♦ ♦

It always sounded funny to people when Chris told them that she was from Croton-on-Hudson. "Like Stratford-on-Avon?" they would laugh. But, aside from the fact that the little village needed to be distinguished from nearby Croton Falls, it was aptly named. You were never far from the river in Croton. Beyond the Municipal Building, where Old Post North began to climb, you could get sweeping panoramas of it, bounded by the majestic hills on the other side. Even at its stormiest and choppiest, the river was a comforting presence, flowing and changing and yet always there.

Chris remembered the time a couple of years ago when she and Rosie and their parents were walking along Riverside Avenue with the Goodings' dog Willie. The dog unexpectedly bolted in the direction of the Hudson, which paralleled the long street. The current was swift that day. Mr. Novac made off like a bat out of hell after the dog, leaping over the railroad tracks and catching Willie just as his paws reached the water. Both dog and man fell together on the shore, and Mr. Novac returned, dripping, with a soggy Willie in his arms.

Chris decided there was no way she would say anything at all about Mr. Novac—Mr. Novac whom she had known all her life and who was her best friend's father. He was like a second father to her.

Then she thought back to last evening. If only she could say with certainty that Mr. Novac had never left his seat! But wait—it was coming back to her. Wasn't there a man who was right behind Mr. Sylvester, who looked like he was heading for the lavatory too? And Mr. Novac was still seated in front of her! If only she could remember something about that man behind Mr. Sylvester! But it was so dark.

It was true that Mr. Novac could be "hot-headed," as her mother liked to say. That hot-headed? Rosie must be beside herself. People knew about the bad blood between Mr. Novac and Mr. Sylvester. And what with Mr. Novac's politics . . . .

It could be anything. Maybe Mr. Sylvester committed suicide, although Chris strongly doubted it. He wasn't the type. He was always so cool and collected. Maybe he fell. Fell? Over the gate? What was he doing out there between the cars anyway?

Look, Mr. Sylvester probably had a lot of enemies, and you could maybe count Mr. Novac among them. That was the bad thing. But it didn't mean that he would kill him.

The Municipal Building, formerly a school, was a three-story red brick structure that resembled the Croton-Harmon High School in style. The police station occupied the first floor; her father's office was on the second.

She announced herself and took a seat on a long wooden bench. She could just picture criminals seated there, heads bowed in shame over their handcuffs. Behind her was a photo of a missing Schwinn bicycle.

"Cristabel Gooding?" A young man the spitting image of Marlon Brando emerged from a doorway. He had pronounced biceps, mahogany-colored hair and deep-set eyes to match. "I'm Chuck Riley," he said, as he ushered her into an office.

"Hello, Chris," said Detective Inspector Charles Mangone, a dark-haired, stocky, middle-aged man who made a feeble effort to get up from behind his desk as she entered. Her father was seated on a wooden armchair in a corner of the room. He smiled at her and then quickly looked away. "You can leave us now, Chuck," Mangone said to the patrolman as he motioned for Chris to sit down.

"Are you questioning everyone who was on the train? Or only the Croton people?" Chris asked as the door closed behind Officer Riley.

Mangone's hint of a smile faded. "I thought I was supposed to be asking the questions. We hope to be releasing definite information shortly." He leaned across the massive oak desk that separated him from Chris. "Now Corey Sylvester was a family friend, wasn't he? Weren't you going to work at the paper this summer?"

"Yes . . . I was supposed to start as soon as school is over." She hung her head and then looked up at Mangone. "I know you found his body. Could he have committed suicide?"

Mangone straightened up in his chair. "O.K., Chris, it's my turn now. Tell me exactly where you were sitting on the 8:56 in relation to Mr. Sylvester."

Chris was still planning it out. Mangone was surely going to ask her if she had overheard any conversation between Rosie's father and Mr. Sylvester. She was not going to say anything about Mr. Novac if she could help it. But if she said she was sitting nowhere near Mr. Sylvester, her statement could be contradicted by the state police, or by Mrs. Sedgwick, who knew very well where she had been seated.

"I was sitting in the row behind him," she answered.

"Sandor Novac was sitting directly in front of you?"

"Yes," said Chris, waiting for the inevitable.

"Was he talking with Mr. Sylvester?"

"I think so."

"Did you by any chance catch anything of . . .?"

"No," she said quickly. "I fell asleep right away."

"But Mrs. Sedgwick, who was sitting right in front of you, remembers talking to you after the train left the station."

"If you already know everything that happened," Chris said, "Why are you asking me?"

"Chris," her father interposed. "You need to cooperate with the inspector."

Mangone pushed at an inkwell on his blotter. "Now look, young lady, we need to check our evidence and to corroborate statements."

"Yes, I did say hello to Mrs. Sedgwick, but right after that I fell asleep."

"When did you wake up?" He was fiddling with the inkwell. If he kept pushing it around, it would probably spill. Chris moved her chair farther back from the desk.

"Not until we got to Harmon."

"You mean to say you didn't wake up when the train stalled just past the bridge and the lights went out?"

"That's right. I was pretty sleepy." She hung her head. She should really say something about that man following Mr. Sylvester to the lavatory. "Uh . . . wait," she said. "I think I remember something. I was really just dozing when the lights went out. I . . . uh think there was a man behind Mr. Sylvester when he got up to go to the bathroom."

"Mr. Novac?" Mangone prodded.

"No, Mr. Novac was still sitting in front of me."

"Can you tell me anything about this other man?"

"I don't think so—it was pretty dark."

Mangone rose to his feet with difficulty and sighed. "And you were very groggy. O.K., Chris. If you should recall anything that might be of interest to us, please let us know." And to her father, "Thanks for your help, Gil."

Her father got up, put an arm lightly across her shoulder, and escorted her to the door.

◆　　◆　　◆

"Mother!" called Chris as she opened the front door to the spacious multi-level house on North Highland Place which Rosie's father had designed. North Highland was a short street branching off woodsy Mt. Airy Road at the top of the first big hill. She raced into the large kitchen-dining-living area where she could usually find her mother when she wasn't teaching drama classes at Scarborough, a nearby private school.

Her mother looked up from a book. "Cristabel, do the police have any new information?"

"Not much."

"What did they want from you?"

Chris explained that whatever it was they wanted she couldn't give them very much information, even though she had been sitting in the same coach as Mr. Sylvester.

"And Sandor," said her mother.

She should have known. Her mother and Rosie's mother must have talked at least several times since last night.

"Yeah."

The phone rang. Chris's mother picked up, listened for a moment. "Of course, Rosie," she said, "here she is."

Rosie sounded distraught. "I'll be right over," Chris told her, barely waiting for her mother's permission to leave the house.

She zoomed down the hill to Rosie's. No one answered the bell, so she let herself in and headed toward the rear of the house. When Mr. Novac had renovated the old place, nestled in the first crook of winding Mt. Airy, he had built two wings onto the kitchen at the rear of the first floor, one for his "workroom" and one for Mrs. Novac' studio.

The house seemed empty, but Chris guessed that Mrs. Novac might be in her studio. Fortunately the door was open. Inside was a tableau: Rosie sitting on the floor, with her face in her mother's lap, sobbing. Mrs. Novac, seated in an old battered director's chair, was stroking the top of Rosie's head.

Around them were stacked paintings, prints, books, and painting materials. Northern light flooded the room from two large skylights, a glass-paneled door to the back yard, and a floor-to-ceiling window. An unfinished painting was propped up on the larger of two easels. Chris coughed, and Mrs. Novac looked up. Her eyes were red-rimmed. "Oh, Chris, I'm so glad you're here. You'll do Rosie good."

Rosie glanced up at Chris. "Can we go outside, Mama?" she asked.

Mrs. Novac looked only too happy at the idea.

Skirting a milk bottle full of freshly-picked black-eyed Susans atop a small, paint-splattered, wooden stepladder, they went out the back door into the yard

Lawn chairs informally surrounded an umbrella-shaded table. After a few minutes Mrs. Novac deposited a tray of lemonade and homemade cookies on the table and withdrew.

Rosie was looking intently at her lap. "You know my father is a suspect," she said.

"Just because they were sitting across the aisle from each other?"

Rosie started crying again. Chris felt like shaking her. She waited several minutes, looking at the ground.

Finally Rosie said, "No. See, they did the autopsy on Mr. Sylvester." She was set to cry again, but Chris grabbed her shoulder.

"What did it show?"

Choking back sobs, Rosie told her that when the police found the body, it was quite mangled. *That severed arm.*

"At first," said Rosie, "they thought it might have been an accident—you know, with the lights out and the confusion. Or else maybe he committed suicide."

Chris shook her head. She had already ruled it out.

"And then . . .," Rosie continued, but she broke down.

Chris waited a while. Rosie was drowning in her tears. Finally Chris touched her elbow gently. "And then . . . what, Rosie?"

"And then . . . when they did the autopsy they found bruise marks on his neck. Someone had grabbed hold of his neck."

Uh-oh. He was pushed. It wouldn't have been too hard to push him over the gate and onto the ground if he was already suffocating. So Mr. Novac was the perfect prime suspect. Rosie had told her recently that her father feared for his job in New York because of his politics. "If you're a liberal, you're a Commie, and better dead than Red," he had said. Mr. Sylvester's negative comments on his work would only make it easier for the firm to fire him.

What the suspicions and accusations would mean for Mr. Novac's future Chris could easily imagine. A lot of people knew that he was trying to open his own business in Croton. Because he wanted to establish a greater local presence, he was planning to run for a vacancy on the Croton School Board.

From the patio they could hear the slam of the front door and Mr. Novac calling, "Lili!"

Rosie looked at Chris in alarm. Chris quickly scooped everything up onto the tray, and they rushed upstairs to Rosie's room.

Rosie sat down on her bed, and Chris on the other twin bed, both covered in sky blue chenille bedspreads. Rosie's violin lay on her small, antique desk, next to a music stand. Her windows were open to the soft, early summer sunshine.

"Daddy's hardly said a word since we heard from the police," Rosie said.

Chris nodded. Poor Rosie! Now of all times her parents should stop fighting and stick together.

"Mainly he keeps complaining about that article by Aline Loucheim . . . ."

"Who's Aline Loucheim?"

Rosie sniffled and reached for a Kleenex from her night table between the two beds. "*The Times*' architecture critic, silly. Anyhow, she was talking about my father's proposal for the Tarrytown Arts Center. She quoted Mr. Sylvester, who said something about how Daddy's design for a dove of peace would look like a monster glass bat."

"How come she interviewed Mr. Sylvester?"

"Who knows?

Chris took her glass of lemonade from the night table.

"Oh, Chris," said Rosie, "I forgot. What happened to you yesterday—was it only yesterday? How come you were so late? Where were you?"

Chris still hadn't made up her mind what to say. For reasons she herself couldn't quite understand, she didn't want to say anything about Mrs. Sedgwick and Bristle-Head, or about the man in the brown suit. She had a vague feeling that she was in some way at fault for getting mixed up in whatever mess she was in.

"Oh, it's just that I lost my notebook and camera, and I spent so much time looking for them that I didn't realize how late it was. And I never even found them."

Voices sounded from below, and Rosie opened her bedroom door a crack. In the past Chris would have told her to close it, but today she sat spellbound and silent, straining with Rosie to catch every word.

"We can forget about the School Board," Mr. Novac was saying, "I can kiss it goodbye."

Rosie's glanced at Chris as if to say "I told you so."

"Plus I'll probably be run out of this goddam town. Because now the police will be investigating all of us *suspects*. And you can bet that I'll be at the top of their list."

They could even hear the clink of the ice bucket as Rosie's father poured himself a drink, probably his favorite, scotch on the rocks. Chris started to wish that she had stayed home.

"So . . . ." Mrs. Novac's voice was so soft that it was hard to hear her. "So . . . do you want to tell me what you talked to Corey about on the train?"

"Not really, but you'll drag it out of me anyhow."

Silence.

"It would be better," Mrs. Novac said, "to try to . . . ."

"All right, all right. Look, you know what I said to him. I told him he was out of line. Asked him why he had it in for me. As if it weren't obvious, the right-wing bastard."

"Did he . . . did he have anything to say in return?"

"He was very smooth. Papered everything over; said his comment about the Arts Center proposal wasn't personal—just an off-the-cuff remark. Just sloughed off the Loucheim interview. Then he tried to sweet-talk me. Said he wanted me to meet someone who was interested in my work. What a crock! He's out to ruin my career!"

They heard the clunk of his glass on the coffee table.

"Did you speak to him again after the lights went out, chéri?"

His voice sounded scratchy. "What is this? Dress rehearsal for an inquisition? No, of course I didn't speak to him after that. I'm not even sure where he went when he got up. Maybe he was going to the toilet."

Ice rattling around in his glass was the only sound that they heard for a while. Mr. Novac resumed. "Gil told me the funeral will probably be held tomorrow or Wednesday. But it will be private, just for the family. There'll be a public memorial service later on."

"To which we're all going," declared Rosie's mother

A loud crack sounded—as if Mr. Novac was hitting the table with his fist. "Oh, for God's sake, Lili! Yes, we're all going! Don't you know when to let up?" The screen door to the back yard slammed shut.

CHAPTER THREE

Even though Chris was an expert at listening in on phone conversations, she could catch only bits and pieces of the gossip that buzzed over the shared "party lines" on Mt. Airy Road. It was all about the Rosenbergs—or Corey Sylvester. The people who lived on Mt. Airy, or what the villagers called "Red Hill," sounded scared. The hill was populated by many of the village's leftists, and they were saying that since Mr. Sylvester's anticommunist views were well known, blame would surely fall on the Reds or alleged Reds. "You'll see," one caller said, "it'll be just like the Rosenbergs."

Joan Sylvester suspended publication of the *Croton-Harmon News* until further notice. Chris had been counting on her three-day a week job there after school let out, and now here she was, sitting around twiddling her thumbs. She knew she should be feeling terrible about Mr. Sylvester, but what would she do if she didn't have her job at the paper? Staying home with her mother was not an option.

She wasn't looking forward to today, when her mother was having Mrs. Novac and Rosie to lunch. Most of the other mothers had lunch parties or played tennis or socialized every day, but Rosie's and Chris's mothers were career women, so they didn't have much time for that kind of thing.

At the front door, Mrs. Novac handed Chris's mother a bottle of Chablis, as Rosie lingered behind her.

"Chablis!" Chris's mother exclaimed. "That's going to be a bit elegant for my tuna salad."

"It will be good for us, Maya."

Chris dried the lettuce, as her mother had requested. "Can't Rosie and I just go to the village?" she asked.

"Not until after lunch," her mother said in that schoolmarm voice she sometimes used.

They all settled into cushioned chairs around the glass-topped patio table. Chris's mother adjusted her long, embroidered blue caftan, which had caught on her chair leg. "That young policeman came to see us yesterday," she said. "He wanted to ask Chris more questions. Chris didn't want to talk to him, but I told her she had to. She was very stubborn."

Don't waste your breath, Chris mentally reassured her mother. You needn't reassure Mrs. Novac. You won't find me discussing anything about Mr. Novac with the police.

Mrs. Novac reached for her glass of Chablis. "Yes, Chuck Riley. He visited us too, with Charlie Mangone. They were both very polite. Almost apologized for coming over. You know, young Chuck is the one who helped me when I got stuck in the car in last year's blizzard—remember? We all chatted a while about Joan and Corey. They asked us how long we had known them and so on. Then they asked Sandor to repeat what he had said at the police station about his movements on the train and about his conversation with Corey. Sandor told him that he had spoken with Corey about his comments in the papers."

"Did they ask you about the power failure?" Chris's mother asked.

"Of course, Maya. When Chuck asked what Sandor was doing all the time that Corey was away from his seat, Sandor said he was just sitting there. And who could confirm that? No one was paying any attention, and Chris was asleep." She drained her glass of wine and poured herself more.

I could confirm it—almost—but no one would believe me.

After a pause, Mrs. Novac leaned across the table and said, "Oh, Maya, I haven't been so afraid since the war."

Huh? Mrs. Novac afraid? Chris always thought of her as very strong. After all, she had been a member of the Communist Youth in France, and she had weathered the death of her parents in the war. Chris and Rosie could never get much out of their parents about that. All they knew was that Rosie's maternal grandparents had died in "the camps" in Europe after Mr. and Mrs. Novac were married in the United States.

"Besides, isn't it convenient that the Rosenbergs are Jewish?"

"So are Kaufman and Saypol," her mother responded.

Rosie poked Chris in the ribs. "Who are they?" she asked sotto voce.

"Judge and prosecutor in the Rosenberg case," Chris whispered back. Aloud she said, "Yeah, they're Jewish. Just proving their loyalty to the United States, aren't they? To show that not all Jews are Commies."

Chris's mother frowned.

"She does have a point," Mrs. Novac said.

Chris's mother was staring at the uncut lawn through the large window. "Well, there were plenty of other Crotonites on the train."

"Yes, but not with Sandor's motive. Anyhow, the police have brought in the Westchester County District Attorney. I don't know how many people here they've already questioned."

Chris's mother toyed with her salad. "Maybe it wasn't even someone from Croton."

"Yes. But I guess they're starting with the Crotonites."

In a low voice, as if she was talking to herself, her mother said, "You know, Lili, last night's rehearsal was awful. People kept muffing their lines. We couldn't concentrate—all we could think about was Corey. Of course a 'Red' will be blamed. Leland finally had to schedule an extra rehearsal. Here in Greenwich Village North . . ."

Chris always hated it when her mother started a sentence like that. She would never let Chris forget that because her father hadn't wanted to raise a kid in the city, they had moved to Croton—her father's home town—when she was a toddler, interrupting her mother's brilliant off-Broadway career. Now her mother taught drama at the private Scarborough School and acted in productions of the Croton Players, the local community theater.

A blacklisted fugitive from Hollywood, Leland Lennard, who had once worked with Orson Welles, directed the group. Chris was left with the guilt.

" . . . non-Equity actors have trouble remembering lines under pressure."

Right. Not like the Actors Equity pros in New York, where the show always goes on.

A scratching sound at the screen door leading from the kitchen to the overgrown lawn reminded Chris to get up and let in the Airedale, panting and scraggly.

"Willie, bad dog," scolded Chris's mother, patting his shaggy head. "Where have you been? You're covered with mud! He's been out all morning," she explained to Mrs. Novac. Willie, a.k.a William Shakespeare, snuggled up to Chris's feet. Chris petted his ears, and his big, soulful eyes gleamed with gratitude.

Her mother persisted. "Did Chuck ask you about other Crotonites at the rally?"

"Yes, of course. But I wasn't about to give him a list. It was beginning to feel a little like the House UnAmerican Activities Committee."

The women lapsed into a silence that in other circumstances Chris would have taken for the comfortable one of longtime friends. Why her mother wanted Chris and Rosie to be part of this lunch was a mystery to Chris. The women were traditionally very exclusive in their lunches. Maybe her mother thought that a family-style lunch would cheer up Rosie and her mother. If so, it definitely wasn't the case for Rosie, whose head was bent over the paper napkin she was shredding. Chris was beginning to feel like a captive.

"Did you know," Chris's mother finally said to Mrs. Novac, "that Sandor has notified Gil he won't accept if he's offered the position on the School Board?"

"He hasn't said anything to me, but I'm not surprised. Since everyone thinks he's a Communist, they would never have appointed him anyway, and certainly not now."

Willie, energized, started prowling about the table, sniffing and whining. Chris tried to feed him some of the salad, but he turned on his tail and sulked.

Her mother got up. "Oh dear, wait a minute—I have to do something about the dog. You know what a fussy eater he is."

She disappeared into a large walk-in pantry. Rosie wandered over to a bookcase and picked up a piece of paper from a sheaf lying on top of some books. She stared at it for a minute and wordlessly passed it to Chris, who was still sitting at the table, wondering if she should start to clear.

It looked like the kind of rough pencil sketch her father habitually did at parties, in a corner, hunched over his sketchbook. Her father did his free-lance comic strips mainly in stolen moments.

Chris, thinking to divert Rosie's mother, passed it along to her.

Mrs. Novac studied it for a moment. "Oh, yes. This looks like it's from the Sylvesters' spring open house. Look!" she said to Chris's mother, who had returned. "Doesn't it look like Harold Lewis and Maria Muller?"

Chris and Rosie giggled. Maybe Chris's father had overheard the conversation in the gazebo from somewhere nearby on the grounds. Or maybe he made it up. Anyway, as everyone knew, it was at the Sylvesters' open house that Harold Lewis's affair with Maria Muller finally got discovered by the other principals—the lovers' spouses. The Lewises and the Mullers had been the best of friends. Now what would happen was anyone's guess. Mr. Lewis might just be capable of divorcing his wife, but Hendrik Muller, Chris's mother said, would never let Maria Muller go, even if Maria did wear the pants in that family.

Rosie and Chris served the ice cream slathered in chocolate sauce and whipped cream. "Chris!" her mother called out. "You've got chocolate sauce all over your shirt. Well, at least you're wearing those awful old dungarees. It won't matter what gets spilled on those." She turned to Mrs. Novac. "I wish that Chris would discover clothes and make-up. Then maybe she'd be more careful."

"You should be happy," Chris said to her mother, "that I'm not a clothes horse and I don't wear make-up—I'm saving you money."

Rosie whispered to Chris that she needed to talk to her in private. Balancing their bowls of dessert, they scrambled off to Chris's room and hunkered down on a fluffy beige rug in front of the twin beds that looked just like Rosie's, except for the color scheme.

"The past few days have been awful," Rosie began. My mother doesn't even stay in the studio. She mopes around the house, playing French records. Do you know how many times I've heard Piaf singing *La Vie en Rose*?" She started to imitate the tough, sexy voice of the French chanteuse:

Quand il me prend dans ses bras
Il me parle tout bas
Je vois la vie en rose. . . ."

"Doesn't she realize how dopey she sounds?" Rosie continued. As if she didn't know that Chris could get the French, she translated: "'When he takes me in his arms . . . I see life through rose-colored lenses.' Some rose-colored lenses. My parents have been fighting all the time."

Chris put a hand on Rosie's arm in commiseration. "Let's go to Silver Lake, O.K.?"

"So listen to what happened yesterday. Mama went out somewhere. I was upstairs practicing. Then I went to the studio looking for her, and there, on her easel . . . ." Rosie looked like she was on the verge of another good cry. "There on the easel . . . you know, on her painting about money . . ."

Chris knew the painting, called "Lucre," very well. On the upper right corner of the canvas, a green-faced George Washington smiled down from behind a large dollar sign, as if from behind bars, at a panorama of shoppers staggering under the weight of the enormous parcels that they were carrying. Towering at crazy angles over the mule-like people were shadowy skyscrapers bunched together. In an inset panel on the lower left, were several scruffy, down-and-out men lying in the littered gutters of New York's Bowery.

". . . on George Washington's face someone had painted a black mustache, and there was a note tacked onto the easel . . ." Rosie faltered. ". . . written in red crayon. It said, 'your husband is a Commie murderer.'"

♦　♦　♦

ERICA HARTH

Except maybe for Black Rock, Silver Lake had the best swimming in town. But it was several miles away, in Harmon. If Rosie went with her, Chris didn't mind the walk, but Rosie said she was going to go home with her mother right after lunch. She didn't want to go swimming, she said, because of a dream she had had the previous night.

It was the first day of the school year. A hush had fallen over the building, as if the walls were padded with huge wads of cotton. As Rosie walked through the corridors, her feet sounding no steps, clusters of students drew back and made way for her with a mixture of fear, respect, and loathing. Their noiseless conversations, like a silent film without subtitles, ceased as she approached, and their bodies congealed into clumsy statues. She waved to Chris, who did not respond, but faded slowly into the background until she disappeared altogether.

"It's only a dream," Chris said. "And I'm not about to disappear on you."

"I don't know who'll be at Silver Lake. I don't want to face anyone."

Today, though, the walk without Rosie wasn't so bad, because Chris needed thinking time. Rosie would be a total wreck if anything bad happened to her father. Already Chris felt a distance opening up between herself and her best friend. She and Rosie were supposed to be sworn allies, and now Rosie was retreating into her own world.

Sometimes Chris thought that she and Rosie and their girlfriends lived in a parallel universe. Unlike the other girls, they didn't wear lipstick. They didn't listen to the Hit Parade on the radio, they couldn't stand Eddie Fisher, and they thought that Patti Page singing "How Much is that Doggy in the Window" was dumb. They didn't date or go to parties with the boys in their class, and they didn't dislike school. Why couldn't her mother understand those things? She wasn't a conformist herself. But she kept harping on Chris to ditch her beloved old dungarees and be more "feminine."

Chris had a good swim out to Third Rock, chatted with a few friends, and soaked up a lot of sun. Afterward, she felt lazy, and she dragged her feet at the start of the long walk home. When she got to the center of what was known as the Upper Village, at the intersection of Old Post Road and Grand Street, she was ready for a break. The Upper Village had displaced the Lower Village as the commercial center of Croton. The older business area, on Riverside Avenue fronting the Hudson and the railroad tracks, had become a bit run-down. On an impulse, Chris decided to make a detour.

Mrs. Sedgwick lived in a modest bungalow on Van Wyck Street, near the Municipal Building. Chris had never actually been inside her house. The closest she had gotten was the summer after fifth grade, when Mrs. Sedgwick volunteered to take any interested students to hear Paul Robeson sing, in neighboring Peekskill. Robeson had a beautiful bass voice, and he was a fine actor. But he was a Negro and pro-Communist, so he had a lot of enemies, including the United States government. The small group of five or six students had met at the teacher's front door. Chris still had nightmares about that day—the burning crosses, people being beaten and stoned. The concert had to be stopped and rescheduled for the next week, when her parents took her to it. She was scared to go, but she did. Never again would she think that the Ku Klux Klan operated only in the South!

The tiny lawn in front of Mrs. Sedgwick's house was freshly mowed, and the privet hedges around it neatly trimmed, but the shades were drawn. Maybe her former teacher, a widow with no children, went away in summertime. Chris rang the bell anyway. She was just about to leave when Mrs. Sedgwick, wearing an apron over a light summer dress, opened the door.

"Oh, dear, how fortunate!" she said to Chris. "I just came back from a luncheon."

She didn't look like she had been out at all. Her gray-streaked hair was mussed up, and her apron was stained with sweet-smelling traces of baking. The house was very warm, and a strong, gingery aroma emanated from the kitchen. Chris, worried that she might drip water onto the wood floor, tried to inspect her footprints, but her bathing suit was already fairly dry under her shorts and tee shirt.

Mrs. Sedgwick ushered Chris in and began pulling up window shades. "I just wanted to keep out the sun," she said, motioning Chris to sit in a thickly-upholstered armchair. Low bookcases swarming with books and magazines were the only sign of untidiness in the little living room. "I've just taken out a batch of ginger snaps from the oven for our Friends' meeting," she said, "may I give you some, with a glass of iced tea?"

Chris, who had worked up an appetite at the lake, accepted eagerly.

"Luscious," she told her former teacher at the first bite.

Mrs. Sedgwick smiled. She made no move to take a cookie herself, but drank from her tall glass of iced tea, laced with fresh mint leaves.

"Mrs. Sedgwick," asked Chris, trying to feel her way into a conversation for which she hadn't exactly planned. "What happened after I . . .uh, left you at the Rosenberg rally?"

There was a hair's breadth of a pause. "Well, Mr. Hanks (that was Burly Beard, Chris remembered) pulled at the F.B.I. agent's arm to keep him from going after you." She smiled again. "You were fast, Chris. The agent was furious, and I thought that he and Jim Hanks would come to blows. Then . . . I don't know . . . the agent went away. He seemed to melt into the crowd."

Chris swung a leg back and forth. "Do you . . . uh . . . remember about my notebook and my camera? I did have them with me when I left, didn't I?"

Mrs. Sedgwick chuckled. "You certainly weren't about to give them up, that's for sure." The ice cubes in her glass clinked. "I don't remember if you had them when you left. I thought I saw you put them in your book bag. But it was all so quick."

"I'm pretty sure I had them. But then . . . well, later I fell—see?" She pointed to the greenish yellow remains of a large bruise on her knee. "And then . . . and then when I got up everything was gone except my book bag."

Mrs. Sedgwick was looking at her closely. "You have to be careful, dear. At least we got to see that agent for what he was. Sometimes you just don't know, especially at these large political events."

"What do you mean, careful?" Chris asked.

"It's not really a good idea to cross them."

"You mean I should have given him my stuff?"

"N-n-no, not necessarily. You were very courageous. But if you confront them the way you did, you can arouse their suspicions. Then they can bother you even more."

"You mean," Chris asked, "that maybe he came after me and somehow got my things?"

The ice cubes clinked again as Mrs. Sedgwick set her glass on a nearby table. "No. I don't know what happened. Probably your things just dropped out of your book bag when you fell. But these agents . . . they can harass you." She popped up from her chair, as if she had just remembered something, went to the front door, opened it, shut it, and returned to Chris. "I thought I heard someone at the front door," she explained.

That was strange. Chris hadn't heard the bell, or even a knock. She put away any thoughts of telling Mrs. Sedgwick about the man in the brown suit. Mrs. Sedgwick changed the subject anyway, to the train ride home.

After she left Mrs. Sedgwick, Chris did something she had never done before. She looked around her. Van Wyck Street was quiet except for three young children playing ball farther down toward the river. Somewhere, though, she sensed an intrusive presence, like a cat in a tree. A few moments later, she looked over her shoulder. A man with wavy blond hair and large sunglasses slipped around the corner of Mrs. Sedgwick's house, as if he didn't want to be seen. He looked like he didn't belong on Van Wyck Street.

Chris was still hungry. She slowed down as she reached the Parkway Delicatessen, on Grand Street, thinking about what she might buy there. The two owner-managers—Joan Sylvester always called them the Parkway Boys—had known both Chris and Rosie since they were little. While those ahead of her placed orders, Chris casually helped herself to a bunch of grapes and nibbled on them as she circled the pot-bellied coal stove and looked out the window at the passing scene. A shadow crossed her sight-line. It was the blond stranger with the sunglasses, making tracks toward Mt. Airy Road.

When it came to her turn on line, Chris held up the bare stalk which moments ago had held large green grapes.

"How much is this, Mr. Naison?" she asked.

He threw up his hands and laughed.

She felt fortified, yet still wary about meeting up with the man in the sunglasses. But as she continued on her way along Grand Street and up Mt. Airy, she saw no one remotely like him.

With relief, she turned onto North Highland Place and let herself into her house. Designed by Mr. Novac to catch the cross breezes wafting through the old maples and oaks on the hill, the house always felt nice and cool on a hot summer afternoon.

"Mother?" called Chris. "Daddy?" No one was home except the dog, and he barely raised an ear at her from under the coffee table. The house seemed forlorn and lonely, with no welcoming aroma of baking ginger snaps. She had lost track of the time. She wandered into the kitchen, where the clock said 5:30. No wonder. It was one of the days her father spent in his New York office. Her mother had probably gone to pick him up at the Harmon Station.

As she did so many times when she was alone in the house, Chris picked out an LP to play on the phonograph. Over the years she had learned a lot about music from Rosie, and had come to prefer classical music to anything else. She and Rosie were about the only kids she knew who listened to it regularly. The familiar sounds of Mozart's Piano Concerto No. 20 comforted her.

The sink was still filled with dishes from lunch. On the table was a pile of unopened mail. Chris sat down and started flipping through it, as if, on an off chance, there might just be something there for her.

It looked like a few bills and a letter for her mother. Then, as she uncovered a ragged piece of paper, her hand froze. Printed in red crayon was the message, "Commie-lover, resign!"

CHAPTER FOUR

"Maybe you really should think about resigning," Chris's mother said to her father at dinner that evening.

Chris swallowed her impulse to shout out, "No!"

Her father frowned. "Are you kidding? I'm the most progressive manager this town has ever had. You think I'm going to leave the job to Gus or Vince? Look, my politics have already cost me plenty. I'm not going to give in to ignoramuses now."

Chris blew her father a kiss.

Her mother glared at her and said to her father, "Look, your august Croton lineage will get you only so far—it may not count for much against anti-Communism."

Her mother was always reminding him that he was a descendant of an old, prominent Croton family, as if that's what got him to be Village Manager. As if he couldn't have gotten there on his own.

"Anyway," her mother said, "let's talk about it more after Wednesday. You remember I'll be in the city then to see a matinee of *Guys and Dolls*."

To see *Guys and Dolls*! How could her mother not include her? "But you know I've wanted to see that ever since it opened! Can't you *please, please* get me a ticket and let me go with you?"

"Can't you find anything to do in Croton that day, dear?"

That was weird. Her mother was usually pretty good about letting her tag along to special events. But this time it took some doing to get her mother to relent and order an extra ticket to the musical for her. The ticket came with the condition that Chris meet her at the Dardanelles Restaurant on University Place at 1:30, only *after* her mother's lunch with "a friend," whose name she did not reveal.

Her father would be working at home that day. Since he had lost his syndicated comic strip, "Kookie Kutt," a couple of months ago, he had been working extra hard at home to come up with politically acceptable ideas for a new series. In the process, he scribbled lots of doodles that Chris would find strewn around the house. Her father filed most of them, even the ones he habitually did at parties to entertain himself. In fact, he had a set of metal boxes in the basement that housed old cartoons and doodles. Chris didn't see what was so bad about the strip that lost him his syndication. It was one of her favorites. She had traced a copy of it, and from time to time she would take it out of her desk drawer and reread it.

Kookie Kutt, Your Friendly Cop

♦   ♦   ♦

On the Wednesday that Chris and her mother caught a morning train for New York, her mother seemed very distracted. She spent most of the time on the train reading the newspaper, so Chris opened her copy of Richard Wright's *Native Son*.

She and her mother parted ways at the Dardanelles. As she watched her mother turn into the restaurant, she had a momentary sense of abandonment, but she shook it off. It wasn't as if she had never roamed around Manhattan on her own. She set out for the Strand Bookstore, where she browsed happily.

By 12:00 she was hungry, so, clutching the second-hand copy of *Catcher in the Rye* that she had snagged—the one she had at home was all tattered from overuse—she headed to Sam's Delicatessen on 8th Street. By 12:45 she had finished her brisket sandwich with potato salad, the best potato salad in New York, and was ready to leave. She hesitated. It would take her only a few minutes to hoof it over to University Place. She'd be early. It was obvious that her mother didn't want her around. But what could it be? An affair? She didn't like to speculate about her parents' love life, but the thought of them sneaking around and meeting others for secret rendezvous disgusted her. Her friend Gail Korngold's parents had both been misbehaving for years, but it bothered Gail every time she found out about a new adventure. Chris tried dragging her feet and looking in the shop windows on 8th Street. No good. She was too curious about what was happening at the Dardanelles.

The restaurant was dimly lit, and Chris could barely distinguish the surroundings when she first entered. Finally, in a dark corner, she spotted her mother with Frank Ewing. Oh, the drama critic—that made sense. They would be discussing theater. But why couldn't her mother just have said so?

Her mother followed Mr. Ewing's reviews and essays in a number of important publications, like *Variety* and *The New Yorker*. He was often a guest on radio and television programs too. Around Croton he had become a familiar figure since he had moved in with Delia Morrison, Mr. Sylvester's assistant at the *Croton-Harmon News*, but he lived there only part-time because of his work in the city.

Her mother's face fell as Chris approached the table. She was too early all right. Two partly filled glasses of white wine and some leftover dolma told Chris that they hadn't gotten very far in their meal.

"Now that you're here, why don't you pull up a chair?" her mother said to her. Was that a note of resentment? "How about some dolma?"

Chris shook her head no and sat down.

Frank Ewing shrugged off his brown corduroy jacket and tossed back his light brown hair, which had a tendency to fall into his right eye. Sitting down, he looked like a much smaller man. Actually, he was about six feet tall and pretty brawny. Chris thought he would be cuter if he just stayed sitting down all the time.

A waiter appeared with the main course.

"Delia tells me that if the paper reopens, you've got a job," Ewing said to Chris.

Her mother didn't join in the feeble effort to include her. She addressed Mr. Ewing. "Delia probably told you about the funeral, didn't she?"

"Yes, a private family affair. Good show that they asked Delia."

Why did Frank Ewing always sound so British? At least he didn't put on a British accent.

Chris cast an envious eye at her mother's shish kebab. "Mrs. Sylvester says that Delia has been a wonderful support to her since . . . uh . . . ." She faltered. Would you say "the murder?" "the accident?"

Ewing's head was bent over his fish. "Delia *is* wonderful."

With her fork, Chris's mother smoothly slid a kebab of lamb off the skewer. "Joan can't do without her now. Delia's been taking charge of just about everything, I understand—from funeral arrangements to legal questions. I'm worried about her, though. She's hardly had time to absorb the shock of Corey's death, because she's been working so hard to help Joan."

"Not any harder than she was under Corey's iron fist," Ewing said.

Huh? Chris hadn't heard of anything like that. Her mother was silent.

"The best thing for Delia," Frank Ewing continued, "would be for the paper to stay permanently closed. Truth is, though, I can't afford to support her yet. It's god-awful."

Well, it wouldn't be the best thing for *me* either, Chris thought.

"Frank! How delightful to find you here!" A large, solidly built man stooped over them.

"I'm shockingly early for my date," the bearish man said, skipping introductions, "the price of hyper-punctuality. May I join you while I wait?" The question was addressed to Frank Ewing.

Ewing pulled another extra chair from the next table and smiled a welcome. "With pleasure."

Chris caught a look of annoyance on her mother's face.

The newcomer relaxed in his chair, which was blocking the aisle in such a way that waiters had to detour around it. Ewing belatedly performed introductions. Philip Raven was a founding editor of the *New Guard Review*. Chris knew from Mrs. Novac that when it started out, in the 1930s, *NGR* had been one of the leading leftist literary magazines. But now, what with the rising anti-Communism and the Cold War, she said, the magazine was no longer so leftist.

"We were all shocked to hear about Corey Sylvester," Raven said to Frank Ewing. "He was such a valued member of our literary fraternity— and such a leader in the struggle against totalitarianism."

With difficulty, Ewing disengaged a fish bone from the tines of his fork. "Yes. He will be widely missed." At last he was able to spear a morsel of fish. "Did I tell you how much I loved your issue on 'Nation and Culture?'"

"What was that about?" Chris put in.

Raven didn't hear her, or else he preferred to ignore her. "Oh yes, "it *has* been a long time since we've met. That was last year's quarrel. Mailer was quite disagreeable."

"Well, I do agree with *NGR* that mucking about with social and economic issues never did much for literature—don't you think, Maya?" Ewing turned to her.

Her mother looked flustered. "I don't know. Shaw's plays are political, aren't they?"

Raven cleared his throat. "Shaw? Yes, he was political, but he saved his bite for his offstage commentaries. What got onto the stage was the witty bark that we all treasure. It can't compare with the kind of agitprop that the Communists regularly smuggle into their so-called art."

Her mother fell silent.

Chris leaned toward the bearish man. "I've been reading *Native Son*, by Richard Wright. It's political all right, and I think it's great literature." She avoided her mother's eye.

Raven turned to Frank Ewing. "I'm doubly pleased that I ran into you like this. I was going to call you about something very exciting. Have you heard about the new review that's coming out—this month, as a matter of fact?"

"I take it you mean *Encounter*?"

"Yes, *Encounter*, precisely."

Mr. Ewing explained to her mother, "It's a new literary magazine from England."

"I was talking to Stephen. . ." Raven began.

"That's Stephen Spender," Ewing interrupted, addressing her mother again. "He's one of the editors. You know, Stephen Spender, the poet."

Her mother managed a smile. "I know."

Chris looked at Ewing. "Oh, I've read Stephen Spender. He's pretty good."

". . . and he mentioned your name," Raven continued, above Chris's voice. "He wondered if you'd like to do a piece on the work of Alfred Lunt and Lynne Fontanne. Something about the Anglo-American acting couple would fit right in with the magazine's mission to introduce England and Europe to contemporary cultural currents on this shore and to show the Old World that we're not the barbarians they think we are."

"Um, certainly. That would be of great interest to me."

"Say, Frank," Raven said, "it seems that Sylvester and your art critic friend Wylie Maxwell had a bit of a dust-up over Maxwell's essay for *Encounter*. Maxwell may have wanted to submit it elsewhere. Do you know anything about it?"

"No. He and Corey were great friends, I thought."

"Well, Maxwell was fit to be tied. Apparently he felt betrayed by Corey." Raven took a step back. "Homer!" he called, waving a hand to a figure framed in the entryway. "Homer Graham Harris," he announced, like a butler at a ball.

"The critic," Ewing said to Chris's mother. "Teaches English at Smith College."

"I must leave you," Raven said. "Homer said it would have to be a quick lunch." He turned to Ewing. "May I ask Stephen to get in touch with you then?"

"By all means." Ewing fished around in his breast pocket for something. "I say, Raven, may I borrow your pen for a minute?"

Raven dropped a silver fountain pen onto the table. It looked fatter than most pens, Chris observed, and it was engraved with the initials "FSS." Not Raven's initials—that was odd. Mr. Ewing picked up the pen and jotted something down in a small notebook before he returned the pen to Raven.

"I assume," Mr. Ewing said, "that contributions for the first several issues are all lined up. I've a lot on my plate just now."

Raven leaned his hands on the back of Chris's mother's chair. "Yes, yes. To be sure. We'll do our best to accommodate you."

Was that a sigh of relief Chris detected coming from her mother as Raven moved away? Whatever did she want to put up with these boring people for?"

CHAPTER FIVE

Just in time. Chris had had enough of sunburn at Silver Lake and hanging out at her girlfriends' houses. When the phone call came asking her to report for work at the office of the *Croton-Harmon News* on the following Monday, she hopped up and down with glee.

That Monday turned out to be a muggy, mid-July day, and by the time that Chris reached the creaky old building on Riverside Avenue, she was feeling sticky and disheveled. Delia Morrison, the "chief editorial assistant," greeted her with a wide smile. "Chris, I'm so happy to see you. You're going to make a big difference around here." Chris looked around, half expecting Joan Sylvester to pop out of a closet.

"Oh," Delia said, reading her mind, "Joan couldn't be here today. I'm your designated office guide."

In the little cubicle that was her office, Delia invited her to sit down on a lumpy armchair and proceeded to tell her about the paper: a brief history, the mission to cover local news, staff structure, production process—always stopping for Chris's many questions. Then she led Chris on an exhaustive tour of the place, which consisted of one large main room divided into separate cubicles, each stuffed with files, books, and papers. It was going on one o'clock when Delia suggested a lunch break, after which she would explain what Chris's duties would be.

"Do you have your lunch with you?" Delia asked.

Chris looked blank. She hadn't given any thought to eating.

"Well, I have enough for two," Delia said. "But in the future you might want bring a bag lunch with you. There really is no good place for lunch around here."

They sat in Delia's cubicle and shared her ham and cheese sandwich and plums. It seemed to Chris like a picnic—as if it were her first day on an extraordinary holiday. Delia wanted to know all about her work on the "Tiger Rag" and what she expected to learn at the *Croton-Harmon News.*

Chris had never really gotten to know Delia, only exchanged greetings with her at the Sylvesters' open houses and other social functions. Why were people always badmouthing this nice lady? It wasn't fair. They gossiped about her and Frank Ewing, who was some ten years her junior, and who divided his time between his own place in Greenwich Village and Delia's. Well, so what if she and Mr. Ewing were "living in sin?" And so what if Mr. Ewing was younger?

No one seemed to know much about Delia's husband, or ex-husband, or whatever he was, who had moved away. She was either a divorcée or a soon-to-be divorcée—Chris was not sure which. Men seemed to find her very attractive, but gossipy women whispered about her strawberry blonde hair. "Does she or doesn't she?" they parroted the Clairol ad. Delia rented a small apartment in a large, single-family house in Harmon, near Chris's friend Gail's house. Somehow Chris had gotten the idea that Delia needed money.

By her second week on the job, Chris was beginning to think that Delia was really an overworked secretary. She mentioned to Chris that she rarely had the time to go into New York and join Frank Ewing on the city's theatrical scene. Ewing, as far as Chris could tell, kept himself pretty much apart from Croton's social life. At home, Chris's mother hadn't mentioned the lunch at the Dardanelles, so Chris kept quiet about it too.

Chris's fantasies about being sent out on assignment as a reporter-in-training were beginning to fade. But she could tell that what she did by way of answering the phone, filing, typing invoices, and running errands was a godsend to Delia. Delia's regular duties had expanded to learning about estate law, taking shorthand for Mrs. Sylvester at her meetings with the family lawyers, and cleaning out Mr. Sylvester's office.

Whenever her schedule permitted, Delia sat down for lunch with Chris in her cubicle. The lumpy old armchair had become a comfortable place. Chris loved listening to all Delia's stories about the various characters in Croton who had complained about news items, sent crackpot letters to the paper, and even attempted a lawsuit or two.

Now, toward the end of July, on a damp Friday, Chris sat at the wobbly wooden table in the front of the office that served as her desk and a reception area, chewing on a licorice stick from Pop Berger's as she tried to sort the various bills and invoices according to Delia's instructions. The table top was covered with wooden filing boxes, which would eventually be returned to a set of built-in wall shelves running along one side wall of the large room.

She liked the alien world of the Lower Village with its ramshackle small store fronts and delivery trucks facing the railroad tracks and the river. It somehow made her feel adventurous, like a real reporter posted in a far-flung place. The residential part of the Lower Village was totally different from the other parts of Croton—Mt. Airy, or the Upper Village, or Harmon. The two- and three-family, wood-frame houses that lined the streets of the wide hill stretching from Riverside Avenue to the Upper Village were occupied by descendants of the Italian and Irish immigrant families who had helped to build the New York Central railroad and the Croton Dam. The fathers and sons in many of these families still worked for the New York Central line.

Joan Sylvester swept in with a bit of breeze from the Hudson. She was professionally dressed in a gabardine suit. "Chris, dear, I'm afraid that you'll have to mind the store for a few minutes. I'm going to borrow Delia for a quick run to the house. After you go through those bills, will you begin sorting the material on the shelves in the large office?"

She never referred to this space, in the center of the floor, as Mr. Sylvester's office. "Office" was anyway not exactly the right word for this larger cubicle in the maze of all the others that filled the store front, which was lit unsatisfactorily by long, overhead fluorescent bulbs. In the back were a little kitchenette and bathroom. Mrs. Sylvester and Delia had been spending every spare minute trying to clear out Mr. Sylvester's cubicle. He had evidently let no one disturb his inner sanctum. Stacks of books, pamphlets, papers, magazines, back issues of *The Croton-Harmon News* and other assorted items were piled up in a dusty bookcase, on top of file cabinets, on the floor, and even on the two sagging, mustard brown armchairs meant for visitors.

The other day Mrs. Sylvester had come across a well-worn copy of *Winnie-the-Pooh* underneath a stack of yellowed issues of the *Citizen Register*, a Croton/Ossining daily. She held up the volume to Chris. "My husband used to read this to our children when they were small," she said to Chris, her eyes filling with tears. Although Mrs. Sylvester and Delia did housecleaning whenever they could, periodically carting off superfluous material to the Sylvesters' house on Quaker Bridge Road, it seemed that they were always discovering more to do. Chris got the overflow.

Now Chris was thankful for the women's absence. It gave her a chance to break the monotony by poking around where she had no business, and goofing off a bit. She was especially intrigued by the old photos lining the office's southern wall. Someone had framed ragged images of nineteenth-century passenger and freight boats docked at what was then called Croton Landing. Men were straining to unload large stone blocks from a local quarry, which were probably used for building the Croton Dam. There were also photos from later on, of the freight and passenger trains that stopped at the Croton North Railroad Station. Now, of course, the big station was in Harmon. In the fading brown and white photos of the many businesses on Riverside Drive, she could recognize some that were still standing today: Powley's jewelry store, Gerstein's Hardware, and Scalzo's Plumbing.

She slogged her way through the bills and invoices and moved on to the next chore. Mrs. Sylvester had given her detailed instructions—even writing out some of them—on how to sort the chaos cluttering her late husband's bookshelves. Now that Joan Sylvester and Delia had cleared his desk and some other surfaces, she could begin.

It was strange to see the office more or less as it would have been if Mr. Sylvester were still alive. It was strange that his space looked so *inhabited.* It looked like someone had just tossed things around so that they landed helter-skelter anywhere. Chris would much rather have let everything be. But she gamely drew up a stepladder and started in on the top shelf. E.H. Gombrich's *The Story of Art* leaned cozily against John O'Hara's *A Rage to Live.* A stash of cheap pens and a bunch of "I Like Ike" buttons fell out of a manila folder. A letterhead envelope turned out to contain photographs of the Starlight Drive-in Theater on Route 9.

She had just gotten to the next shelf when a piece of paper fluttered out of a coffee-stained copy of the *Best American Short Stories* of 1951. She climbed down from the little ladder to retrieve it.

It was dated March 1953.

Corey: Your unflattering editorial on my participation in the plans for the Tarrytown Arts Center was gratuitously nasty. First of all, I am not in it alone, but am working with colleagues in my firm. So why personalize it? Secondly, the project is now in such an early planning stage that you'd think it wouldn't even be worth your attention let alone the effort you must have put into writing your appraisal. Or maybe it costs you no effort to be cutting? Thirdly, what do my politics (which you thoroughly misunderstand) have to do with this project? I deplore your entirely inappropriate tone. This is not the first time you have attacked me in print, but I hope that it will be the last. In the meantime, an apology, preferably a public one, would certainly be in order. Don't forget—I have plenty of influential friends. Sandor

She stood holding the note between her thumb and forefinger, as if it were a dirty rag. If the cops ever got hold of it, they would rake Mr. Novac over the coals.

Sometimes Chris felt destined to be an observer. She often thought of the play she had seen with her mother, "I Am a Camera" by John van Druten. She had also read Christopher Isherwood's *Berlin Stories,* which inspired it. She would always think how strangely she herself resembled a camera. "I am a camera with its shutter open, quite passive, recording, not thinking," Isherwood said. Wasn't she always watching other people's lives, rarely participating? Well, wasn't that what reporters did? But when would she start to lead her own life?

A scratching at the door pulled her back to the present. Willie! She had forgotten all about him. No one wanted him inside the office, so she had left him outside. With her mother again in New York for the day and her father at work in his home office, she couldn't avoid taking the dog with her. But it was such a long, unaccustomed walk from home to Riverside Avenue that she hadn't wanted to bother with a leash, and Willie had finally tired of running about by himself. She stuffed the piece of paper into her bag.

"Well, come on in then," Chris said, opening the door to admit the dog. His tongue was hanging out of his mouth, his eyes bright with anticipation.

"Okay." Chris dug a dog biscuit out of a pocket. "Here. And if you're good you can stay inside for a few minutes, but then I have to kick you out."

Willie chomped and growled with contentment, his tail wagging.

What to do with Mr. Novac's letter? Should she take it home and hide it? Burn it? If he was the chief suspect, wasn't this evidence? And wasn't there some kind of law about withholding evidence? Dick Tracy probably wouldn't approve of her. But evidence of what? Of motive, that's what. No, unconvincing. So Mr. Novac got upset. It didn't mean he killed Mr. Sylvester. She didn't remember the editorial Mr. Novac mentioned, and besides, she hadn't really started reading the village newspaper until very recently. Mr. Novac was probably right that Mr. Sylvester could have written about something else. On the other hand, Mr. Novac's letter did sound threatening. The butterflies in her stomach that had been quiet since June 19 began to flutter again. She had to make a decision. All she knew was that she wasn't going to get Mr. Novac into deeper hot water.

She took another piece of licorice and forced herself to return to her task. What else would she find? Willie, who loved Kleenex, helped himself to one from a box that was on the floor. When Chris snatched the box from him he howled in frustration and jumped to retrieve it from the desk, over-turning a letter tray in the process. A few papers scattered onto the floor. On top was a note from Wiley Maxwell—didn't those boring men at the Dardanelles mention him?

As if in haste, Maxwell had scrawled his note, dated June 10, on *Time Magazine* office memo paper. *Happy to accept the invitation for a visit with you and your family the weekend of the 19*th. *See you at the rally first? I'd like to finish picking that bone with you before our visit in Croton. I still can't believe that you would go behind my back and com-promise my career.*

At that moment Willie growled and pawed at the box of Kleenex, knocking it to the floor.

"That's it for you, doggie," she said. As she opened the door to shoo out the dog, she saw a pair of blue trousers moving along Riverside Avenue toward the intersection with Brook Street.

"Oh, Officer Riley! Sir!" she called out.

Chuck Riley turned and smiled his appreciation. Chris understood. Not many of the Croton kids called him sir.

"Hi, Chris. Are you a reporter in training now?"

"Don't I wish! I'm just helping out around the office."

"Good for you." The policeman with the deep-set eyes stood awkwardly in front of the door frame, his hands in his pockets.

Chris tried to block Willie, who was doing his best to get inside the of-fice. "Officer Riley, have you finished questioning everyone?"

"You mean on the Sylvester case? Nowhere near. We have a lot of work to do."

"Do you think the red letters have anything to do with it?"

"Red letters? Oh, you mean those anonymous notes," Riley said. "We've had quite a few complaints about those."

"Well, will people who got the letters be suspects?"

"I really can't say, Chris." He prepared to move on.

Willie was nuzzling Chris's knees. "So since I'm working here on the paper, can I help you with anything?"

He smiled at her. "Sure, sure, Chris. Just keep an eye out for anything unusual."

"Okay." She stood on one leg, rubbing it with the other. Officer Riley was so nice. He'd be shocked to know that she might be committing a criminal offense. Right at this very moment she could be "obstructing justice" by not giving him her "evidence"—if that's what it was.

"Do you know someone named Wylie Maxwell?" she finally asked him.

"Why do you want to know?" There was something very charming about the way he half-smiled at her.

"Oh, I overheard Delia mentioning him on the phone, and I just wondered if he lived in Croton," she lied, uneasy at the thought that maybe she had said too much.

"*Wylie* Maxwell? Hm-m-m. There's Peter. . . and his son Tobias. No Wylie that I know of in Croton. What do you know about this Wylie Maxwell?"

The Airedale snuggled up to Chris's calf and then darted past her into the office. It was one of his favorite tricks, and this time she could have hugged him for it. Saved by the dog.

"Uh-oh—Willie! Sorry, Officer Riley, I have to go," she apologized, as she lunged after the Airedale.

CHAPTER SIX

What was that bone that Wylie Maxwell had to pick with Mr. Sylvester? Was Rosie's father threatening Mr. Sylvester with the power of his "influential friends?" It got so that Chris couldn't stop her mind from churning her "evidence." She had to shake herself into paying attention to Rosie.

"Can you imagine?" Rosie said, as they sat on their towels at the small, pebbly beach at Silver Lake. "My mother actually asked me to pay a condolence call to Mrs. Sylvester tomorrow with your mother. She says it's 'seriously overdue.' She's really nervous about it. I think it's a terrible idea."

A pebble landed at Chris's feet, and she looked up to see their classmates Marty Kruger and Pete Dawes waving from a distance. "Hey, wanna swim out to Third Rock?" Marty called.

Even though Pete was in the chess club Chris had started at the high school, she made a practice of ignoring him elsewhere. He and the boys in their class were such babies. Rosie hadn't even turned her head. Their small crowd of girlfriends didn't deign to associate with them.

"No," Chris called back. "We have something to discuss."

"Private business," Pete shouted to Marty for their benefit. "They always have private business."

"Couple of weirdos," Marty shouted back.

"Yeah, I'm going on the condolence call too," Chris answered Rosie. "It won't be so bad. Joan is really O.K."

"Oh, you call her 'Joan' now?"

Well, she didn't, but Mrs. Sylvester had asked her to. She hung her head and mumbled, "Sometimes."

The next afternoon was warm and muggy. Her father wasn't accompanying them, because as Village Manager he had paid a separate visit to Joan Sylvester, in part to discuss the public memorial service for Mr. Sylvester that would be held after Labor Day.

"Sandor finally agreed with me that I can represent him today," Mrs. Novac said from the passenger seat in Chris's parents' battered Volkswagen Beetle. "It would have been very awkward for him to come with us."

Chris had heard more than she wanted to about Rosie's mother's musings on the subject. There were so many precautions to take now that Rosie's father was a suspect.

"Chris says that Joan's been her usual self from the beginning," her mother said, from behind the steering wheel.

"Yes, "Mrs. Novac agreed, "She is a stoic, that woman." She pushed back a stray lock of hair from her French twist.

"Either that, or she's putting on a great act."

Her mother seemed keyed up. Chris waited.

"I can't go swimming with you tomorrow," Rosie said to her. "I have to . . ."

Chris put a finger to her lips and craned her neck forward.

It came out as they turned onto Route 129 from Grand Street. "Lili, I've been asked to audition for the part of Maggie in *What Every Woman Knows.*"

That was a surprise. It was the first time that Chris had heard anything about it.

Her mother sounded breathless. "I found a letter in my Scarborough mailbox yesterday, when I went in for a meeting. It was from Viktor Cornelius—the director." Her mother swung onto Quaker Bridge Road. The windows were open to the warm sunshine, and Chris could barely make out the conversation over the breeze ruffling the Croton River. "I haven't even told Gil yet."

"Now, Maya," Mrs. Novac said, "you wouldn't be afraid to tell him, would you? *You, my feminist friend!*"

Chris's mother swerved to avoid a squirrel. "Well, yes, I suppose I am a little hesitant. We need my salary. This is an off-Broadway production, and off-Broadway isn't exactly a gold mine."

Yes, they would definitely need the money if her mother was going to leave Scarborough. They were already trying to economize, what with the loss of her father's syndicated comic strip. Okay, Chris could always cut down on the books she liked to buy and start a college fund. But maybe soon she'd have to contribute the money to household expenses. And maybe they wouldn't even be able to afford college for her. She'd have to give up her allowance and start saving her wages from the newspaper.

As they pulled into the Sylvesters' driveway, Chris flashed back to the afternoon of the last open house, less than a month ago. The big news had been the discovery of Mr. Lewis's and Mrs. Muller's affair. It was a different world then.

Joan Sylvester bustled out of the open French doors and greeted them as if hosting one of her parties. "Hello, dears," she smiled, throwing her arms around the two adults and escorting them all inside. "So lovely of you to come over. Delia is just bringing tea."

Chris bit her lip to keep from commenting. Delia bringing tea? Was Delia moonlighting as maid-of-all-work?

Delia didn't look like a housemaid in her cream-colored satin blouse and wide black slacks. She sat down at the dining table with Mrs. Sylvester and her guests in front of a big silver tea service and a platter of petit fours.

Delia poured the tea into smallish porcelain cups as Mrs. Sylvester passed around pastries. Mrs. Sylvester chuckled as she looked at Chris's mother and Mrs. Novac. "I'm not offering you girls cocktails at this early hour. I don't want you returning to your husbands with liquor on your breath." Mrs. Sylvester herself passed up on the pastry. "Delia and I have finally started in on the closets. I couldn't move an inch without this kind lady."

"Each decision is difficult," Delia said, as if from far away and in awe of her new set of responsibilities.

"Oh, darling, you make it so much easier for me with your wonderful wisdom." She reached over to pat Delia gently on the shoulder.

Rosie's mother broke the silence. "It is much better not to have to take the decisions all by oneself. Corinne must be a great comfort too."

The Sylvesters' daughter Corinne had flown in for the family funeral from Hollywood, where she had been working at bit parts in the movies, and she had remained with her mother for several weeks. The Sylvesters' son Jack and his family, who lived in Connecticut, had been back to visit a few times after the funeral.

Joan Sylvester moved her chair closer to the table, as if getting down to brass tacks. "Now tell me, all of you, how do you think the paper has been doing?"

Mrs. Novac coughed politely.

"Your feature on Corey and the history of the newspaper was just right," said Chris's mother. "I really liked that photo of the original staff."

"Very fair and balanced coverage," said Mrs. Novac.

Wait! It sounded like Mr. Sylvester himself on the day of the vigil talking about the paper's "objectivity."

Mrs. Sylvester turned directly to Rosie's mother. "I'm so glad that you think so, darling."

How could Mrs. Sylvester be so cool? It was almost as if nothing at all had happened. And could Mrs. Novac really mean what she said about "balanced coverage?"

Mrs. Sylvester's guests—except possibly Rosie—knew that there had been no coverage of the ongoing criminal investigation except to say that it was taking place. Mrs. Sylvester's eyes went moist very easily these days.

"I've promised myself that I would try to follow Corey's example and maintain the tradition of good journalism."

What a joke! Is she serious? What would Mr. Novac say?

Chris's mother set down her empty cup on the glass-topped table and accepted a refill from Delia. "I'm happy to learn that you and Gil have come up with a plan for the memorial. The high school auditorium should be just about large enough."

"I think so, yes," said Mrs. Sylvester. "We're not quite done with the list of speakers. Gil will be the M.C., of course, and Ralph Carr has said that he will speak." Ralph Carr was the editor of Ossining's *Citizen Register*. At least one former Village Manager would be speaking, as well as a number of other village notables and a few of the newspaper's chief advertisers. Some chamber music was also planned. Rosie had not been asked to play.

Delia excused herself, and the three women chatted a while about the Sylvesters' children and grandchildren and about various local friends who had been especially helpful to Mrs. Sylvester. Chris munched on some petit fours, and Rosie sat stiff and silent.

A slight chill descended on the room.

Mrs. Sylvester rose from her chair. "Let me show you," she said, "a bit of gardening I've done."

Chris and Rosie followed their mothers as Mrs. Sylvester shepherded them past the gazebo and a few yards into the woods, where they spied a clearing. The hostess smiled at their surprise. "Of course, I didn't move the earth—I got the De Lorenzo Brothers in. But I did plant that sapling." Around the sapling, she said, she was planning to plant some bulbs and lilac bushes. "It's a spruce. Corey always loved spruces, even though he never did remember the name. Eventually I may put a bench or two around the tree, and maybe a stone fountain."

They stood quietly for a minute or two. In the presence of this living memorial Chris found herself shivering in the afternoon sun.

As they headed back toward the house, Delia intercepted them.

"Joan," she whispered, "Mr. Maxwell is here."

Wylie Maxwell? What a stroke of luck!

Mrs. Sylvester wrinkled her brows momentarily. "He wasn't supposed to arrive until dinner time."

"He apologized. Said the 5:49 would have gotten him here too late, so he took the 3:32."

"Oh, well, he'll just have to keep me company while I cook."

Crunching weeds underfoot, they approached the house to see a tall young man waving a greeting from just outside the French doors.

The man bent over to give Mrs. Sylvester a hug. "Sorry I turned up early. But I thought it would be better than arriving an hour late."

"I'm pleased to see you, Wylie," she said. "Thank you so much for taking the trouble to come."

"Wylie is a friend of Jack's from college," Mrs. Sylvester explained by way of introduction.

With his crew cut, navy blue blazer, and white bucks, Wylie Maxwell looked quite young. Still very much the Yalie.

"Oh, Mrs. Novac," said Maxwell, as Chris winced for her, "how opportune. I've been eager to meet you and your husband. I've heard so much about you."

What had he heard, Chris wondered, that Rosie's father was a prime suspect?

Mrs. Sylvester smiled up at her latest guest. "Wylie is on the arts staff at *Time Magazine*. Corey had spoken to him about doing a feature on Sandor and his firm."

Wylie Maxwell turned to Rosie's mother. "And I still hope to do it."

Delia offered to show Maxwell the memorial tree. She had retrieved a wide-brimmed straw hat and fixed it on her head.

The remaining guests watched Delia and Maxwell retreat into the woods. Mrs. Sylvester turned to Chris and Rosie's mothers. "Wylie and

Jack hadn't seen each other since college. But not long ago they met up at a fund-raiser for Prescott Bush." She was met with blank looks. "Prescott S. Bush. You know, the senator from Connecticut who defeated Abe Ribicoff last year. Wylie married a girl from his wife's side of the family."

Chris racked her brain. Prescott Bush . . . oh yes, he was already on a few Senate committees. But then, there was something else. What was it?

"Jack and Wylie vaguely knew his son, George Herbert, at Yale. Wylie says that young George is going places fast."

Rosie's mother was looking more and more uncomfortable. But finally Delia and Wylie came into view, giving the other guests a chance to make their exit. A few leaves from the Sylvesters' lush Japanese maple clung to Delia's hat.

Chris could see that once they got into the car, Mrs. Novac began to relax. "What is it about Prescott Bush?" she asked anyone who would answer. "I think I've heard something funny about him." As the car descended toward the bridge over the Croton River, she answered her own question. "Oh, now it's coming back to me. Something about the Nazis. Something about his bank's connections with the Nazis. Yes, that's it. Quite a scandal."

Chris's mother was concentrating on the sharp turn onto Route 129. "M-m-m. So many awful rumors floating around these days. You never know who turns out to have supported Hitler."

"Had you heard of Mr. Wylie Maxwell?" Mrs. Novac asked.

"Yes. I've met him here and there, in New York," Chris's mother said.

"Really? What puzzles me is how he knows I'm married to Sandor. He called me Mrs. Novac."

Rosie's mother tolerated "Mrs. Novac" only from Rosie's friends and local merchants.

◆　◆　◆

The next morning, a mailman came into the newspaper office with a special delivery letter for Delia. Willie, who had been napping under Chris's table, sprang into action, barking excitedly. Chris was once again the only one minding the store. Delia and Joan Sylvester, who were at the Sylvesters' house for the day, might come back briefly before noon, her boss had said, or they might not. Chris instructed the mailman to leave the letter on Delia's desk.

Special Delivery! What could that be? Maybe it had to do with Mr. Sylvester's death. She told herself that that was dumb. If it was about Mr. Sylvester, wouldn't they have written Mrs. Sylvester? But she couldn't be sure, and she had to do everything possible to protect Rosie's father.

As soon as the mailman was out the door, Chris raced to examine the letter. It was from a Dr. Leopold Kamm on Nordica Drive, in the Harmon section of town. Kamm! He was that creepy cult psychiatrist who had attracted a crowd of followers to Croton. Her friend Gail's family had been members of his group once. Chris held the letter up to the light, but it was opaque. She dropped it on top of the desk and, like a bird of prey, circled around it. She was consumed with curiosity. What to do? Steaming it open was the only way, but she didn't dare risk being interrupted by Delia herself.

"C'mon, doggie," she said to Willie, "we're going for a walk." Delia's house, right down the street from her friend Gail Kornberg's, was a hike, but it would be worth it. She dropped the letter into her green book bag, leashed the dog, and locked the door behind them.

She hadn't come up with a plan. Delia wouldn't be there, she knew, and so maybe she could just go in, steam open the letter there, reseal it, and leave. On the other hand, if Frank Ewing were there, maybe he would open it right in front of her and spill some beans.

It was very warm at midday, and it took her almost an hour to reach Delia's house. She had to keep stopping for Willie, who insisted on sniffing around every other tree.

Delia's apartment was in a small wing of a modern, white stucco house with a flat roof. Chris had never been inside it, but it was an object of her speculation. It was the only such dwelling in the neighborhood, which was filled with spacious, sturdy wood-frame houses of two and three stories. The stucco house was constructed of what looked like modular rectangular boxes irregularly arranged. On top of the biggest one was a terrace with plantings and small trees, graced by an umbrella-shaded table and various lounging chairs. In the good weather she and Gail often glimpsed people drinking or dining or just having a good time up there.

Chimes sounded when she rang the doorbell. No answer. After several more tries, she tied Willie to a tree and gently pushed open the door. She was in a kitchen. Voices seemed to be coming from a room beyond the kitchen. Directly opposite the door where she had entered was another door open to a dark, narrow hallway, at the end of which, presumably, there was a living room.

She sat at the square Formica-topped table squeezed into the middle of the kitchen and strained to make out what was being said. Next to the sugar bowl on the table was a fat silver pen. It looked familiar. Chris picked it up and saw the initials "FSS" engraved on it. FSS—where had she come across that before? Oh yes, at the Dardanelles. It was a pen identical to Mr. Raven's. Was he here too?

The talking had ceased. She heard a rustling, as of papers being shuffled.

"Here, Frank. Here's my draft for the piece on Croton artists. You know it was supposed to go to *The New Yorker*."

"M-m-m, yes, you did tell me." Pause. Probably Frank Ewing was reading something. "Now that's a good opening—perfect for *Encounter*. Wylie, you call her 'Mrs. Novac' here. It's an unpardonable gaffe."

Wylie Maxwell? Was he still here? Chris held her breath.

"Oh, yes, what is it again? Carrera? Cardera?" Maxwell's voice was maddeningly soft and velvety.

"Carrière. You must get it right, Wylie. You'll make an utter fool of yourself if this gets by the editors."

"Okay. It's just that I don't know her work at all. Never been interested. My tastes run more to the New York School."

"I sympathize, old chap. But her name is Liliane Carrière."

"I'll try to get it through my noggin. What do you think of my plan?"

Ewing's voice was scratchy. "Killing the proverbial two birds with one stone, one might say. Now that we've lost Corey, you'll need to find another route to Sandor. I don't think that Joan will be inclined to get you two together."

Why not? Because Mr. Novac is a suspect, dummy, that's why.

"Well, it just so happens that I met her yesterday, at the Sylvesters' house."

"Oh, good," said Ewing. "Sandor's very proud of his wife, so he'll undoubtedly be no obstacle to the double feature. Of course you will have to read up on Lili's work before your first interview."

"And visit the Latham Gallery, which I intend to do right away. Look, Frank, I know how much Corey wanted the piece for *Encounter*. And that you agreed with him. But I had already talked to the people at *The New Yorker* about it. Then they reneged. I strongly suspect that Corey talked them out of it. I wouldn't have thought he'd do that to me. He was my mentor, my second father. You know Corey had connections everywhere. He could quash a deal with a phone call if he wanted to."

They went on talking, but their voices were drowned out by Willie, who had begun to bark. At first it was a plaintive whine, but as the dog realized that Chris wasn't going to come back immediately, he emitted staccato, yapping reproaches.

Shut up, Willie. Please?

When she could tune back in, she heard Frank Ewing clearing his throat. "I don't know anything about Corey's plans for your piece, Wylie. But it really *is* ideal for *Encounter*. Since you're writing about *Croton* artists, you can emphasize just how far Sandor, Lili, and their crowd lean to the political left."

"Corey wanted me to do that. But I want to make the political point without getting too personal. What I want to get across is how political art undermines the very notion of art."

Ewing's voice: "Oh good. So it will be an expansion of that essay you did for *Time Magazine* on abstract art and politics."

Maxwell: "M-m. That's the general idea."

What is? I don't get it.

Ewing: "Y-e-e-s. I can see the title now: 'Beyond Politics: The Abstract Expression of Pure Art.' You'll make Sandor, Lili, and our local crew of artists look very retrograde."

Whatever they're talking about, it doesn't sound good for Mr. and Mrs. Novac.

Ewing: "It's hard to separate political art from leftists, isn't it? It seems that political art these days comes almost exclusively from the left. Now you may know that Corey eventually wanted to write something about Gil's work."

"Gil Gooding?"

Oh, no.

"Yes. Gooding hasn't been producing many comic strips since his syndicated strip was suspended, but he will most surely try for a comeback. He's someone to watch. And now that he's Village Manager, he has a certain amount of influence in these parts."

Maxwell: "Funny you should mention Gooding. I'd been thinking of writing something about cartoonists. Look what I have by Gooding. I found it in our files. It's from last year. Needless to say, *Time* didn't publish it."

Ewing: "Oh yes, the McCarthy cartoon. It circulated around Croton. A bit crude, I think."

Must be the one about McCarthy and modern art. I love that cartoon. I remember Daddy saying that anti-Communists don't make good art critics.

Ewing: "Quite. Would be excellent for an essay on political cartoonists."

Willie was now howling piteously.

Maxwell: "Confound that dreadful dog. Listen, we better get going. We don't want anyone to see that you didn't leave Croton yesterday."

What was that supposed to mean? Why were they meeting secretly?

Chairs scraped noisily. Would they come out this way? No time to get to get outside. As the footsteps approached, she opened the outside door and then slammed it shut, as if she had just come in.

The two men stopped short at the sight of her.

"Uh, excuse me," Chris said, "uh . . . I work with Delia, and I was looking for her."

Frank Ewing's stare was distinctly unwelcoming. "Oh yes, you're the Gooding girl."

"I rang the bell, but no one answered, so I thought I'd leave Delia a note." There was no way she'd hand over the letter now. She held up the pen that was on the formica table. "Oh, by the way, does this pen belong to either one of you?"

Maxwell picked it up and grinned at her. "Yes, thanks—it's mine. Don't want to forget it."

"What does "FSS" stand for?" Chris asked.

"'From Stephen Spender,'" Maxwell said with a note of pride. "Remember, Frank? He passed them out to all of us at that anniversary party for the *New Guard Review*."

Willie let out a loud, piteous howl.

Ewing ran an impatient hand through his hair. "Is that infernal beast yours? Did you have to come by with him? Haven't you heard of the telephone?"

He was right. She didn't have an answer.

"Now, if you'll excuse us, we have an engagement. Perhaps you'd like to tend to that hound of yours."

CHAPTER SEVEN

It was 12:30 by the time Chris got back to the office. No sign of Delia or Mrs. Sylvester. She would just have to risk it. She took the teakettle from the shelf in the kitchenette, filled it with water from the tap, and set it on the hot plate. If Delia and Mrs. Sylvester should walk in, she'd stuff the letter away and say that she was making tea. She had never tried to steam open a letter before. It wasn't as easy as it sounded in the mystery stories. But soon the flap started to unfurl, and she was able to pry it open without tearing it. Clutching the envelope in one hand and the letter in the other, she raced to the nearest desk.

Dear Delia,

I am very distressed that you have not responded to my letters. Your decision to leave us seems to have occurred quite abruptly, and I do think that you owe me an explanation as to what is going on. Why don't you take some time to think about everything and then come to our annual Labor Day party? Come early, so that you and I can have a little talk. To break off in this manner is not at all advisable. You know that it will leave many unresolved issues.

Please reply to me as soon as possible. I would prefer it if you would telephone me at my office, but you may also reply by return mail.

Yours sincerely,
Dr. Leopold H. Kamm

It sounded sinister. Why did Kamm want to hold onto Delia? What was he afraid of? The note could be evidence, but for what Chris had no idea. Just in case it was, she scribbled a copy of it before refolding it and returning it to the envelope, which she resealed in what she considered a professional glue job. She sat still for some minutes, puzzling over the words. Dr. Kamm had a large following in Croton. Recently not only Gail's family but a number of others had left the group, or what her father called the cult. Her parents had told her that many of his followers moved to Croton to be near him. But she never could extract much more information from them. Chris's father often repeated his little riff on Kipling: "Oh, Communists are Communists, and Kammunists are Kammunists, and sometimes the twain shall meet."

◆　　◆　　◆

On her way home, Chris stopped at the Municipal Building to get a copy of *The Jungle* at the library. A teacher had said that it was a classic tale of muck-raking. Leaving the reluctant Willie outside, she had reached the landing of the second floor when she heard voices coming from her father's office. She rapped on the frosted glass window, and without waiting for permission, opened the door. The small office was packed with a group of men sitting around her father's desk. Her father looked straight through her for a second.

Almost directly in front of her was a short, wiry man with hair like a bristle brush. It couldn't be! Yup, no doubt about it—it was the guy she had given the slip to at the rally, who had wanted her notebook. Bristle-Head! What was *he* doing here? She had interrupted him in mid-speech. She could catch only enough to recognize his high, squeaky voice. With him were Detective Inspector Mangone, Chuck Riley, and four other policemen. That was just about the entire force! There was also another man, a tweedy-looking fellow with a pipe, whom she did not recognize.

"Hi, Daddy!" she ventured on the off chance that she might rate an introduction. Her father shot her his "Beat it!" look, but she wasn't going to leave until she had taken in the scene.

Bristle-Head's feet barely reached the floor from the seat of a rickety swivel chair. He was wearing a brown fedora that was too big for his head. As he favored Chris with a brief stare, his hat slipped to the floor. He nearly tipped over in the chair as he bent to retrieve it. Then he sat it on his knees. The hat didn't go at all with that same old black jacket, worn to a shine at the elbows. He dropped his cigarette into the nearest ashtray without extinguishing it, and coughed.

"My daughter," Chris's father announced apologetically. "Chris, I'm afraid that we're very busy just now."

Okay, she could take a hint. Outside, she stood next to the door and perked up her ears. She was becoming a first-class eavesdropper.

Through the open transom, she could hear Bristle-Head's high, squeaky voice surprisingly clearly. "We've got some of the Reds in this town covered, even ones who weren't at the rally. A .. uh . . . conspiracy is still not out of the question. We try to keep track of their movements. Those poison pen notes have helped us track them too. We've learned a thing or two about Corey Sylvester that may be of interest. He used to be in the Communist Party. If he wasn't in it, he was damn close. When he went to work for Batten, Barton, Durstine & Osborne he figured he'd try to make just enough money in advertising to support himself as a writer. He hung around with a few literary wannabes, people he had met in college and so forth."

An unfamiliar voice: "Pike, please get to the point." Probably the tweedy pipe-smoker.

"These writers were all pinkos. But Sylvester's literary career fizzled. He met a girl, got married, had a family, and kept on working at the ad agency. All the time he maybe had the Great American Novel stashed away in a desk drawer—who knows? Anyhow, he finally gets disgusted and quits the Party, in 1939. By this time he's made a name for himself in the advertising business, and some of his pals have become major eggheads on the New York scene. Now here's the meat: some of these pals—most of them in fact—drop out of the Party too. But, see, they're still big-time eggheads. They hang around small magazines and larger ones even; they give lectures and do poetry readings. Sylvester gets a short story published. These guys, we figure can be helpful to us. Why? Because they can help fight the Commies."

Was Bristle-Head saying something about Mr. Sylvester and the F.B.I.? Chris could hear a window creak open.

Pipe-smoker: "Pike. We don't have all day."

Cough. The squeaky voice continued. "How can they help fight the Commies? Well, for one thing, the ex-Communists have information on their friends who are still in the Party. For another, these people are writers, so they can write about the Commies they knew and still know, even if they're not best friends with them. A lot of these people are now with the Congress for Cultural Freedom. We need the Congress to help fight the Commies, no doubt about it. Former American Commie eggheads can discredit the eggheads who are still in the Party, and they can help spread the message of freedom around the world. So the ex-Communists are useful, very useful."

Pipe-smoker: "Get back to Sylvester, please."

"O.K., Sylvester. So Sylvester moves to Croton in 1946. Why? For one thing, he's made a pile of money, so he can afford to leave the ad agency. Croton is a nice place to move to—picturesque. For another, Croton is filled with writers and artists, and he likes writers and artists. Sylvester decides to buy the *Croton-Harmon News,* and he becomes valuable. My outfit hopes that he'll get information on his neighbors for us, maybe write some unflattering things about the ones who are Commies. Get the picture?"

"So . . ." That was Chuck Riley's voice. "Mr. Sylvester had a lot of enemies?"

Bristle-Head: "You got it, sonny. At least, he may have had a lot of friendly enemies."

Another cough, as Bristle-Head goes on. "So Wylie Maxwell turns up at the Sylvesters' open house in May. He's a friend of the son, Jack Sylvester, but Jack wasn't there. So maybe Maxwell and Sylvester have some items to discuss. Maxwell has connections in the Congress for Cultural Freedom, we think, but we haven't confirmed that yet. *Time*, Maxwell's employer, doesn't like the Commies either. What you guys here can do is to keep tabs on this Wylie Maxwell whenever he comes around Croton. He turned up here yesterday to visit Joan Sylvester. Courtesy call to the widow. That makes sense. But first he gets chauffeured around by Frank Ewing, who takes him to his place, and then Maxwell shows up there again, the next day. What do we have on Ewing? Not much, but we're working on it. You can help us there too."

Pipe-smoker: "What do you know about Joan Sylvester's politics?"

"Mrs. Sylvester? Aw, she's his wife."

Pipe-smoker: "So what? I'm a Democrat; my wife is a Republican. So far Joan Sylvester hasn't established any clear editorial policy for the newspaper."

"I don't know. We don't know much about Mrs. Sylvester. She's not mixed up in the murder, so what difference does it make?"

Pipe-smoker: "Do we know if she was on the train—or if she had a friend on the train?"

Bristle-Head: "Aw, nuts. She's a *woman*."

Pipe-smoker: "Women *have* been convicted of murder, Pike." Loud sigh. "What you've told us is all very well. But as I see it, your information adds up to nothing more than a tale of political camaraderie among three literary types. How do you get from there to murder?"

Silence.

Pipe-smoker again: "Were Sylvester, Maxwell, or Ewing paid informants? Or did they cozy up to you for the sheer patriotism of it?"

"I don't know everything, Stewart. But we'll keep you up-to-date."

So the pipe-smoker is named Stewart. But who's Stewart?

Stewart: "You bet you will. Information is your business, isn't it? But don't let's forget our basics. We haven't moved forward an inch on motive, and all we have for a suspect so far is Novac. There's a lot of legwork that still needs to be done. You ask for reinforcements here, I'll send them up. You want my help? I'm on twenty-four-hour call."

◆   ◆   ◆

Chris was waiting for her father to bawl her out once he came home. But he went unexpectedly easy on her. "Chris, how many times have I told you not to interrupt me at the Municipal Building? And please—never come into my office without waiting for my say-so."

Chris got out the dishes and began to set the table. She felt emboldened to ask about something that had been on her mind for a while. "Daddy, how come the F.B.I. guy and the police let you in on those meetings? Don't they worry that you're Mr. Novac's friend? I mean, you could be a subversive too."

Her mother jumped in from behind the stove. "Chris, use your head. Your father wouldn't have gotten to be Village Manager if a lot of people on all sides didn't trust him. His old Croton family lineage gives him a lot of standing. As Village Manager he has to be in on these things. Besides which, we're not C.P., you know."

"Well Mr. Novac isn't a Communist Party member either, is he?" Chris sometimes found Croton politics hard to follow.

"Sandor and Lili were both in the Party in the past," her father said, "but neither one is a member now. A number of people think, though, that they're close to the Party."

"Close to the Party? What does that mean exactly?"

"There's no 'exactly' about it. It's vague. It means you have friends in the Party or you seem to sympathize with Party positions."

"And you and Mother aren't 'close?'"

"No, not like that. It's known that we're liberals, but not Communists and not close to the Party. We have friends of varying political stripes, although, as you know, we don't much sympathize with anti-Communist witch-hunters."

Dinner was tense, another of those times when Chris felt like a third wheel, although nothing much had been said. Her mother had been unusually quiet. Only at dessert did she pull a note from a pile of papers and hand it to her father.

"What's this?" he said, as if an insect had needled him. He glanced at the piece of paper and put it down, frowning. Chris grabbed it from the table before her parents could stop her.

Maya, my dear, you were superb. Will you be our Maggie? Rehearsals commence on January 3, 1954. Yours, VC

So her mother had auditioned and gotten the part! Her father wasn't going to like it. He had been on edge ever since Corey Sylvester's death. Now there was the money issue at home. Also, the School Board's decision. The Board had moved quickly to replace its late member with a strictly non-controversial dentist. Mr. Novac was totally out of the picture. But her father had said that he felt uneasy about this Dr. Mills. The Board member who had pushed Mills called him "apolitical." "Apolitical," her father said, was often a euphemism for "reactionary." The plan for Mr. Novac's proposed elementary school annex had been shelved, pending a new study of enrollments.

Her father was silent for a minute. Chris could feel her mother tensing up. "Why don't you explain, Maya?"

"Viktor Cornelius has offered me the lead in his production of *What Every Woman Knows.*

Her father picked a grape from a bunch in a ceramic bowl and examined it as he might a diamond for flaws. "You could at least have told me that you auditioned for the play."

"I was too nervous. You have a lot on your mind right now."

Her mother's face was shadowed by the dimming natural light. The shorter summer days were becoming noticeable.

At first it looked like her father swallowed the grape whole, but no; he was chewing. "So how much will they be paying you?"

Her mother pushed back in her chair, as if in alarm. "I . . . I don't know. I haven't talked to Viktor Cornelius yet. Frank Ewing put in a word for me, so I got to audition. And then I just got this note."

Frank Ewing. So that was what all that hush-hush in New York was about.

"You haven't asked? Does Cornelius think that you're going to volunteer your services?"

"Oh, Gil, I thought that you'd at least be happy for me. Maybe even congratulate me."

Her father reached across the table and patted her mother's hand. "Of course I'm happy for you, sweetheart. I really am. And I'm proud of you. This is a big feather in your cap. But it's just not the greatest timing in the world. I'm going to have to be looking for more work right now."

Huh? Since when?

"More work?"

"I got a call from Herb today. Rodgers and Meacham is beefing up our 3 to 6-year-olds department, and they're planning to cut back on illustrators and editors in the adult line. So many infants and toddlers around these days."

"Well, you can illustrate for that age range."

"Yes, but Herb told me they have enough staff for the small kids line. Some of the full-timers in adult are going to split their time with the children's department."

Her mother wrinkled her brows. "Tell me what all this means."

"I'm not sure just yet, but probably I'll be going from three-quarters' time to half-time."

Another silence. A long one.

Her mother finally broke it. "Cornelius knows I'm Actors' Equity. He'll have to pay me the Equity rate."

"Why don't you have a chat with him and clear up this matter?"

"You mean that you're asking me not to accept unless he meets your conditions?"

"No, no. But I *am* asking you to find out the terms of your contract before you sign."

"Of course." She got up to do the dishes. Her father sat for a moment, then left the room.

As if to no one in particular, her mother said, "I know what your father is thinking. *If it happened to Sandor, it could happen to me. First the cutback at the press; then the suspicion of neighbors . . . .*" She looked like she was on the verge of tears. Chris had seen her mother cry mainly in Croton Players' productions.

Her mother attacked the dishes so fiercely that she accidentally dropped a plate on the floor. It smashed shrilly to smithereens.

"Maya, are you okay?" Chris's father called from across the room. Chris could hear the irritation in his voice.

The phone rang. Her parents made no move, so Chris picked up. Her father was sitting on the sofa, nursing a brandy.

"But, Rosie, everyone's scared of the bomb, not just you. . . . Who? Molotov? . . Oh, not just them—the Americans talk about dropping the bomb, too, but that doesn't mean that anyone's going to—not after Hiroshima. Each side keeps the other scared. It's called brinkmanship. You just get panicked because you don't know anything about what's happening. . . . You couldn't *sleep*? Really?"

Chris jumped as she felt a tap on her shoulder. Her father held a finger to his lips and motioned for her to cradle the receiver.

"Okay, gotta go. I'll talk to you tomorrow." She replaced the receiver and glared at her father. "Why did I have to hang up? It's still early."

"Because I said so. I don't want to hear your discussion of world affairs right now."

CHAPTER EIGHT

Rosie was so nervous about everything. How could she not be, with her father the prime suspect? Each time Chris thought about her phone conversation with Rosie last evening, she put off making a visit to her. Somehow she just didn't want to. But whenever she needed to make a decision about something she didn't feel like doing, she played a little game. How would it look in her biography? Not visiting Rosie when she was in trouble would look pretty shabby. In the late afternoon, she walked down the hill. Rosie answered her knock with a tear-stained face and led her into the kitchen-living area without a word.

Mr. Novac was sitting on the sofa with a highball in his hand. Rosie's mother, in an armchair, picked up a martini glass on the side table next to her. Neither of the parents looked up when Chris came in with Rosie.

"Let's go . . .," Chris began, but Rosie put a finger to her lips. She pulled out a pitcher of lemonade from the refrigerator.

"I didn't know what to say to him when he called," Rosie's father was saying. "He's like a vulture."

Mrs. Novac looked at her martini. "Well, why refuse? It's a wonderful opportunity for me."

"You're no fool, Lili. Why get mixed up with *Time Magazine* and Henry Luce's right-wing politics? I don't have to tell you how cozy Luce is with the C.I.A. Why have anything to do with Maxwell? He's glib, he's not trustworthy, and he's not all that knowledgeable."

Wiley Maxwell again. Chris's antennae quivered.

"But, Sandor, he's requesting a *double* interview, so when you put him off for you, you put him off for me too."

Mr. Novac took a swig of his highball. His voice went up a few decibels. "So call him and arrange a separate meeting if you want."

Maybe Mr. Novac was right about Maxwell? But he could be nicer to Rosie's mother, Chris thought.

Rosie removed a platter from an overhead cabinet, and filled it with some of her mother's homemade cookies from the cookie jar.

"Even if you don't like his work or his magazine, it would still be fine publicity," Rosie's mother said. She got up to refill her martini glass.

Chris was distinctly not in the mood for another of Rosie's parents' quarrels. But it was worth it to learn more about this Mr. Maxwell.

"Yeah, publicity. Maybe I'm better off being obscure. What did Corey, the great P.R. man, want to introduce Maxwell to me for? Was Corey looking out for my welfare?"

"Maybe he was genuinely wanting to do you a good turn after being so nasty."

Sandor snorted. "Fat chance. Anyway, I'm willing to sleep on it for a few more days. Maxwell can wait. In the meantime, if you're so eager for the publicity, call him up. Feel free."

Chris, riveted at the patio door, felt a nudge from Rosie.

"Come on, Chris," Rosie whispered, "Let's get out of here."

On the patio, Rosie pulled off her headband, letting it drop next to her chair. Her eyes were dripping, and she wiped them with a Kleenex. "It's just that it's one thing after another. First that policeman questioning my parents, and then Sal and Joey at the lake."

"Rosie, those guys are just stupid. You can't pay any attention to them."

"I don't want to hear my father called a . . . a Commie kike."

Chris thought that Rosie was going to choke on the words. "So just tell them to get lost and forget about them."

"It's bad enough that we're so different from everyone else. But now all the kids seem to hate me."

"They don't. And *I* don't—but I'm worried about you."

"Well, forget me. I just want to be left alone."

It occurred to Chris that recently Rosie had said nothing about her practicing. Usually in the summer she practiced around five hours a day. "Rosie, were you practicing earlier today?"

"No."

Chris took a mocha cookie. "No? How come?"

"Miss Schultz is away for a few weeks, so I'm taking a break."

A break? It was unheard of. Rosie never missed her practicing, even when her teacher was away or sick. Chris knew better than to pursue the matter. Every once in a while Rosie had a way of folding up her shutters and closing off the outside world.

The patio door opened noiselessly, and Mrs. Novac leaned out. She looked very pale. "Girls, do you need a refill on the lemonade?"

"Oh, no thanks, uh . . . ." Chris's voice trailed off. She had to stop herself from calling her friend's mother "Mrs. Novac." Last year, after both girls had turned thirteen, the four parents announced that they wanted the girls to call them by their first names. But Chris and Rosie had trouble getting used to the change, and they generally ended up calling them nothing or reverting to the old habit.

The door closed as noiselessly as it had opened.

Chris wanted to take her friend's hand, but Rosie was sitting beyond reach. "Rosie, I'm going to do everything I can for you while I'm working for Mrs. Sylvester."

"Oh, please," Rosie said with a sob. "Just don't talk to me about it, okay? I don't want to hear anything more about it. Nothing—all right?"

◆　◆　◆

The visit with Rosie left Chris feeling deeply uneasy. Maybe her friend was having a nervous breakdown. What exactly was a nervous breakdown anyhow? If Rosie were having one, wouldn't she just stay home in bed?

As Chris walked back up the hill to North Highland Place, she shook these thoughts from her mind and returned to her current preoccupations. What exactly did Dr. Kamm want from Delia? What was Delia's relationship with the doctor? Delia never said anything about the letter, which Chris had left on her desk at the office, with a note, "This came for you earlier today."

The familiar jingle of the Good Humor Truck sounded as if from very far away. It turned out to be right across the street. Chris wandered over absent-mindedly and purchased her favorite, a toasted almond stick. Crumbly bits of almond clinging to drops of ice cream splattered onto her shirt as she pondered the meaning of the letter.

When she got home, she found her father in the living room, absorbed in *The New Yorker*. As if to signal that she'd leave if asked, she sat down at a remove from her father's place on the couch.

"Tell me about Dr. Leopold Kamm," she demanded, without preamble.

Her father looked up, startled.

Her mother, in the wing chair, peered at her from above a copy of *Variety*. "Chris," she said, staring at Chris's shirt. Chris self-consciously shook out a few more crumbs from it. "Chris, have you been snacking again?" Lately she had been taking to telling Chris that she needed to lose more of her "baby fat." Just when she had gotten down to a size 12.

"We've told you about Kamm," her father said.

"Yeah, you said it was like a cult. But I don't really understand. Does he shrink all these people together? Do they all lie down on couches in one big dormitory and tell him their thoughts?"

Her parents laughed, and the atmosphere got friendlier.

"Well," her mother said, "He's a psychiatrist, although as far as we know not a very well-known or respected one, except among his Croton patients."

"So what do you know about him?"

"In fact, very little," her father joined in. "You see, it's like a closed society. You get information only from people who leave. But the people who leave don't like to talk about it, and besides, we're not really chummy with that crowd."

"Because they're French clerks?"

When Chris had learned the word for "clerk" in her French class, she had giggled, because *commis* sounded so much like "Commie." She had shared the joke with her parents, and "French clerk" had become a standard code name.

Her father was flipping pages of *The New Yorker*. "No. You know that our friends don't have to pass a loyalty test. It's true that a lot, if not most, of the Kammunists are also Communists, but they're mainly people whose values are very different from ours. You have to have certain values—or lack of them—to join a cult."

"So if it isn't mass shrinkage, then what do you think it is?" Chris persisted.

Chris's mother picked up the issue of *Variety* as if to resume reading. "Always the reporter, Chris, aren't you?"

"I want to know."

Her mother put down *Variety* again.

Her father was trying to answer seriously. "There is certainly some form of psychotherapy going on. Whether it's individual or group, or a combination of both, we don't know."

"Group? What's that?"

"Sometimes a family goes together to seek help, or sometimes a group of unrelated people—maybe five or ten—will work together on their interpersonal problems."

"So then why is it a cult? Why isn't it just plain old shrinking?"

"Because the patients—or members—," her father said, "live in Kamm's compound, or nearby. And because it seems that Kamm has almost complete control over them."

"For example," her mother added, "some of them become financially dependent on him. We're pretty sure that he put one man through college and another through medical school."

Chris opened her eyes wide. "I thought that people were supposed to pay their shrinks—not the other way around."

"Exactly," her father said. "That's why it's like a cult. Kamm gets a hold over you one way or another. It's not always about money. But if you owe him a lot of money, you're not about to leave."

"If it's all so secret," Chris asked, "how can he have anything over people who leave if they don't give him checks or sign an IOU?"

Her father smiled.

"Psychiatrists take notes and keep records, my darling." He waved his *New Yorker* at her. "Haven't you ever seen cartoons in here with a patient lying on a couch, and the psychiatrist behind him with pad and pen in hand?"

Right. Did Dr. Kamm not want to lose control over Delia? Chris had now practically memorized the letter to Delia that she had copied out, and she had saved it in her desk drawer. She was compiling evidence for she knew not what. Something very weird was going on. "Ugh. I'm never going to a shrink."

"Why do you want to know so much about Kamm?" her mother asked.

Chris stood up. "Oh, Gail mentioned him again. That's all."

CHAPTER NINE

The pace of Rosie's telephone calls to Chris picked up. It was time to give her extra moral support, Chris decided, to go over to dinner there more often, to listen to her more.

It used to be that Chris could count on an exotic soufflé, or *blanquette de veau*, or some other great French concoction at Rosie's house. At dinner, Mrs. Novac would answer Chris's questions about Europe during the war or about her paintings, and Mr. Novac would sometimes talk about the latest architectural news. Now it was different. Tonight they had a mushroom omelet (which Mrs. Novac pronounced French style, 'uhm-*let*, with the accent on the second syllable) and a green salad. Chris and Rosie chatted mainly about school, and Rosie's parents were mostly silent.

After dinner, Chris and Rosie did the dishes, as usual, and Rosie's parents sat in the living area, each deep into a book.

Finally Rosie's father broke the silence in a gruff voice. "Don't be a fool, Lili. "You're just letting yourself in for it. The man is not at all sympathetic to your work."

Rosie stopped short in her conversation with Chris.

"It's not like you to stifle me like this, Sandor. What is it? Are you worried that it will cost you commissions?"

Rosie's father's voice rose. "This isn't about me, Lili. When will you get that through your head? I'm not one for compromising my principles, you know that. I just don't want to see you get creamed."

"Well, what makes you so sure that I will? Perhaps by the time he next interviews me, Mr. Maxwell will have learned a thing or two."

Mr. Novac' voice rose once more. "Your Mr. Maxwell is an idiot and a reactionary. He can't stand any art that isn't abstract, much less any kind of socially conscious stuff. Your problem is that you've never bothered reading *Time* magazine, where he's become a big-shot. It's beneath you. All fine and well, but the price you pay for being so hoity-toity is that you don't know your own critics."

"So *what*?" Rosie's mother fairly shouted. "If he's hostile, it doesn't matter. His article will come out right before my Chicago exhibit. So what if it's controversial? It will be great publicity." She pronounced "publicity" the French way, *publicité*.

Rosie hugged her arms together. She always said that when her mother reverted to French pronunciation it was a bad sign.

"It *won't* be controversial," Mr. Novac contradicted her. "It will be mendacious."

"What is mendacious?" she asked.

Rosie suppressed a nervous giggle.

"Lying"

"Ah, yes *mensonger*." Chris had to lean forward to catch it.

"Mama," Rosie began.

But her mother ran right on. "I do not like Mr. Maxwell. I do not feel that he understands my work. But I would like to have this interview just to give him another chance."

"Give *him* a chance?" Rosie's father pounded a fist on the side table so heavily that his brandy glass would have tipped over if he hadn't quickly retrieved it. "What is he, a charity case? No, you're not being altruistic, you're being greedy. Even negative publicity is fine for you, just as long as it's publicity. Why don't you go to an ad agency, for God's sake?"

Rosie's eyes were reddening. She whispered to Chris, "You better just go home. I can't stand this. I'm going upstairs."

♦ ♦ ♦

The opening of Mrs. Novac's annual Labor Day exhibit at the Croton Free Library always attracted a crowd. This year, as usual, it would feature a gallery talk by the artist. Chris never missed the talk and the exhibit. Mrs. Novac offered the event as a good will gesture to the village of Croton. Special screens were set up on which she could hang her canvases, and the exhibit spilled out into the hallway. The Village Manager always said a few words of introduction. This year's exhibit would be somewhat special, because Mrs. Novac had removed the damage to her painting "Lucre," and many people knew the story.

Chris and Rosie arrived at the Municipal Building before the introduction. Rosie's mother, wine glass in hand, was standing in front of a few paintings from her barge series, which was currently being shown at the Trish Latham Gallery in New York. With her was the man Chris now recognized.

"My husband is very flattered, Mr. Maxwell. But this is just too busy a time for him."

Chris scratched her head. Too busy! Flattered! Hah! Rosie's father wouldn't go near Wylie Maxwell with a ten-foot pole.

Volunteers swirled around them, laying out refreshments on one of the long rectangular reading desks for patrons.

Wylie Maxwell's tone was soothing. "Of course I'm disappointed not to be able to write about your husband too. But I'm very happy, Miss Carrière, that you've given me this brief time before the exhibit today."

"Well, I'm happy to chat with you," Mrs. Novac murmured. She gestured toward "Lucre." "The paint is scarcely dry on this one."

Maxwell peered at the painting from all angles, as if to examine it in greater depth. "Hm-m-m (from one side)." "Hm-m-m (from the other). Uh . . . you use your greens very strategically." Stroking his beardless chin, he stood back for a full view.

"I had trouble with them," Rosie's mother admitted. "But if you can see how the green in the upper right-hand images gets picked up in the panel of the Bowery bums on the lower left, I'll be satisfied."

"Yes," said Maxwell, "that's exactly what I meant."

She had started out, she explained, with a misty blue effect in the lower panel, but had later decided to suffuse it with a greenish glow, as if a miasma had penetrated the early morning light. The result was that ghostly, pale green vapors enshrouded the figures lying on the ground only to blend in with and be absorbed by the cloudy blue-gray of morning light above.

Maxwell gestured to a copy of her print for the Rosenberg rally and squeezed his eyes at it, as if engaged in profound reflection. "Hm-m-m. Reminds me of Käthe Kollwitz."

Chris had seen reproductions of work by the German artist. She tried to remember what she saw, but she didn't think that the Rosenberg print looked much like a Kollwitz. Was Mr. Maxwell trying to tell Rosie's mother that she lacked originality? Anyhow, he didn't seem too enthusiastic about her print.

"Let's look at your barge series," Maxwell suggested.

It seemed that he had at least glanced at Mrs. Novac's exhibit at the Latham Gallery—oil paintings of tugboats and barges plying the Hudson River. There were scenes off the shores of New York City as well as from the banks of the Hudson in the Croton area. Chris loved that series. Mrs. Novac had borrowed only a few for the Croton exhibit.

"How did you get the idea for this series?" he asked.

"I look out the window when I take the train to New York. I rarely read, unless the windows are too dirty for good viewing. And I see the wonderful boats on the river. Sometimes I can see crew members too, so you will find paintings with people as well as a few without. I like the river in all weathers, so you will see sunshine, rain, fog, and snow in the series. I wish I could find a way to suggest the foghorn."

"Do you always carry a sketch book with you?"

"I try to, yes. When I don't have one I ask my memory to store the image. Sometimes it cooperates, sometimes it doesn't."

More chin-stroking, as Maxwell inspected the paintings. "These," he said, "are probably the closest to conventional landscapes you get, wouldn't you say?"

"Landscapes? Maybe. I hadn't thought of them that way. I am interested in the muscle of the boat and the crew, their tension with the water, sometimes their battle with the water. I try to get more movement into them than I would with what you call a conventional landscape. If I do landscapes, they tend to be lithographs."

Maxwell was still absorbed in one of the series. "And of course you are especially known for your portraits."

"Portraits? I suppose so, but I don't think of them that way." She averted her eyes from his face.

Mrs. Novac definitely did not do portraits—or landscapes, for that matter. Was Maxwell at all familiar with her work?

They moved to a canvas that took up most of a screen. A head of Paul Robeson dominated it. The head was overlain with shafts of stones in flight. The canvas was a chaos of movement and violence—spurts of blood, splinters of glass, people fleeing, grimacing or staring in horror. In a corner of the painting, perspective gone flat, sat a police car with two policemen lounging in front of it.

"The Peekskill Riot," Maxwell said.

"Yes. Just so. I was there."

Mrs. Novac once told Chris that she had dashed off her Robeson painting in an intensity of anger and sorrow right after those two awful September days four years ago. Every time Chris saw the painting, those days came back to her: after the fiasco of the first concert, her parents took her to the second one, a week later. This time, 2500 men arrived to protect the performers. The rescheduled concert passed off without incident. But at its conclusion all hell broke loose. "Cover your heads!" Chris remembered her father yelling over the sound of car windows being smashed. She had tried to open an eye, but quickly shut it as glass spewed forth in every direction. She scrambled into the back seat of the car and ducked. Stones were pounding all sides of the car. Her father managed to pull it out of the parking area to shouts of "White nigger!" "Jew! Jew!" When Chris dared to take a peek out of the car window, she could see policemen standing idly by. Luckily she and her parents escaped serious injury.

Mrs. Novac had later commented that the decision to hold the concert in Peekskill, a notoriously reactionary town, was a mystery to her. Chris remembered thinking how terrible it was that Robeson had so many enemies. Of course he had a double count against him: he was a Negro and he had been interrogated by the House Un-American Activities Committee. The riot pretty much spelled the end of his singing and acting career. The government revoked his passport.

Maxwell was visibly struggling to find a response to the Robeson painting. "A powerful statement. Not very flattering to the police."

Mrs. Novac smiled. "You may be too young to remember well. The police . . . um . . . really just let it happen."

Maxwell's face was a blank.

Chris was beginning to think that Mr. Maxwell didn't like Mrs. Novac's work at all.

♦   ♦   ♦

Chris left the reception early, for a visit with her friend Gail in Harmon. As she rounded Old Post Road South where it intersected with Morningside Drive, she jumped at the wail of a siren. Ever since Mr. Sylvester's death she had been living on the edge of nervous excitement. Every siren was a police siren; every shadow that of an assassin. A fire truck zoomed by. It was only then that she noticed a spiral of smoke. It seemed to be coming from the Croton River. Instead of turning right onto Truesdale Drive, where Gail lived, she decided to continue on Old Post Road South toward the river.

It was the wilder part of Harmon. On her left were weed-grown hills, which looked largely uninhabited. To the right, incongruously, was a warren of tree-lined streets on which houses sat neatly side by side and lawns were always groomed. That part wasn't at all like the barely domesticated wilds of Mt. Airy. But especially beyond Morningside Drive, where Old Post Road meandered toward the river, the houses became more sparse and the vegetation more lush.

Chris's parents remained at the Municipal Building to toast Mrs. Novac. They would pick her up at Gail's after dinner. After the loss of her camera and notebook at the Rosenberg rally, Chris had taken to carrying a small note pad and pencil in her handbag, as if to be at the ready for the next catastrophe. She trotted in pursuit of the fire. The spiral had ballooned into a black cloud. As she crossed Truesdale Drive onto Nordica she began to smell the smoke.

When she got closer to the river, she lost sight of the vista that she had had on the higher ground of Old Post Road South. She decided to follow her nose, which caught a strong whiff of smoke. People were raising a ruckus somewhere on Nordica Drive. She could hear shouts and cries and agitated conversation just before a fire truck came into view.

Chris didn't know this part of Harmon well, even though it was quite close to Silver Lake. But she never took Nordica Drive to get to the lake, choosing instead to cut through an overgrown path that led directly to the small, rocky beach.

Last year when she, Rosie, and Gail went rock hopping in the river, they ventured farther toward Ossining than they usually did. Chris remembered stopping to look up to the top of a steep boulder on her right, where two ill-matched structures were perched side by side. One looked oriental, almost pagoda-like. Its sharply sloping roof rose from behind a wide, flat, porch-like section sitting on piles driven directly into the rock. The entire side of the section visible to them from the river was made up of floor-to-ceiling windows—or were they doors?—crisscrossed with small, traditional panes. The other structure was a handsome but oddly constructed fieldstone house, with a low-lying, horizontal wing that seemed almost tacked on to a more conventional two-story main section. The two structures together, both overshadowed by a grove of evergreens, looked as protected as a fortress. This view was about all you could get. From Nordica Drive the buildings were almost totally hidden by trees.

"Is that Dr. Kamm's place?" she had asked Gail, knowing full well that it was, and pointing to the top of the cliff.

"Yes." It was rare that Chris could get much more out of her on the subject.

Like everyone else, Chris knew the outlines of the story—a real Hollywood-style legend. At the beginning of the twentieth century, the real estate mogul Clifford Harmon had started an artists' colony in the neighborhood. Painters, entertainers, writers, and others flocked to the place. Its center was the Nikko Inn, very Japanese-looking, and the Playhouse next door to it. Harmon built the fieldstone Playhouse for his mistress, the beautiful and internationally renowned diva Lillian Nordica (née Lillian Norton in Farmington, Maine), and he also built her a lavish mansion on nearby Alexander Lane. The pupils of Irma Duncan, the adopted daughter of famed dancer Isadora, came to dance on Lillian's lawn. The diva sang in the Playhouse for the likes of Irving Berlin and David Belasco. The motion picture duo Mary Pickford and Douglas Fairbanks were among the many well-known people who partied at the Nikko Inn. And every once in a while, if you knew where and when to look, you could see locals dressed up as gondoliers ferrying the celebrities up and down the Croton River. During the Prohibition, the Nikko Inn thrived as a speakeasy, but after the repeal, the long party wound down. Dr. Kamm acquired the property in the 1930s, before Chris was born, and a new chapter began.

Kammunists and Communists, huh? Delia's letter came to mind. Were Dr. Kamm and his people mixed up in Mr. Sylvester's murder? Since a lot of people seemed to think that there was Communist foul play at work in Corey Sylvester's murder, maybe there was also a link to the Kammunists. Chris felt as if she were literally on the scent of something.

A police car and an ambulance, along with the fire engine, blocked access to the area. As Chris headed for the house, one of the firemen called to her, "Hey, Miss, where do you think you're going?" She had never seen him before. He was probably new.

"My parents are in there," she lied, and kept going.

Firemen were furiously spraying flames that had begun to lick what seemed to be a new wing of the fieldstone house. The fire was confined to that side. Chris inched closer to the source of the fire, but she found herself overcome by a fit of coughing.

"Back! Stand back!" shouted a fireman.

Still coughing, Chris wheeled around and joined some thirty-odd people who were assembled on the lawn, watching. On the stone and concrete patio that overlooked the river she could see tables laid out with refreshments. A few people stared at her, so she tried to melt into the crowd, backing up as inconspicuously as possible toward the patio. While managing to snag a canapé, she spotted Harold and Bella Lewis, amazingly together and even holding hands. Didn't her parents say they were getting a divorce? Both Lewises were short and chunky. Through Mrs. Lewis's dyed blond hair faded brown roots were visible. Munching on her canapé, Chris squeezed through the crowd and approached the couple.

They quickly let go of their clasped hands.

"Why, Chris," Mrs. Lewis said, clearing her throat, "What are you doing here?"

"I was on my way to my friend Gail's house," Chris answered, deciding that the truth was best, "and I saw a cloud of smoke. So I followed it over here."

Mr. Lewis did not greet her. He looked annoyed.

A middle-aged woman standing nearby chimed in, "You'd think you'd want to stay away from a fire, not visit it."

Mrs. Lewis said, "Yes, Chris, this isn't really a good place for you."

Chris planted her feet more firmly on the ground. "Oh, I'm not afraid. It looks like the firemen have things under control."

The flames were in fact diminishing, and a few guests applauded. One or two wandered over to the patio and helped themselves to refreshments amidst the billowing smoke.

"Of course," she said, "I don't want to crash the party."

If it were her parents' friends, they would simply have laughed and told her to get something to eat and drink. But apart from the Lewises, who were not really friends of her parents anyway, she didn't recognize a soul.

The guests had evidently calmed down and were talking among themselves in hushed tones.

"It was just a kitchen fire, I heard."

"A grease fire, huh?"

"Mary was scared out of her wits."

"Is Dr. Kamm here?" Chris asked Mrs. Lewis, who ignored her. She spied a slim, bearded young man in jeans who had just slipped in through the brush and the evergreens that hid the house from Nordica Drive. Rats! It was Nick Salvucci, come to scoop her. He was the only full-time reporter on the *Croton-Harmon News*, and he had graduated from the high school only a couple of years ago. He was saving up to put himself through college. Chris moved farther into the thick of the crowd.

It was then that she caught sight of Delia Morrison, darting out of the main house, and up a path that led to the wooded grove, her red hair streaming behind her. She seemed to be hugging something close to her chest. Delia! So she had accepted Kamm's invitation to the party. Was she returning to the group? Chris would have dearly loved to talk to her, but she was even more eager to observe unobserved. If Kamm spotted her, she'd be sunk.

When the firemen emerged from the house and announced that it was safe now, a general cheer went up from the guests, who started to disperse, leaving her easily visible to those who remained. Exposed! Nick sauntered over.

"Well, Chris! Good for you! You know where to find the action, I guess."

To her surprise, she was grateful for Nick's appearance. He could be useful to her. "Nick," she whispered, "which one is Dr. Kamm?"

He spent a few seconds surveying the scene.

"Not here, kid. I don't see him."

"What happened, anyhow? Is there much damage? Was anyone hurt? Maybe Dr. Kamm got burned."

"Nope. No chance. It was no big deal. Kitchen fire that started to spread, but the Fire Department was right on it."

"Do you know where the kitchen is located?" Chris asked.

"You can see for yourself—where all the smoke is."

"It looks like that whole wing of the house."

"Yes, that's their new wing, with a big kitchen just for large parties, I was told."

"Do you think it was arson?" Chris tried to keep the anticipation out of her voice.

"Arson? Listen, kid, if you don't watch out, you'll turn into a yellow journalist."

She half-heartedly searched for a response, but she didn't want to get sidetracked. "How do you know it's not arson?"

"I don't know for sure. But Mary came running outside, saying she'd started a fire in the oven. Maybe it wasn't an accident, but I doubt it—Mary doesn't seem the arsonist type."

Chris pawed the ground with a foot. "Does Dr. Kamm often give parties?"

"I think he does, but this is special. It's Kamm's annual Labor Day shindig. Throws a cocktail and dinner party for all his . . . er, patients."

"So all these people are his patients?" Even Bella and Harold Lewis!

"Yeah. Confidentiality doesn't matter inside his group. You know, with shrinks it's all supposed to be very confidential and secretive. If you're seeing one, you don't want anyone to know, much less to learn anything about your private life. But Kamm doesn't care about formalities. These people are like a large family that keeps to itself."

"Wow! It's a big crowd!"

"Yeah, and more to come."

Sure enough, at that very moment a small stream of people was trickling in from the street. They had probably been detained by the police or firemen, and had just been let through the roadblock.

Nick moved on, notebook in hand. Chris saw him go into the house.

Where was Delia? Maybe she had returned and was on the porch. Chris circled the house, searching.

In the meantime, there was a general movement toward the tables on the patio. Glasses clinked, laughter bubbled up, and the party resumed. Standing on the patio, but obscured by a very large man, was that little F.B.I. man in his old black jacket. Pike! Wasn't that his name? He certainly did get around.

A gentle poke in the ribs distracted her. Nick had reappeared and was by her side. "There's Kamm," he said in an undertone.

She followed the direction of his eyes and saw a compact man of middling height with a generous shock of salt-and-pepper hair, a ruddy complexion, and large beetle brows beneath steel-rimmed spectacles. As he entered the patio from the inside, at least a dozen people swooped down on him, like a gaggle of fans clamoring for autographs. It was "Dr. Kamm" this and "Dr. Kamm" that, embarrassed giggles, exclamations. Kamm emerged from the group with difficulty, his suit rumpled, people literally hanging onto his arms. Precariously balancing his drink, he made his way slowly across the lawn to the patio.

Chris listened for snatches of conversation. Next to her, an older woman was saying to a younger one, "Dr. Kamm saved my life. He really did. You're lucky that he's taken you on, dear. He's so busy now; it's a wonder that he can add any new patients at all."

It was only when she saw Kamm in person that Chris realized how very different he was from the man she didn't even know that she had been picturing. Her fantasy-man was regally tall. He had black hair and a mustache to match, and he wore a black sorcerer's cape. The real Dr. Kamm looked more like a disheveled professor.

He made straight for her, before she could escape. His eyes bored right through her. "*What,*" he snarled through clenched teeth, "are you doing here?"

Chris backed away.

"I was just walking by, and I saw smoke."

"Don't you know better than to walk into a fire?" he roared. "You are trespassing. You were not invited to my house. Now just get out, before I have the police throw you out!"

CHAPTER TEN

Chris was bursting to tell her parents about her adventure at Dr. Kamm's. But when their VW Beetle pulled up in front of Gail's house and she saw Frank Ewing in the front passenger seat, she realized that she would have to take a back seat to the conversation.

"So kind of you to give me a lift home," Ewing said, twisting toward her mother, who shared the back seat with Chris. "Can't think where Delia could be." Of course! Delia was at Dr. Kamm's.

Ewing, still contorted in the front seat, continued, "Have you clinched the deal, ducky?"

Her mother lowered her voice. "Um-m, maybe."

"Oh, so you know about Cornelius's offer to Maya?" her father asked. He sounded testy.

Chris's mother looked over at her, but Chris turned away in annoyance to stare out the window. Don't worry; I'll keep your secrets.

A tad too late, Ewing replied to her father, "Gossip simply abounds in theatrical circles, you know, Gil. I saw Viktor at a cocktail party a few days ago, and he was positively glowing about Maya. Thinks it's a real coup to have gotten her."

"He hasn't," Chris's father grunted, "*gotten* her yet. There's still a lot to be worked out."

Her mother bit her lip. Frank Ewing fell silent.

They stopped in front of the white stucco house on Truesdale Drive that Chris knew so well. The windows in Delia's small wing were completely dark.

"Looks like Delia hasn't gotten home yet," Ewing said. "I should have thought she'd be here by now." He hopped out, offered his thanks, and disappeared. Her mother clambered up front to take his place.

"Guess what . . .," Chris began.

"So," Chris's father said to her mother, "have you thought any more about what to do?"

Useless to try to break in. Third-wheel time again.

Her mother turned to face him. "You know that Cornelius offered me $50 for the rehearsal period, going up to $60 for the performances. That's really a respectable weekly salary for someone who's been away from professional theater as long as I have."

"And he'll give you an Equity contract?"

"Of course, Gil. I'm a union member. I thought we already discussed that."

"H-m-m. Not bad. Just about as good as what you're getting at Scarborough."

"Yes."

Chris still could not get used to her father's worry about money. First the loss of the comic strip, then the reduction of his work hours. What next? Would she have to apply for a scholarship to college? Chris never had to think about money before.

"You can probably get him to go higher. How long do you figure your leave would have to be?"

"Cornelius and I covered that. A couple of months rehearsal time and then—well, we don't know about the run—a month? But of course we'll hope for more."

"So let's say two semesters. You know, you're in a good bargaining position. Scarborough can hire a cheap replacement for you and at the same time have the prestige of a faculty member on the professional stage. Maybe you could even get Cornelius to reserve bargain rates for groups of Scarborough students. We'll have to see what we can arrange about your benefits."

"Gil, you know I'm not good at bargaining. I don't like it. Now if you want to represent me . . . ."

"I wish I could," her husband said. "But I'm afraid it has to be your solo performance, honey. And you know, it may mean having to give up some of your other activities. Like the League of Women Voters, for instance. I don't see how you can go on as V.P. of the chapter while you're commuting to New York."

"Well, what do you want me to do? Cornelius won't wait forever. He'll give me about a week."

Her father, Chris thought, was being a bit tough. Her mother, after all, had given up an acting career to move with him to Croton. And all because of her, Chris! The old feelings came back with an ache. Why couldn't they have just stayed in the city? And why couldn't they have had a child before her? An older sister who could take care of her. Probably her mother had been too busy with her career.

Her father offered his coaching services for a second meeting with Cornelius and for an upcoming discussion with the headmaster of Scarborough. "Funny," he said to her. "You have so much confidence on stage and so little with your employers. Can't you try to pretend that these interviews are scenes in a play?"

Silence.

It was clear that her father was feeling a lot worse about finances since his meeting with his boss Herb. She had heard the story yesterday. Herb and her father went back a long time, and they were on very good terms. Herb had told her father that he was feeling increasingly under pressure to bring a colleague, Saul, up from quarter- to half-time. Herb had given Saul employment when he was blacklisted by Twentieth-Century Fox.

Her father had waved a dismissive hand. "Of course I was blacklisted too. But Herb said—probably he was right—that it wasn't the same thing. That the syndicate did drop me, but that I was able to get plenty of other free-lance work, and that I had my job at the press. And he pointed out that we have only one child whereas Saul has two and a third on the way."

In the end, the boss had said that he'd see what he could do. Herb couldn't formally bring her father up to three-quarter time, but maybe he could find him a fair amount of paid overtime. "It wasn't anything firm," Chris's father had said. "He's going to go back to his flow charts and speak with me again in a few days."

Time for another try. "You'll never guess what happened today," Chris sang out from the back seat, learning toward her parents.

Her father was observing her through the rear-view mirror. "Sit back, Chris."

She did as she was told, and repeated, loudly, "So guess what happened today."

Silence.

"There was a fire, and the fire department and the police and an ambulance all came out for it. And guess where it was." No response. "It was at Dr. Kamm's!"

Her mother did not turn around. "How do you know?"

"I was there. I was right there, and I got to see the famous Dr. Kamm."

"What on earth," her father asked, "were you doing at Kamm's place?"

"Well, when I was walking to Gail's I saw smoke, and I followed my nose and eyes."

No one asked about injuries, or damage, or what might have caused the fire.

Her father, his voice rising with irritation, said, "Chris, you can't go butting in to everything. Don't you know you're heading straight for trouble?"

♦ ♦ ♦

When the phone rang at 6:00 the next morning, the first day of school, Chris was already in the kitchen fixing her breakfast. She picked up to hear a muffled, indistinct voice. She barely made out the urgent request to speak to her mother, who padded downstairs in her slippers and bathrobe, rubbing her eyes.

"Frank? What? Did you call the newspaper? What were her plans for yesterday evening?"

Chris poured her cornflakes over some fruit as quietly as possible so as not to miss anything.

"No, I don't mind calling Joan. I'll just say that I tried Delia at home and at the paper, and didn't reach her. Then I'll call you. If you get any information before that, please let us know."

She hung up. Chris was at the table, digging into her bowl of cereal. "What was that all about? Nothing bad has happened to Delia, has it?"

Her mother's tone was weary. "Later, Chris." She turned to go back upstairs.

Chris rose in a flash, tugging at her mother's elbow, just as she had done when she was little. "No, Mommy, please, please tell me."

"I really should go consult your father." Chris had not let go of her mother's elbow. "All right. When Frank got home last night, no one was there. He waited up for a while, and finally went to bed around 11. Not that he could sleep. Delia didn't come back. Frank says he's been up almost all night, and he waited until now to phone us."

Chris chewed her lip. "I saw Delia yesterday, at Dr. Kamm's."

Her mother's eyes widened. "At Dr. Kamm's? What could she have been doing there?"

Chris was about to tell her when she remembered that she wasn't supposed to know anything about it. "I saw Mr. and Mrs. Lewis there, too."

"Was Delia with anyone? You know how people talk around here."

Right. Delia had a bad reputation. People might think she had run away with another man. But Chris knew that Delia wouldn't do anything like that.

"No, I just saw her for a second and then she disappeared. I didn't see her again, and I didn't even say hello to her. I don't think she saw me."

Her mother frowned and went upstairs.

The family rarely breakfasted together during the week. Her mother generally had coffee and doughnuts with her colleagues before classes, in the teachers' room. Her father's schedule was variable, so you couldn't count on him.

The phone rang a minute or so later, and Chris picked up again. Without announcing himself or waiting to find out who was on the other end of the line, Frank Ewing asked, "Do you think I should call the police?"

"Wait, I'll get my mother," Chris said into the receiver, but before she could turn around, her mother took the receiver out of her hand.

"I would, Frank. What harm could it do? And it will make you feel better to know that as many people as possible are looking. I'll call Joan immediately. By the way, Chris said that she spotted Delia for a moment at Dr. Kamm's yesterday." She put her hand over the mouthpiece. "What time would you say it was when you saw Delia, Chris?"

"Oh, I don't know—maybe a little after 5, maybe 5:30."

In a minute or two they were all assembled in the kitchen, her father in trousers and an undershirt, shaving brush in hand. It would have been like a holiday if everyone weren't so down in the dumps.

Her mother picked up the phone just after she hung up with Frank Ewing and dialed. She seemed to be listening to what Mrs. Sylvester had to say for a very long time. Finally she put her hand over the mouthpiece again and whispered to her husband, "Let's meet Joan at the office. I don't think that she should go in there alone."

They agreed to meet in the twenty minutes it would take Joan Sylvester to get to the newspaper office. Her mother would just have to miss the teachers' meeting.

Chris stood up, leaving her cereal unfinished. "I'm getting dressed right away."

"Oh, no, young lady," said her father, "you're not going to start off school by skipping out on it. You're going to feed Willie and then you're on your way."

At the sound of his name, Willie, who was curled up under the kitchen table, roused himself and pawed at the door. Chris let him out. "I can walk to school from the newspaper. It's nearer than from here anyhow. So I'm a little late. What's the difference? It's not like I'll miss some world-shaking event in history class."

Her father's frown turned into a half-smile. "You have to have your way, don't you? But we're not letting you inside the office. And we're dropping you at school on the way back."

Chris and her parents got to the newspaper office before Joan Sylvester and sat waiting in the car.

"Delia is definitely trouble," said Chris's father. "I could have told you."

Chris and her mother were quiet. Chris had heard her father gripe about Delia before. Her mother always said she thought that Delia had had a difficult life and that people shouldn't gossip about her. How hypocritical the gossips were, she would say—as if they themselves were so virtuous! Delia had never to her knowledge hurt anyone, her mother would argue, and she had a right to lead her life the way she wanted.

The Sylvesters' Nash drew up just behind them. Mrs. Sylvester was crisp and smart, in a navy blue jacket dress. She embraced Chris's mother and nodded at Chris and her father. Chris followed the three adults to the office door, where her father seemed to become aware of her presence.

"No, Chris," he said. "You're waiting outside—remember?"

It was unfair. If something horrible had happened, she wanted to know about it. Anyhow, her parents—at least her mother—would be just as shocked by something grisly as she would.

She paced back and forth in front of the building for a few minutes. Then something occurred to her. Around the back of the building was a door that delivery people used. The front door key opened both doors. Shifting into a casual saunter, she meandered back to her parents' car and retrieved her book bag. Somewhere on the bottom of the notebooks and books was her key ring.

Very few people were out on Riverside Drive at this hour, but Chris decided that a business-like air was a good idea. She hastened to the back door, trying at the same time not to crunch twigs noisily on the gravel path. The back door led to a very small mudroom, beyond which were the kitchenette and bathroom. Whew! The key turned noiselessly in the lock. She put her head to the inside door and finally could hear faint voices. It seemed that they were all searching. But for what? Signs that intruders had been there?

"Everything looks fine to me," she heard her father call. And then footsteps. Uh-oh! They were probably going to check the kitchenette and bathroom. She heard the screech of a siren. Quickly she turned tail and let herself out.

She zoomed around the gravel path and made it to the front just as a police car pulled up. Officer Riley was in the passenger seat and Mangone was at the wheel. At that moment her parents and Mrs. Sylvester emerged from the front door.

"We got a call from Mr. Ewing about Mrs. Morrison," the chief said to Joan Sylvester. We came right over, but it looks like you beat us to it. Have you been inside?"

"Yes," Mrs. Sylvester answered. "Everything seemed to be in order."

"Mind if we have a look around?" Mangone asked her.

She opened the door for him.

Chris's parents stood awkwardly on the sidewalk, as if not sure that they should remain there or go back inside. Chris scooted over to Riley.

"Did Mr. Ewing tell you that I saw Delia yesterday afternoon?"

"Yes, he said you told him she was over at Dr. Kamm's place. We were planning to go up there after we leave here." Riley considered her for a moment. "Wait here. I want to have a word with the chief."

Chris watched as he and Mangone conferred at the front door. Riley returned in a few minutes. "The boss agrees with me. You can help us reconstruct the scene and Delia's movements at the party. We'd like you to come with us to Dr. Kamm's."

Chris's father hastily scrawled an excuse for her and told her to get to school as soon as possible. Her parents had their arms around one another as they watched her get into the police car and drive off with Mangone and Riley.

CHAPTER ELEVEN

The day had dawned cloudy, but the sky brightened when Mangone braked in front of Kamm's compound. Without guests roaming around the lawn and refreshments on the patio, the place looked forlorn. A twinge of nervousness unsettled Chris's usual composure. That Kamm was a spooky guy. He would undoubtedly recognize her as the intruder at his party, and he wouldn't be at all pleased to see her.

Mangone pounded a fist on the front door of the fieldstone house. He whispered to Chuck, "Just let me lead the questioning, son." Finally a stout, out-of-breath woman in an apron appeared at the door. She was slapping dough from her hands. With a heavy Irish brogue, she said, "May I help you? If it's Dr. Kamm you've come asking for, he's in the consulting room. Can't be disturbed."

"Sorry," Mangone spat out. He tapped his badge. "Police. Let us in."

They waited in a cramped foyer with a parquet floor. The woman disappeared behind an inner door. Chris was close enough to Riley to catch a whiff of something that might have been shampoo or after-shave lotion. It had a light, citrus-y scent. Ordinarily, Chris didn't like artificial scents, but this one made her want to draw even closer to the young patrolman. The two officers stood awkwardly, not exchanging a word. The house was soundless.

After what seemed like ten minutes to Chris, but was probably more like two, the inner door opened. It was not Dr. Kamm, but a diminutive woman in a silk kimono. Her gleaming black hair, streaked with white, was coiled into a neat bun. "Yes? Mary says that you were asking for the doctor. May I help you? I am Mrs. Kamm."

"We're waiting to speak with Doctor Leopold Kamm," Mangone said.

"He is never to be disturbed," Mrs. Kamm said, "when he's in the consulting room. May I have him get in touch with you when he's done?"

Mangone put a foot down on the threshold of the inner door. "Ma'am, we're the police. We don't wait. We can speak with the doctor here or in my office."

Mrs. Kamm's frostiness dissolved into what looked like fear. "One minute," she said, and closed the inner door firmly, leaving them once again in the dark foyer.

Mangone arched his eyebrows at Riley, withdrew a large handkerchief from a pocket, and honked his nose.

Kamm opened the door, rubbed his hands together, and smiled. He half bowed and ushered them through the door with a gesture. Then he saw Chris. "You!" he cried. "What are you. . . ?" Then he caught himself, and addressed the policemen. "Come in, come in. Sorry to have kept you waiting. This foyer isn't made for more than two people."

Chris detected a very slight, indefinable accent. Or maybe his speech was just what they call "clipped."

They followed Dr. Kamm into a large living room with a set of floor-to-ceiling windows. It was the largest living room that Chris had ever seen. She edged closer to the windows. There was no way directly to the Croton River from here. They were atop a cliff that looked even more precipitous from the interior than it did looking up from below. The perspective of the house from the river was, she realized, skewed, making the building look somewhat squat. But the sloping ceiling was dramatically high. No wonder they called it the Playhouse!

Kamm motioned for them to sit. The furniture consisted of thickly cushioned chairs and an extra-long sofa, all upholstered in a faded sepia flowered print, and a set of low-slung, contemporary black leather chairs. The highly polished, chocolate brown hardwood floor looked as if no one ever walked on it. In various corners, plants were stuffed into fat blue and white porcelain vases. Chris noticed that many of the green leaves were turning brown. It was strange how dark the place was, considering the huge windows. But when you looked outside almost all you could see was giant evergreen trees. Probably the room never got much sunlight.

Mangone sat at the edge of one end of the couch, which did not give with his weight. Chris took the other end, and Chuck Riley and Kamm each took a leather chair. A very un-cozy room. The guests were like base-ball players occupying their respective bases in the field.

"What can I do for you, gentlemen?" Kamm asked in a honeyed tone. "Gentlemen" obviously didn't apply to Chris.

"We're looking," Mangone said, "for a woman named Delia Morrison. She's been missing since yesterday."

The honey dropped from Kamm's voice. "And why does that concern me?"

"This young lady, Christabel Gooding, tells us that she saw Mrs. Morrison on your property yesterday afternoon."

Behind his spectacles, Dr. Kamm's piercing eyes fixed on Chris.

"Ye-e-s, my uninvited guest," he said to Chris. "What, may I ask, were you doing on my property, at a private party?"

"I, uh, ..."

Mangone cut her short. "We're the ones asking the questions, Dr. Kamm. Miss Gooding is a credible witness."

"That may be," Kamm replied, "but she had no business at my party."

Riley broke in with a grin. "Once the Fire Department arrived, Doctor, your private party got very public."

Mangone silenced Riley with a look. With exaggerated patience he said, "Dr. Kamm, I'm afraid we'll have to ask you for the guest list. We'll need to question the people who attended your event."

Kamm removed his spectacles, arched his thick, beetle brows, and blew away what might have been a speck of dust on a lens. "My guest list? The guests here yesterday were my patients. I can't divulge their names."

Mangone snorted, "Your patients were your guests? I thought there was some rule about confidentiality. Did each of your guests know that the other guests were patients, too?"

Kamm was silent.

"Okay, Doctor," Mangone continued. "Let's begin with you then. About what time did Mrs. Morrison arrive?"

"Ah, I'm not sure. Cocktails were called for 4. Maybe she got here sometime around 5:30 or so."

"No!" Chris blurted out. "It had to be before then. I got there around 5, and I saw her come out of the house while the fire was still going."

Mangone didn't take his eyes off Kamm. "We can check that with the Fire Department. Now, Dr. Kamm, did Mrs. Morrison come to your party alone, or was she with someone?"

"I can't tell you that. My housekeeper answered the door."

"And when did you see Mrs. Morrison last? Do you remember what time she left?"

"Well, there were so many comings and goings. Let me see. . . She did stay for dinner, I think, and we served the buffet at 6:15. But when she left I cannot say precisely."

Chris opened her mouth and then shut it again.

Mangone went on, "Did she leave by herself, Doctor?"

"Yes, I think so. I don't recall that anyone else left with her."

Mrs. Kamm entered so noiselessly that all four people in the living room started when she spoke. "Doctor," she said softly to her husband.

"Doctor?" Did Mrs. Kamm call her husband "Doctor" when they were alone, too? On the other hand, Chris couldn't imagine anyone, not even his wife, calling him "Leo."

"Doctor, there's a patient to see you. She says it's urgent. You know, she telephoned this morning."

"I have to see this patient," Kamm said to Mangone.

Mangone jumped to his feet, as if to block Kamm's way. "Oh, no, Dr. Kamm. Not until we're done. He turned to Mrs. Kamm. "Tell her to wait."

With an openly frightened look, Mrs. Kamm withdrew.

Mangone eased himself back onto the couch and then leaned forward.

A minute later the same door flew open, and Bella Lewis rushed past the protesting Mrs. Kamm. In her eagerness to get to Kamm she seemed not to notice Chris or the men in uniform.

"Doctor!" she cried, as Mrs. Kamm looked on in horror. "Doctor! How could you not see me? You know what I'm going through. This is the most terrible conflict of my life!"

Kamm silenced her with a word. "Bella."

She wiped her eyes with a lace handkerchief, but some tears dropped to the floor.

Embarrassed, Chris averted her gaze. It always bothered her to see grown-ups shed their veneer of control. It was as if she had caught Mrs. Lewis taking off her clothes. Her mother saved such behavior for the stage.

"Bella," Kamm repeated in a low tone, as if he were soothing a child. "You can see that I'm with these gentlemen now. I'll be with you as soon as possible. Now let Mrs. Kamm take you back to the waiting room. Try to collect yourself." He nodded at his wife.

Mrs. Lewis's body relaxed, her shoulders slumping forward. Sniffling, her head hanging low, she let herself be led out.

Mangone had not moved. He continued as if there had been no interruption. "Can you tell me, if Mrs. Morrison talked to any particular individual or individuals?"

"Frankly, no, I can't tell you. I wasn't mingling at all with the guests at first, because I had important calls to respond to in the consulting room. I make it a point to return patients' calls within twelve hours, if at all possible. Then there was the fire."

"When you came out, did you see her?"

"No, but I wasn't looking for her. There was a fire in my house, as I think you are aware."

Riley stretched, and Mangone straightened his spine. "Now, Doctor," he said, "about that guest list. . . ."

Kamm shifted his look to Chris. Was it the spectacles, or were his charcoal brownish eyes glittering at her and at her alone? *You keep away from me, or else . . .* those eyes said. "I'll ask my housekeeper to get it for you." He crossed to the other side of the room and said to the wall, "Mary."

Oh, it was an intercom, so small that Chris had completely missed it.

Two minutes later, Mrs. Kamm reappeared, with Mary behind her. "Was it this you were wanting?" Mary asked Kamm, handing him several sheets of paper.

Kamm passed them to Mangone.

"Mrs. Kamm, Mary. Please sit," said Mangone.

They did as they were asked. Kamm remained standing.

"I was not at the party at all," Mrs. Kamm volunteered to the two policemen. "I had a frightful migraine, and I was lying down in a darkened room in the Playhouse."

Mary huffed and puffed to Mangone, "See here, I had a lot of work to do. I went to answer the door, but I was mainly in the kitchen. Don't ask me about none of the guests."

"Speaking of the kitchen," Mangone said, "we'll just take a quick look around the premises, Dr. Kamm."

Kamm removed his spectacles and wiped them. "You think I've got Mrs. Morrison stuffed into a closet?"

"Look," Mangone said. "A lot went on here yesterday. We'd like to inspect the fire damage. It's in your own interest."

"You're welcome to look around when you show me a warrant."

"All right, Dr. Kamm. "We'll be speaking to the Fire Department any-way."

At that moment the doorbell rang, and Mary hurried away. When she returned, she trotted to keep pace with a distraught Harold Lewis.

"I know my wife is here," he said to Kamm, "Please ask her to come out here at once." A herringbone jacket with worn leather elbow patches hung unevenly over his muscular torso. His greying brown hair was a bit messy, and his light blue eyes were noticeably bloodshot. Chris thought she smelled whiskey.

There was a pause, as Mr. Lewis looked around, taking in the presence of others. Mangone waved him to a seat. "While you're here," he said, "let me ask you a few questions. You and your wife are friendly with Mrs. Delia Morrison, I believe."

Harold Lewis passed the back of a hand over his brow. "Yes, my wife especially. She and Delia and a few of the other girls sometimes have lunch together."

"But you and Mrs. Lewis didn't go to Dr. Kamm's party with her?"

"No, Delia went directly from her office, I think."

Chuck Riley intervened abruptly. "Mr. Lewis, do you have any reason to believe that Mrs. Morrison might have run away? Did she seem unhappy?"

Lewis lowered his head. "Well, she was of course upset by Corey Sylvester's death. But, no, I'd say that she was holding up very well. She seemed to enjoy working more closely with Joan. She's very attached to her, you know." He looked up eagerly toward the door, as if willing Bella to appear.

Riley was on cat's feet now, ignoring Mangone. "Do you know of any romantic complications in her life?"

Did Mr. Lewis actually chuckle? Or was it just a cough? "You're all so prejudiced against Delia, aren't you? Well, you're wrong. She's completely devoted to Frank Ewing. The fact that they don't live together seven days a week means nothing."

Mangone asked Mary to bring Bella Lewis. The cook promptly vanished. Several minutes later she reentered the room, Bella Lewis in tow.

"This is intolerable," Kamm snarled, "interrogating my patients."

"I won't take up much of your time, Mrs. Lewis," Mangone said to her. "Please sit down. We need to clear up a few things."

Mrs. Lewis sat on a leather chair, lit up a filter-tip Parliament cigarette, and blew smoke from her nostrils. Despite her chunkiness, Chris thought, there was something sophisticated about her. Maybe it was her sultry, dry drawl that reminded her of the actress Tallulah Bankhead.

Kamm remained standing.

Yes, Mrs. Lewis said, she and her husband had heard, and they were both very concerned about Delia's disappearance. So unlike her. She was so *conscientious*. It was hard to imagine her walking out on Joan Sylvester, much less on Frank.

Mangone questioned them closely about Delia's movements at the party. Neither one had been paying much attention, because they were trying to work out their own problems. Bella Lewis knitted her brows. "But I did see her, I did. Let me see—it was after the fire began. She seemed to be rushing out of the house. There was something odd about it." She paused, knitting her brows even more deeply. "I know. Right after she rushed out, I saw a man who nearly tripped trying to catch up to her."

"Do you know who it was?" asked Mangone.

Mrs. Lewis was thinking. "No. . . . Of course I only saw him for a moment, and from the back. But I didn't recognize him."

Dr. Kamm escorted the policemen and Chris to the front door himself.

Kamm opened the front door and swept an arm toward the lawn in a gesture for them to leave. "You've been very civil," he said, as the three prepared to depart. His brows beetled. "But—his eyes flashed on Chris again—I do consider your visit an invasion of my privacy."

"We'll be back," said Mangone, "with a warrant."

Kamm shut the door, and Chris heard the click of a lock. She turned to Mangone. "Maybe Dr. Kamm was wrong about when Delia left the party. He said he thought she stayed for dinner. But I'm pretty sure she left the house before dinner was served."

They started up the winding path to Nordica Drive. The grass around it was overgrown and spilled onto the gravel. Mangone swerved off the path into the high grass splashed with ferns, signaling to Chuck and Chris to stop there with him. "Now Chris, see if you can repeat Mrs. Morrison's movements as she left the house."

Delia had definitely been going toward the woods. Putting one hesitant foot before the other, Chris made her way to a cool, shady grove of spruces. The ferns were thicker here. Through the trees she could glimpse the edge of the cliff. You could get to Nordica Drive from the spruce grove, but it would have been a roundabout way of going. Mangone and Chuck waited by the side of the path, watching her. What was that glint of metal she spied through a clump of ferns? It was something silver. She got as close as she could, not wanting to call attention to herself by bending over and picking it up. She could see, however, that it was a brooch she had often seen Delia wear. A clue! She would have to come back for it. But why was she on the lookout for clues? Chris wondered. And then it hit her. Of course! She wanted to be the first to crack the case and break the story.

"Is that it?" called Mangone.

"That's all I can remember," Chris said.

Mangone turned to Chuck Riley. "Hm-m-m. We won't get anything out of Mary or Mrs. Kamm—that much is clear. And Ewing seemed surprised when I told him that that Delia was last seen at Dr. Kamm's party. But Nick Salvucci told me he saw Delia dash out of the house shortly after the fire was extinguished—sometime around 5:30, and he didn't see her return. She had evidently stayed inside the main house during the fire."

Following Mangone's lead, Chuck and Chris got back on the path and headed for Nordica Drive. Mangone lit up a cigar. Chuck Riley leaned against the cruiser. "So why did Mrs. Morrison rush out like that? Who or what did she want to get away from?"

"Good question, Chuck. Another interesting thing is that Hendrik and Maria Muller and the Lewises were all there at the same time. I thought that the two couples were avoiding each other since they discovered the infidelity. So for the four of them to turn up at Dr. Kamm's—it was unexpected."

"All the guests were Kamm's patients?" Chuck Riley asked. "And aren't they Communists?"

"Yes, they're all his patients. And many are Communists. But they're slippery folk, and you can't always tell their politics. That's why it's good to keep an eye on them."

Mangone opened the driver's door of the cruiser, and the two men climbed in.

Chris stood rooted to the ground.

"O.K.," said Mangone. "We'll get a crew to come out and go over the grounds. Time to shove off, young lady."

Chris's mind was elsewhere. It was on that bit of silver in the ferns. The image of it made her realize that she didn't want to get in the car with the policemen. She didn't want to go to school at all.

"Coming, Chris?" Riley called from the front seat.

"No," said Chris. "I'm just going to walk to school from here."

The two men looked at one another. "We can't leave you here alone," Riley said. Mangone nodded.

"Tell you what," said Chris. "Why don't you drop me off at the corner of Morningside Drive and Old Post Road South? I'll walk from there."

Mangone threw her a hard look. "We're taking you back to school where you belong, and that's that."

They dropped her off in the school's parking lot. As soon as she saw the cruiser turn around and disappear down Old Post Road South, she ran around the back of the school onto Old Post Road South in the opposite direction, toward Nordica Drive. She had to get back before the police crew did. Luckily, no one was on the high school lawn.

Now how was she going to do this? She was dressed for school, in her purple felt skirt with a crinoline, a white blouse, and loafers. Not exactly ideal for the expedition she was planning.

Her visit to the Kamm compound confirmed her impression that climbing down to the river from Nordica Drive was impossible. The only way to get there was from Silver Lake. If her mission was successful, she wouldn't even have to return to Kamm's to retrieve the brooch. At least not today. She picked up her pace. Luckily the day had turned out so warm and summery that when Chris reached the pebbly beach at Silver Lake, she was tempted to take a swim. Shaking her head at the quandary she was in, she removed her socks and loafers. The damned skirt and crinoline were too long. She could break her neck over them. There was no help for it, though. She'd just have to hop over on the rocks. It was slow going. It was hard to keep her balance with her book bag, into which she had stuffed her shoes and socks. At one point she slipped and felt a stab of pain as her sole met a pointy stone in the river bed.

Past Silver Lake, the rocks got larger. Some seemed more like small boulders. From here on Chris needed to wade. The river was high, and the cool water lapped at her legs. Soon she realized that her skirt and crinoline had gotten wet almost to her knees. They were dragging her down.

Oh, rats! I'm going to have to take them off. At least no one's around.

She undid her cinch belt, stepped out of the skirt and crinoline and laid everything carefully on a rock. But what if a breeze came and blew them off? She could wade around in her slip back here, but how would she get home? She bent down and scraped the river bed with her hands, finally coming up with a small rock, which she placed on top of the skirt and crinoline.

What if, after all this, I'm wrong? I'll really be in hot water. From cold to hot water! That's a laugh.

All along her eyes had been combing the river. But when she reached the bottom of the cliff on which Kamm's compound sat, she waded close to the shore to get another view of the old Nikko Inn. She tried to imagine it on a misty day. It would look like a Japanese brush painting, only not beautiful. Grim and . . . sort of like a witch's castle.

Then she looked down. From a distance of several feet the first thing that leapt into her view was a patch of strawberry blond hair.

CHAPTER TWELVE

There was no first day of school for Chris that year. Instead she returned to Kamm's grounds with the police and the Medical Examiner. The M.E. was scary—asking her to compare photos of Delia with other women, asking her about the shape of Delia's nose, the color of her eyes. Chris pointed the police to the brooch. When she got home, exhausted, she skipped dinner, flopped onto her bed, and fell into a deep sleep.

She was falling from a gigantic, rocky cliff. At the bottom, Delia was waiting to catch her. But when Chris landed in Delia's arms, she saw that Delia didn't have a face. Her eyes were two black pits, her mouth a shapeless gash, her nose like a squished wad of gum.

When Chris woke, it was with a vision of Delia as she last saw her alive, the woman whose absence was so bottomless it took the tears away. Delia—always so ready to help Chris, so interested in her activities, always rooting for her—Delia respected her opinions and listened to her seriously. Chris and Delia could giggle together like pals, but somehow Delia was always her mentor. Her mentor—or mother? Maybe that's what a real mother was like. Chris wouldn't know.

◆　◆　◆

It wasn't her byline, and it wasn't the headline that Chris had imagined, but there she was, the next day, in the *New York Times*: "Teen-ager Finds Body of Missing Newspaperwoman." The cause of death was as yet undetermined, the paper said. Chris pushed away her bowl of cornflakes. She'd have to put them back into the box. She couldn't swallow a flake.

As she got up she nearly collided with her mother, who was studying her script as she came into the room.

The script dropped from her hand. "Oh, Chris, you startled me. I thought you'd be in bed. What are you doing up this early?"

"Going to school. I'm just going to get dressed."

Her father had entered the room and was glancing at the open newspaper on the table. "Oh no, young lady, I think that you deserve a day of rest at home. And maybe other kids have seen this article, too. I don't want people bothering you about it right now."

"Yes, Chris," her mother added, "Didn't we all decide that you'd stay home today?"

Chris stared first at one, then at the other. "Yesterday all you wanted was for me to go to school. I don't want to stay home today. I want to go to school and have a normal day."

"Now how can it possibly be a normal day?" her mother said. "That's the whole point. Is it normal that you should be in the *New York Times*? None of this is normal, and you need some time to recover."

"What are you going to do—lock me in? I'm going to school, and that's that." She marched out of the room.

But as Chris started her walk to school, she had to admit to herself that her parents may have had a point. She forgot to look both ways at the intersection of North Highland Place and Mt. Airy, and a car, its brakes squeaking, honked, swerved and missed her by inches. Once she got to school, kids buzzed around her with questions, like hungry bees. This is what it must be like to be popular, Chris thought. Classes were just a jumble of letters and numbers. She had the vague sense that she was being treated like some kind of heroine. Teachers were letting her out of quizzes and homework.

After classes, she dragged herself to the first weekly staff meeting of the "Tiger Rag" thinking she might try to leave early. Mark Radetski, the editor-in-chief, said, "We need to jazz up this rag." Mark was a sixteen-year-old senior and very smart. "How about some cartoons?" Mark asked. "One cartoon per issue, maybe? On some hot topic at school."

Clay, the layout person, didn't like the idea. Of course—it would mean more work for him. He grumbled all the time about the old mimeograph machine. What he said, though, was that he thought it would be hard to come up with ideas, and the illustrations they already had were fine. Clay did the illustrations. "Anyway," Clay said, "I am not a cartoonist. Who would we get to do cartoons for us?" Silence. Eyes fell on Chris. Everyone knew about her father.

"Yeah," said Patty, a junior and, some people thought, next in line for editor. "Chris, I bet you'd do a fabulous job."

"I don't do cartoons," Chris said, without thinking. "That's my father's thing. I write." She had doodled a lot, though, since she was a little kid, and she still liked to draw. As chatter arose around her, she reconsidered. Maybe she should give it a shot. Maybe she was ready for something new. "Well," she finally said, "I guess I could try one cartoon. But even if I end up doing cartoons, I'll still want to write articles."

"Great, Chris!" said Mark. "We all know that you're a girl with many talents." There was some snickering from the back of the room. Mark was in Chris's chess club and one of the few kids who had something interesting to say about politics. Was it only last week that he had asked Chris to go to the movies with him? But he was about four feet tall.

Late in the afternoon, when Chris left the building, she was hit by the thought that on Saturday she would be expected at the office of the *Croton-Harmon News* to help Joan with the next issue. She'd have to force herself to go. What would it be like to walk in there and not be greeted by Delia? On

Sunday Delia would be buried. Chris planned to go to the Croton cemetery for the ceremony, but her parents said she should wait and see what Delia's family wanted.

She turned onto Old Post Road South, wishing that she didn't have to walk all the way home, wishing that someone would come along in a car, offer her a ride, and tell her that the whole thing was untrue.

"Hey, wait up!" Rosie waved from the lawn of the high school. For the past several days Chris had barely seen her. Rosie hadn't shown up for their morning walk to school.

"I know I should be home practicing," Rosie began. "I can't, though, How could I have said I'd play in the Shostakovich Piano Trio for the recital? It's the hardest thing. I'm so afraid I'm going to mess it up."

"You won't." Chris was sure that Rosie could play just about anything. Yet how could Rosie even think about her recital after yesterday?

Rosie stopped in her tracks and put a hand on Chris's arm. "Chris, I just can't go home. I *can't*. Can I come to your house for a while?"

"Of course." Chris longed to say no. But they had an unspoken pact that each of their houses was always open to the other. "What's going on? What's been happening?" Chris asked. No mention by Rosie of what happened yesterday. Well, if Rosie wouldn't mention it, neither would she.

"Oh, it's just everything. My father is still yelling at my mother about that Wylie Maxwell. I think Daddy is getting more and more worried. Last night he said he had a tail."

Chris looked at her.

"Right. My mother didn't know what he was talking about either. She looked at his rear end and said, 'What do you mean, a tail?' But then he explained to her that someone's been following him."

Chris arched her eyebrows.

"I know. It sounds crazy, and Daddy's been drinking a lot lately. But he said that one of these days he would confront whoever it is that's tailing him. And now Daddy thinks if it turns out that Delia was pushed, he'll be the one they go after. My mother said he was being paranoid, and that he had an alibi because he had been at the Municipal Building for her exhibit all that afternoon. Then Daddy shouted that he was the perfect fall guy. 'They'll find a way to break my alibi,' he said."

So Rosie was too distracted even to ask her about finding Delia's body.

A tear splashed onto the Peter Pan collar of Rosie's blue gingham blouse. "Maybe he's right, Chris. Maybe he *is* the perfect suspect. They still think he killed Mr. Sylvester, you know. And look what happened to the Rosenbergs."

Chris tried to shake off the image of Delia's water-eaten corpse in the Croton River. "It's okay, Rosie. They still don't know a thing about what happened to Mr. Sylvester. They have to investigate."

"Didn't they investigate the Rosenberg case? Fat lot of good it did the Rosenbergs."

"This is different," said Chris. Even as she said it she wasn't sure why.

"Maybe. Maybe he *is* paranoid. When my mother said that, he just blew up some more. 'Me paranoid?' he said. 'That's a good one. What about our government? Huh? And those House UnAmerican Activites Committee bastards and McCarthyites who look under their beds every night for Commies. You think maybe I'm hallucinating?'" Rosie pulled out a much-used handkerchief and buried her face in it. "He called my mother naïve and self-centered."

Rosie abruptly sat down on a curb and began to cry, quietly at first and then in earnest. "I hate them, both of them," she sobbed. "I can't go back to that house, Chris. I can't live with them."

Chris sat down next to her and waited until her tears subsided.

When Rosie lifted her head, it was to ask, "You don't think he's guilty, do you, Chris?"

"I hope not. How can we know, though, until they do the investigation?"

Rosie stood and glared down at Chris. "You don't *know*? You don't *know* my father, what kind of person he is? You think he would kill someone?"

Chris got up and put a hand on Rosie's shoulder. "It must be terrible for you at home, Rosie. Your parents must be really hard to live with now. But listen—we have to do whatever we can to help him. He's in an awful position."

Rosie shook off Chris and turned away. "You talk just like a reporter. That's right—find out the truth. You don't understand a thing. It's not *your* father. You don't know what it's like. It's bad enough being called a weirdo all the time. But now people think my father is a murderer. Even you." She started up the hill at a clip.

Chris followed closely behind her. When they got within view of Rosie's house Chris moved up alongside her. "Are you coming over to my house?"

"No," Rosie said. "Just go away and leave me alone."

♦　　♦　　♦

Once Chris got home, she walked around the house in circles, trying to figure out what to do. She was longing to apologize to Rosie for whatever she might have said to offend her, to make everything O.K. between them. Finally she picked up the phone and dialed Rosie's number. No answer.

At dinner she could barely swallow. What had she done to Rosie? Now even her best friend wasn't there for her.

Chris's father, who as Village Manager was in the loop, had news to pass on to her and her mother.

"We didn't learn all that much from the autopsy. At this stage of decomposition, you can't get all that much information."

Chris shifted in her chair.

"What the M. E. found was consistent with a fall from the cliff. But we won't know anything more until the forensic team from White Plains comes up."

"Do you really think you should be telling us all this?" her mother asked.

Early that morning, her father continued, he had gone to a meeting of the Police Department. Mangone wouldn't commit himself on the question of the relation—if any—between the two deaths.

"The chief's right, you know, to hold off drawing any conclusions," Chris's father said. "Someone—we don't know who–was there when Delia fell, but the chief wants to wait for the conclusion of the forensic examination before involving any other law enforcement agency. First he wants to compare the guest lists from Kamm's party with the list—such as the police have it—of the people who were on the train home from the Rosenberg rally."

Between bites into the drumstick, her father looked over at Chris. "Here's where you come in. The police want your help, and I've told him that your mother and I have no objections so long as it doesn't interfere with school."

Huh? Then why didn't they want her to go to school today? Great that the cops were asking for her. Except that right now she felt lousy. She couldn't stop thinking about Delia—Delia in the water, Delia in the office, Delia who would never be in her life again.

From a distance she heard her father say, "Chuck Riley said the force was counting on you, that you've shown great intelligence and courage."

A small thrill of pride broke through Chris's sorrow.

"And Mangone praised you too. Said you have quite a head on your shoulders. He wants you to check their list of Kamm's guests."

◆　◆　◆

Early the next morning, Chuck Riley telephoned and asked Chris to come to the police station. Before he could suggest a time, she said, "I'll be right over." It was more important than school.

Remembering her close call of the other day, she paused only for inter-sections.

Riley offered her a Coke, which she accepted to be polite. He was drink-ing coffee from a large mug that said "Chuck" on it, his eyelids heavy with fatigue. "Chris," he began, "I'm sure that you're very upset. You've been through a lot."

She picked up the coke bottle, thought better of it, and put it down.

"We want to keep track of all the guests at Dr. Kamm's party. Because of the connection between Mrs. Morrison and Mr. Sylvester, we're interested to know which of Dr. Kamm's guests may have been at the June rally in New York."

"What can I do to help, Officer Riley?"

He smiled at her. The smile woke up his face. He handed her a copy of Kamm's guest list. "What you can do is try to remember the people you saw at Dr. Kamm's. Were any of the guests also on the train home from the Rosenberg rally?"

She scanned the list. "Mr. and Mrs. Lewis," she said. "I tried to talk to them at the party. They didn't seem too happy to see me, though."

"Anyone else?" Riley pressed.

"Well-l-l, the Mullers."

"Anyone else, Chris? Even people whose names you might not know? People you could describe?"

She propped up her elbows on his desk and cupped her chin in her hands. It was becoming very hard to reconstruct that afternoon. Through a haze she saw the image of Bristle-head. Should she say anything about Pike? She still hadn't told anyone about her run-in with the F.B.I. agent at the Rosenberg rally. She continued to feel guilty and confused about it. Maybe she should just have given Pike her notebook when he asked her for it. Wasn't she evading the law? She shut her eyes tightly.

"Chris?"

Better not to say anything. But maybe she could give a hint. "Uh-h-h, wait a minute. . . there was someone, some man. . . . I don't remember very well. I guess I didn't get a good look at him. Anyhow, I wouldn't know his name. I think I've seen him somewhere else, though—not on the train."

"Could it have been in New York?"

She scrunched up her face again, closing her eyes and furrowing her brow.

"Uh-h-h, I don't know. Maybe." Pause. "Well . . . no, I don't know."

"Okay, Chris, thanks a lot for your help. If you do remember anything about this man, you'll let us know, all right?"

CHAPTER THIRTEEN

Sitting at the kitchen table, her unfinished breakfast set aside, Chris stared at the *Croton-Harmon News.* It looked like the issue that had announced Corey Sylvester's death, the paper edged in black. Edged in black for Delia! It was still hard to believe. Chris pushed back the spasms of loss and devoured the article.

It was all there: the party at Dr. Kamm's, Chris's discovery of the body; and, finally, the ambiguous conclusion: forensic experts from New York City had found signs of a struggle on Delia Morrison's arms. But there was no firm indication that she had been pushed over the cliff. Because of her links to the victim of the crime committed on June 19, which remained unsolved, the local police were once again working together with the Westchester County D.A., Cobb Stewart, and with the F.B.I. Chris was praised for her quick thinking and her courage. There was a photo of a younger Delia She was even prettier then.

Frank Ewing had notified Delia's landlord that as of November 1 he would cease to occupy the apartment. Delia's ex-husband had taken a night train back to Pennsylvania immediately after coming up to identify the body. According to the articles in the *New York Times* and the village newspaper, Delia's connection to Dr. Kamm was not known.

Something had been gnawing at Chris's brain until it could no longer be ignored. Shouldn't she go to the police with her copy of Dr. Kamm's letter to Delia? Probably no one but her knew anything about the doctor's displeasure at Delia's decision to leave his group. Why did Delia decide to go to Dr. Kamm's party anyhow if she had already told him she was quitting the therapy? Wouldn't the police want to look into the matter? But somehow it felt wrong—wasn't it an invasion of Delia's privacy to make that letter public? And what if it incriminated Delia in some way?

The trunks of the old oaks in the back yard were blackened and slick against a grey sky with low-slung storm clouds. With a pang she thought of Rosie. At least Mr. Novac didn't have anything to do with this case. He wasn't even at the party. But things still didn't look at all good for him in the Sylvester case. Absently, Chris riffled through a pile of papers on the table. Oh, here was something that was probably meant to be part of her father's latest idea, a comic strip modeled on the television show, "Candid Camera," with Croton local Allen Funt. After trapping his victims in an embarrassing situation, Allen Funt would say, "Smile—you're on Candid Camera." Her father was planning to call his series "Candid Crayon." The comic strip looked like an earlier one that he had drawn.

The idea of "Candid Crayon" intrigued Chris. People eavesdropping and spying on their neighbors and in the meantime being spied on by the F. B. I. She inspected the comic strip again. She was sure she had seen it before. Oh yes, it was the one from the Sylvesters' open house, maybe about the Lewises and the Mullers. But this one was different; she couldn't say how. Why would her father redo it?

She had to see Rosie. She picked up the phone and dialed her number. Rosie herself answered.

"Are you going to walk to school with me?" Chris asked.

Rosie sounded as if she were talking from another state.

"No. I'm getting a ride from my mother on her way to the station—she's going to New York today."

Chris's stomach went hollow. Rosie didn't even ask if Chris wanted to ride with them.

♦ ♦ ♦

Chris forced herself to go through the motions of sitting through class after class. At lunch time she was on her way to sit with Mark Radetski and some others from the school newspaper when she realized that she had no appetite. So she wandered aimlessly through the Upper Village. What was happening to Rosie?

She skipped the after-school volleyball game with Gail and some other girls, and took off as soon as classes were over, figuring she wouldn't run into Rosie, who had orchestra that day. Chris's parents wouldn't be home for at least an hour or two. She was aching to talk. To divert her attention, when she got home, she picked up the phone for some eavesdropping on the party line. Nothing doing. Besides which, she didn't want to tie up the phone. What if Rosie was trying to call?

Deciding that she'd get an early start on her homework, she sat down at the kitchen table and opened her geometry book. No use. It was a bunch of dancing triangles and circles. Pushing them out of the way was the special delivery letter for Delia. That letter again! She had to do something about it.

With shaky fingers she dialed the number of the Police Department and asked for Chuck Riley. He was there! The butterflies got going again.

"What is it, Chris?" Riley could be very gentle when he wanted to.

A pause. She was thinking. "Well . . . there's something I think I should tell you. But, uh, I'm a bit worried about it. I could get into trouble."

"I can't help you, Chris, unless I know what it's about. Does it have anything to do with Delia Morrison's death?"

She took a breath so deep that Riley probably heard her. "It might."

The policeman said nothing, and the pause lengthened.

"Okay," she said. "But if I tell you, will you promise not to get me into trouble?"

She could almost hear him smiling.

Slowly she confessed to having opened the special delivery letter from Dr. Kamm to Delia Morrison. She felt her face flushing crimson. Lucky he couldn't see her!

"Chris, this may be important. Can you remember what was in the letter?"

Chris summarized it to the best of her ability. She hesitated before adding, "I . . . uh, I copied down the letter before I delivered it to Delia. I have the copy."

It was tampering with the mail. Was she stupidly confessing a crime? But the letter was from Kamm, and, no matter what, Kamm had a part in this awful story. If she said nothing, she was pretty sure she'd be withholding evidence.

Riley's voice was warm. "Well, thanks for telling me about this, Chris. Bring me your copy of that letter first thing tomorrow morning. And don't go opening anyone else's mail, okay?"

♦   ♦   ♦

Just as she cradled the receiver, there was a bustling in the front hall. Her mother and father came in chattering with that critic, Frank Ewing. Him again?

Frank Ewing nodded a greeting at her as her father ambled over to the liquor cabinet. Oh no, was Mr. Ewing going to stay for dinner?

Her father passed around drinks.

"A toast to you, Maya!" said Ewing. His voice was flat.

What did they know that she didn't? And when was she going to get to talk to her parents alone?

"Thank you, Frank. I'm having trouble believing it, but this is a nice way to be convinced."

"I couldn't hold out any longer, Frank," her father said. "Cornelius is going to match Scarborough's salary, even improve on it a little."

Oh, that was it—her mother was going to be a star! Chris had been hoping that her father would consent. If she weren't so tired, she'd be excited. But even the prospect of going to the first night and maybe writing an article on it didn't interest her right now.

"So," said Ewing, "Wylie and I are going to have to compete over who can produce the best review."

Her mother took a sip of the martini she was holding. "Wylie Maxwell? "I didn't know that you knew him."

Wylie Maxwell . . . Why did he keep popping up?

"Oh, certainly. We're invited to the same cocktail parties, after all. He's the golden boy at *Time*. How do you know him?"

"I met him at the Sylvesters," her mother said.

"So Wylie Maxwell knew Corey?" Her father asked.

Ewing's worry lines deepened into a frown.

"Yes, he was friends with Corey's son at Yale."

Her mother fished for the martini olive with a swizzle stick. "So Joan said. But . . . isn't it strange that Mr. Maxwell was at the Sylvesters' open house when their own son wasn't?"

After the briefest of pauses Frank answered, "Jack Sylvester leads a very busy life, so I'm told. And besides, Corey took a journalist's interest in Wylie. He was hoping to help nurture a career for him at the new journal, *Encounter*."

"Did he want to get Maxwell to write for the Croton newspaper, too?"

"He was always on the lookout for good writers." He stared into his martini glass. "Speaking of good writers, I believe that your friend Liliane Carrière has sacked Wylie."

Her mother swallowed the olive with a small cough. "Oh, you mean that article he wanted to do on Lili for *Time Magazine*? Well, she must have had her reasons for bowing out."

"My opinion," Frank Ewing said, "which I know is entirely gratuitous, is that at this stage in her career it's a serious mistake. Maxwell's photographer would have gotten beautiful shots of her work."

Ewing stood up. Her father stood, too.

The critic clapped her father on the shoulder. "Well, it was good running into you," he said. "Very opportune meeting. And congratulations again, Maya."

Her mother rose and gave Frank a hug. "Frank," she said, "just tell us before you leave, how are you? I know that we're not going to see you much around Croton anymore."

"Well," his voice broke, "you can imagine. Delia was . . . everything to me." He cleared his throat. "But I'm getting along, on my trusty combination of scotch and Miltown."

Chris's mother grasped his hand. "Gil and I feel terribly bad for you. Is there anything that we can do?"

He withdrew his hand abruptly and turned his head away from her. Was his body shaking? If so, he rapidly regained control of himself.

"Have you heard," her mother asked, "about the program for Corey's memorial service?"

"Yes. Joan called me."

"Will you be coming up for it?" she asked. "Or for Delia's funeral?"

"I doubt it."

"Too painful?"

"Much too. And I don't know what Hugh Morrison's plans are. Besides…" His voice trailed off, and there was an uncomfortable pause.

Chris thought that her mother should stop pestering Mr. Ewing with her questions, but she continued, "Are you . . . are you following the investigation?"

"I prefer not to," Ewing said. "If the police need me for anything, they know where to find me. Otherwise, I'll settle for ignorance."

◆　　◆　　◆

Chris was just getting ready to go to bed when the phone rang. "For you," her mother called to her. Thinking it might be Rosie, she sprinted to the phone. Her mother, smiling, handed her the receiver and mouthed, "It's a *boy*."

Chris frowned at her and took the receiver.

"Oh hi, Mark."

"Hey listen, Chris," Mark Radetski said. "We didn't decide when you'll be giving us your cartoon. How about for the next issue?"

Chris thought a minute. Too much to do between now and then. Besides, she just wasn't in the mood to think up a cartoon right now.

"How about for the issue after?" she asked. "For two weeks from now?"

Mark sounded disappointed. "Oh, okay, Chris, if you really can't do it before."

He paused, and Chris waited.

"....Uh, maybe we can talk over some ideas together. Could we walk to school together tomorrow morning?"

She looked around to make sure that her parents weren't within earshot.

"The thing is, Mark, that I have to go over to the police station early tomorrow—before school."

"The police station?"

"Yeah. You know, since I found Delia's body (it felt weird to say that), they keep needing to talk to me. Besides which I have to give them something."

Uh-oh, why did she say that? She should have kept her mouth shut.

Fortunately he didn't pick up on it. "So let's find another time to talk."

Was that Mark clearing his throat, or did she hear a funny click on the phone?

"Mark," she asked, "did you just hear a kind of click on the phone? Like someone on the party line hanging up?"

"No. No, I didn't. Well, maybe I'll see you later in school then."

It was strange. That funny click didn't really sound like someone hanging up on the party line. Come to think of it, it was more of a light tap than a click. Living on Mt. Airy had taught her that a tap on your phone was not something you were eager to hear.

CHAPTER FOURTEEN

What a different world it was at 6:30 in the morning! There was practically no traffic on Mt. Airy, so the chirping of the birds came through undisturbed. But the stillness did not seem peaceful to Chris. The darkened sky held the threat of rain, and an autumnal chill gave her a shiver or two. She felt weighed down by the knowledge of what was in her book bag. She was dragging her feet, pushing herself to keep going. What would Delia think? Wasn't turning over the letter a betrayal?

As she turned from the foot of Mt. Airy onto Grand street, where it curves into the center of the Upper Village, a creepy sensation crawled spider-like up her spine. Someone, somewhere, had fastened eyes on her. She wished that she could have taken Willie along. He wasn't exactly protection, but he had a very off-putting bark.

At the still shuttered Parkway Delicatessen on Grand Street, she allowed herself a look over her right shoulder. The empty streets were like a ghost town. Most stores wouldn't be opening up until shortly before nine. It was too early for students to be walking to school. There were only two parked cars on Grand Street, and not one person.

She reached the intersection of Grand Street and Old Post Road when she felt a drop of rain splash onto her head. A wind was coming up. It was time for her old Shetland sweater, which she had tied around her waist. She set down her book bag on the sidewalk and was slipping on her sweater, when, swift as Superman, someone came up from behind, grabbed her book bag, and made a run for it.

"Hey!" she called, "Hey, you! My book bag!"

The man, whose features she had barely seen, was off and running. She started after him at a clip, her sweater half off and dragging at her feet. In middle of the street her sweater caught at her right foot and sent her hurtling toward the stop light at the center of the intersection. She heard a thwack as her head hit the base.

The next sound was of Willie whining into one of her ears, more and more shrilly and insistently, until, as she came to, it turned into a siren. Looming over her was a head so large that she could barely make out its features. "Chris! Chris!" she heard, "Can you hear me?"

She looked up to see the features slowly shrink and resolve themselves into a face she thought she knew. It was a policeman.

"My head hurts," she said.

Chuck Riley drew back a lock of her hair. "Yeah, no wonder. You must have hit the ground running. No, don't get up. We've called an ambulance."

"I can't see too well out of my right eye."

He called to the rookie to get out the first aid kit. Riley knelt by her side and dabbed at her right temple. It hurt. Not so much as the top of her head though. He gently placed his jacket over her legs. He was holding a Shetland sweater that looked torn.

She tried to ask, "Where's my book bag?"

Riley must have understood her, because after what seemed like a few minutes he answered, "I'll have someone go get it."

"I'll go," Chris mumbled.

Chuck Riley held out an arm, as if to restrain her from getting up. "No you won't. Just wait a few minutes."

When she saw another policeman approach empty-handed she choked back a sob. "I'm sorry," she said.

"For what?" Riley asked.

"Oh, Officer Riley," she wailed, "Someone took my book bag."

With the whine of another siren, Mangone leapt out of a cruiser and bent over Chris. "We've called your father. He'll be over right away."

"Um, okay." She thought she was speaking, but it came out a whisper. The blinking lights of the cruisers were making her dizzy. She could taste the blood that was pouring out from somewhere on her head. Her eyes were closing. "My right eye is funny."

Mangone, squatted down over her, leaning forward almost into her face. "Was Kamm's letter in your book bag, Chris?" She heard the chief say something to Chuck Riley about Delia maybe defecting. "Defecting, defecting . . . ." Isn't that what Iron Curtain people did?

"Yeah, the guy was probably after Delia's letter," Riley said, his voice coming through to Chris in something like a wind tunnel. "I think Chris was on her way over to the station to bring it to us." He turned back to Chris and dabbed her face with gauze.

She felt something like the swish of a paintbrush on the other side of her face. Willie! He was licking her cheek.

"No more first aid, Chuck," Mangone said. "Wait for the ambulance."

"Aw, sir," Chuck said, "just look at her."

As her eyelids drooped, she heard someone say, "She's passing out again."

♦   ♦   ♦

When she woke up, several heads were spinning around her. A woman in a white cap, a man in a white coat, someone . . . her father!

Her father was sitting at her bedside, holding her hand. "You're going to be fine, missy," he said.

The white-capped lady handed her a glass. "Here, honey, drink this."

She couldn't manage it alone, but the nurse helped her. "I'm in a hospital?" she asked her father. It was no use trying to hoist herself up a bit. Her head and her chest hurt too much.

"You've had a bad accident, little lady," the man in the white coat said to her. "But we're taking care of you here in the Emergency Room. Do you remember what happened?"

She had lost something. What was it? It was something very important.

Her father squeezed her hand. "Chrissie, do you know why you're here, in the hospital?"

"Because my head hurts. And my eye is funny. And there's ringing in my ears. Will my brain be okay?" she asked no one in particular.

"Don't worry about your brain, kiddo," her father reassured her. "I've always told you that your head is hard as a rock."

Chris tried to turn her head more toward her father and grimaced. "Is Mommy here?"

"No, she's in the city." Gil glanced at his watch. "She's going to be coming home soon. Do you know how you got here?"

"Uh-uh."

"The ambulance came. I drove behind it, with Willie. Soon I'll go back and get your mother, and we'll both drive down here together."

Chris's eyelids felt heavy again. "I'm in Tarrytown?"

"Yes," said her father, and she was asleep.

◆ ◆ ◆

The hospital corridors were painted a peach color, and the lighting, although bright, was not harsh. They were transferring her from the emergency room to a regular one. Her father was walking along with them. At the elevator Mangone and Chuck Riley were conferring in undertones. What were they doing here? Her father stopped to talk with them.

Mangone was muttering something about a stranger and checking the Harmon and Croton railroad stations. The chief was saying something to Chuck about stepping up surveillance of Kamm. Kamm? Huh? The last thing she heard before they wheeled her onto the elevator was Chuck Riley saying, "The poor kid. Poor little kid."

In her room, the doctor explained to Chris's father that they would keep her under observation in the hospital for a few days. She would need to be extensively tested. She had suffered a vitreous hemorrhage in her right eye, and her vision would probably improve with eye drops. If something more serious than a concussion had occurred, such as a sub-dural hematoma, they might not know it for at least several days, maybe weeks.

Vitreous hemorrhage? Subdural hematoma? What was going on?

So far so good, the doctor told her father. In the ER, the bleeding from the head injury seemed to have slowed, which was a good sign. She needed only ten stitches. And also, she hadn't lost consciousness again.

♦   ♦   ♦

When she next woke up, Mangone and Chuck Riley were with her father in her room, talking quietly. The door to the room was open, and the little man with the squeaky voice was there. That man was every-where!

"Shit!" he exploded. "Excuse my French. Those guys! This is out of bounds. Out of bounds!" He caught his fedora, which had slipped sideways off his head, just in time to keep it from landing on the floor.

"Look, Pike, why don't you wait outside?" Mangone said to him.

"They're on our turf again. They're always where they're not supposed to be. They shouldn't even be in this country. And they're dumb! They always bungle things. Bungle them!"

The room was quiet.

"Who?" asked Mangone.

"The Agency. The goddam Agency! They're not supposed to interfere with us, but they always do. Think they're G-men. Wanna play tough. But they've got their heads up their ass. Excuse my French."

The officers waited.

"So we've got your thief. I recognized him at the train station. If you're still looking for him, you'll find him with the Agency. They really botched it, those bastards."

"If you mean the C.I.A.," Mangone murmured soothingly, "We've seen them before. It isn't the first time they've been around Croton."

"Yeah, but now they've seriously injured a kid. For nothing. For nothing!"

Oh, why didn't they all just go away and let her sleep?

"Did they get the wrong person?" Riley asked.

"No, it was Chris Gooding they were after, all right. But they clammed up about what they wanted from her. I couldn't get any information."

"Would you kindly get to the point?" Mangone said.

"Yeah. The point is they harmed the Gooding kid for nothing. They must have known she was on her way to see you guys with something of interest for you."

Mangone leaned in toward Riley and Pike. "Chris had phoned Riley to tell him she had a letter that had something to do with Dr. Kamm and Delia Morrison. What was that all about? Did it have anything to do with what happened at Kamm's party?" He moved closer to the agent and Riley. "Next. We'll need to talk more to Frank Ewing about Delia. We also need to work on our overlapping lists from Kamm's party and the Rosenberg rally. There's the Lewises and the Mullers, we know that. I'll start in on them myself."

"You won't get anything out of them," Pike said. "They don't mind letting everyone know about their sex lives, but when it comes to details about Kamm, they shut their traps."

"Please, gentlemen," Chris's father said in a raised voice, "Kindly conduct your business elsewhere."

He bent over to kiss Chris's forehead, and they all filed out, still talking.

CHAPTER FIFTEEN

It was getting to feel claustrophobic. In the three—or was it four?—days that she had been hospitalized, at least one of her parents was always around, hovering over her.   Chris was allowed no other visitors except for their family doctor from Croton, Dr. Carroll, who peered into her eye and told her that she was a brave girl. Not a word from Rosie. Chris could now sit on a chair in her room for short intervals. She was sitting with her mother when the door opened to admit a visitor. She could see a little better out of her right eye now, but things were still blurry. She could just barely make out Mrs. Lewis, of the marriage-partner-switching foursome.

Was Mrs. Lewis allowed to visit?

Her mother let go of her hand and stood up. "Bella! How kind of you to come! How did you get past the guards?"

"Oh, I just breezed by, you know, saying that I had something to deliver and would be right back. They didn't bother to chase after me." She looked blonder than usual. At the sight of Chris's swollen face, she shook her head with a brief tsk-tsk. The bandage around Chris's head had been replaced by a large rectangle of gauze covering the stitches on the part of her scalp where they'd removed her hair. With a "Chris, dear, you poor thing," Mrs. Lewis handed her a box.

Chris's hands were unsteady, and it took her time to unwrap the package. The sight of her favorite chocolates made her stomach feel queasy. "Lindt chocolates," she said politely. "Thank you!" Why was Bella Lewis being so nice?   She tried to remember why she thought that Mrs. Lewis didn't like her. Was it something that happened at Dr. Kamm's party?

Without waiting for an invitation, Mrs. Lewis took the chair that her mother had vacated. She had heard about the accident only yesterday, and she felt terrible, just terrible. What an awful thing for Chris's parents to have to go through. At that she nodded a look at Chris's mother, who had to remain standing, the only two chairs in the room being occupied. She and Gil must have been scared to death. She wanted to know how Chris was doing, if they had gotten any news about her attacker. These questions were aimed at Chris and her mother in rapid-fire succession, leaving little room to respond. Chris hoped that Mrs. Lewis would state her mission before her mother found a way to shoo her out.

But Mrs. Lewis seemed to have other ideas. She looked up at Chris's mother. "Maya, they keep these hospitals impossibly hot. Would you be a dear and get me a glass of ice water? Chris seems to have run out of extra glasses."

By her sweeping exit Chris could tell that her mother was exasperated.

When her mother was out of earshot, Mrs. Lewis whispered, "Chris, dear, I do owe you an apology. I was quite rude to you at Dr. Kamm's. Harold and I were distraught. I was so traumatized by the fire that I was incapable of uttering a civil greeting."

Chris ransacked her mind for a memory. "That's okay."

"And then this horrible business of Delia's death, so soon after Corey's— Joan must be beside herself."

Only Mrs. Lewis had brought it up with her. Her parents seemed to know that she didn't want to talk about it.

"Harold and I didn't even know she was at Dr. Kamm's that day, didn't even see her. We were all talking about leaving Kamm's group, you know. First Delia—I thought she had already left him before the party—and then Harold and I, and Hendrik and Maria. But the four of us hadn't come to a decision yet." She paused to look at the half-open door. "We went to the party anyway, knowing full well that it might be our swan song."

Swan song? What was the woman talking about? The throbbing in Chris's head had become a pounding.

"You would think that Dr. Kamm might be sorry to lose so many patients at once. But then he's not in it for the money, you know, dear. He has pots of money. He throws it around all over the place. He gets quite wild, though, if people desert him, and now people are starting to leave in droves." She dropped her whisper even lower. "I wanted to say . . . I've seen you with that nice young policeman, Chuck Riley. You know, dear, there's no reason to mention to him that you saw Harold and me at Dr. Kamm's. I wouldn't want. . . ."

Why is she asking me this?

Footsteps approaching. Uh-oh. Her father, with her mother following. He was an even stricter watchdog than her mother. He handed Mrs. Lewis the glass of water without a word.

Mrs. Lewis took a small sip of the water. "Oh, thank you, Gil. This is so refreshing. Well, I'm relieved to find your daughter on the mend." She patted Chris's hand. "I'm sure you tire easily, dear, so I'm not going to stay." She got up and faced Chris's father. "All I wanted to do was bring Chris a little something to cheer her up." She threw Chris a meaningful look. "I'm so happy I got to have a chat with you, dear."

"It's very kind of you," her mother said, as Mrs. Lewis wriggled into her cashmere cardigan and left the room.

Once the three of them were alone, her mother was at her bedside in an instant. "Chris, darling, you must be exhausted."

"I'm okay."

Her father pulled his pencil from behind one ear and twisted it in his hands. "What did Bella Lewis want from you?"

"Oh, Gil, don't bother her now," her mother pleaded.

"That woman is up to no good," he said. "I don't want you to have anything to do with her, Chris. In fact, I don't want you to have anything more to do with the police and their investigations. When you feel better we'll talk about your work at the newspaper."

Chris felt her eyelids drooping again. Sleep was good.

♦   ♦   ♦

The problem was waking up. Chris was supposed to be discharged the next day, but then a strange thing happened. She had a dream that she was walking home from Silver Lake by herself. *When she rounded the bend on Mt. Airy and Rosie's house came into view, she heard someone calling her. She couldn't tell where the voice was coming from. Chris, Chris, the voice repeated. Was it Rosie?*

She woke up to find white-coated people surrounding her. Someone was tapping her shoulder, no—rubbing her shoulder. The whole bunch of people was staring at her.

After what seemed like a very long time, her mother was there. And one of those white-coated doctors was saying, "It happens sometimes, Mrs. Gooding. They can fall into a very deep sleep, and then it's hard to wake them up. She is not comatose. But we still have to stay on the watch for a hematoma."

The sun was in her eyes, making everything even more blurry. Her ears were ringing again. She understood that she'd be in the hospital for a while longer.

♦   ♦   ♦

Flowers from well-wishers crowded the window ledge and left little room on the bed table. Nothing from Rosie. When the petals started to brown and curl at the edges her mother wanted to discard them all. But Chris begged to keep them. They brought in the outdoors, and they kept summer alive. She could sit up for a bit longer now, even walk in the corridor a bit with the nurse. It was difficult. Her limbs didn't want to obey her.

On an afternoon when the sun was gently baking the room, Chris slowly awoke from a nap to find bright, multi-colored balloons dancing in front of her eyes. Was it her mother standing by her bed? "Mother?"

A voice came from far away. "No, it's Rosie."

She wanted to shout, "Rosie!" But it came out a whisper.

The balloons swayed back and forth on their strings. No, not balloons! Flowers—beautiful, beautiful wildflowers.

"Oh, Rosie—they let you come in?"

"Yes, my mother's waiting downstairs. She said I can't stay longer than ten minutes. Your mother is with her."

Chris winced as she pushed herself up to a sitting position. "Rosie, it's wonderful to see you! And you brought me flowers!"

"Yes, I picked them for you this morning."

With the bunch of slightly faded wildflowers, Rosie had brought her a breath of Mt. Airy. Chris was transported to the hill, climbing it alongside of Rosie on a cloudless day, with the tiger lilies in full bloom, and she was happy.

"We've been so worried about you, Chris. Are you okay? How's your head?"

"Better."

"When you get out of the hospital, I'm going to help your mother take care of you while she's busy with the show. It's all arranged."

Chris grinned. She hadn't grinned for a while. With the movement of her mouth she could feel a stretching of her scalp under the bandage.

"Rosie Nightingale. What are you going to do for me, bake me a chocolate cake?" Rosie didn't know how to bake. For that matter she didn't even know how to cook.

"You'll see. I *am* going to cook for you and your father when your mother won't be able to. I really am. Mama is teaching me."

Mrs. Novac teaching her? Rosie? What Rosie liked to do was to eat her mother's delicious food. She never had the slightest interest in learning how to make it. Rosie was very blurry in the sunlight, and everything looked slightly green. Were those tears in Rosie's eyes?

Rosie had closed the heavy wooden door to Chris's room, and now it opened wide. Chris's favorite nurse came in with a fresh pitcher of water and a thermometer. "Temperature time!" she called. "Clear the decks!"

To Rosie she said, "Are you from Croton too, dear?" In answer to Rosie's nod, she added, "Well, I'll give you a minute more together. Then I need to draw the curtains and take Chris's temperature." She padded quickly out of the room.

Rosie took Chris's hand. "I wasn't allowed to visit you until now. I feel so much better now that I've seen you. You don't look nearly as bad as I thought you would, and you're awake and talking."

Of course I'm awake and talking. Whatever is Rosie thinking?

The nurse lost no time in returning and promptly drew the curtain around the bed, giving Chris hardly the time to say goodbye to Rosie. Her mother slipped into the room and sat in a chair. Chris could see her through a space in the curtain. After taking her temperature and vital signs, the nurse drew back the curtain to reveal her mother approaching the bed.

"Mother, guess what! Rosie was just here. She said she's going to take care of me, cook meals for me and Daddy when you're busy. Isn't that wonderful?"

"She'll be a big help," her mother said.

CHAPTER SIXTEEN

As she peeled the carrots for the pot-au-feu that she was learning how to make, Rosie nicked her finger.

"Ow," she said, worried that an injury might affect playing her violin. She put down the peeler and faced her mother. "Listen, I don't really want to go to the memorial tomorrow. Do I have to?"

In return she got the kind of frosty look that always made her wonder if she was adopted.

Her mother slid a few onions her way. "Yes, you do have to go, *ma fille*. You know how important it is that we as a family appear there together. Now if you would just peel these onions."

The only thing that consoled Rosie was that she was able to get in a few hours of practicing before the beginning of the ceremony. Still, as she and her parents filed into the high school auditorium along with the other early arrivals, she was wishing that she could have been keeping Chris company at the Goodings' house. It would have been different if Chris could have come along to the memorial with them.

The service was scheduled for 7:00 p.m. Mr. Gooding was already there when they arrived, because of his duties as Village Manager and M.C. So Rosie and her parents and Mrs. Gooding all went together. Nick Salvucci, acting as newspaper photographer, stationed himself around the midpoint of the outer right aisle, near Mangone and Riley, who were on duty, guarding the auditorium. It was an unseasonably cool September evening. People who had initially removed their jackets soon put them back on, or wrapped them around their shoulders.

The musicians—a trio of graduates from the Bennett Conservatory—arranged wooden folding chairs for themselves on a corner of the stage to which an upright piano had been moved, next to the American flag. The stage was draped in black crepe, and a large, framed photographic portrait of Mr. Sylvester was propped up on a chair.

By 7:15 the auditorium was nearly full. People were squirming to find a comfortable position on those immovable, hard, wooden chairs that Rosie disliked. All the prominent local merchants were there. In the front row sat the dignitaries: Chris's father and the Village Board members, police Chief Charles Mangone, the chief of the Fire Department, the village clergymen. The staff of the Croton newspaper sat in the second row.

People picked up copies of the mimeographed program, piles of which were stacked on a table at the auditorium's entrance. Rosie recognized the Mullers and saw that they were separated by some rows from the Lewises. The musicians struck up the slow movement from a Mozart trio, and a hush fell over the auditorium, broken only by the occasional squeaking of seats.

At the close of the movement, after a respectful pause, Mr. Gooding mounted one set of the two pairs of steps flanking both sides of the stage. His eulogy was brief but lively. "Corey Sylvester elevated our little weekly to the level of serious journalism. Too serious for comic strips by the likes of me," he added, getting some subdued chuckles.

As Mr. Gooding left the stage, Rosie recognized Wylie Maxwell from the day of the condolence call to Joan Sylvester. He was sitting next to the Sylvesters' son in the front row. All she could see of Maxwell was his crew cut and navy blue blazer. Oh, if only Chris could have come along, too! She would have been so interested to see Mr. Maxwell.

The clergymen's eulogies were impossibly boring, as she knew they would be. She amused herself by trying to decide which selections of music she would have made for the ceremony. In the "musical interlude" that followed the clergy's eulogies, the trio gave a passable rendition of the first movement from Dvorak's "Dumky." They were a bit out of tune. With both pleasure and annoyance, Rosie reflected that she would have performed much better than the violinist.

At the conclusion of the movement, Joan Sylvester mounted the steps. She brushed back an invisible wisp of hair. She was wearing a forest green dress in that mid-calf length, New Look style. Rosie didn't like the new style, but it was hard to find shorter skirts now.

By the time the Sylvesters' son and daughter delivered their eulogies, Rosie was almost dozing. In the next musical interlude, the trio's rendition of the slow movement from Beethoven's "Archduke" made Rosie want to cover her ears.

Mrs. Sylvester mounted the steps again in order to, as she put it, "pay honor to Delia Morrison."

That's all? Rosie wondered. Surely Mrs. Morrison deserved more. Maybe they'd have a separate memorial for her, but somehow Rosie doubted it.

Mrs. Gooding whispered to Rosie's mother, "See Dr. Kamm over there?"

"Where?" said Rosie, who wasn't supposed to be listening. Her mother ignored her. "Where?" Rosie demanded.

Her mother nodded her head to the right at a gray-haired man sitting two rows in front of them.

"That short man? Is that his wife next to him?"

A matron directly in front of them turned her head and put a cautionary finger to her lips.

At that moment Rosie missed Chris more than ever. If she were here, Rosie would have passed her a note. Something like, "Looks like Mr. Lewis, only worse." They would have had to stifle their giggles, and the lady in the row in front of them would have been even more annoyed.

After Mrs. Sylvester's comments, Mr. Gooding introduced Mr. Caspar Worthington. Worthington was president of Worthington and Greene, a stationer's supply company headquartered in White Plains, with a large re-tail outlet in Ossining. He was a faithful advertiser in the *Croton-Harmon News*.

"Now, my friend Corey Sylvester and I," Worthington drawled, with a very faint Texas twang, "go back many years, many years before he turned the *Croton-Harmon News* into a first-class little paper. He was one of the finest publishers and editors I've had the privilege to know. And he was a mighty fine individual. It was an honor to call yourself his friend. Now the tragedy is . . . ." He looked up from his notes, directly at the audience. "The tragedy is that some folks around here resented his success. They didn't like his patriotism. Thought he was too hard on the Reds. So they griped in their letters to the editor, and Corey Sylvester had the decency to publish those letters. And now, the tragedy is that Corey paid for his decency, paid with his life because some folks just didn't like . . . ."

"Shame!" someone called out.

"Some folks just didn't want to see anti-Communism in the press . . . ."

A ripple went through the auditorium.

"Shame!"

"No politics!"

"Next speaker! Next speaker!"

In a flash, Mr. Gooding was at Worthington's side.

"Please, everyone," he called out. "Let him finish. Let's be respectful."

"Let *him* be respectful!" someone in the audience shouted.

People ostentatiously rose from their seats in protest and spilled into the aisles on their way out of the auditorium. Rosie waited to see if her parents would leave too. They were both frowning. She knew they would think that Mr. Worthington was Red-baiting.

She who was indifferent to politics was somehow pleased to see Worthington retreat from the stage, leaving Mr. Gooding in charge. Mr. Gooding conferred briefly with Mrs. Sylvester, and then gave a signal to the trio.

As the musicians began hastily tuning up for their final selection (the slow moment from Beethoven's "Ghost"), Rosie saw that Dr. Kamm was among those preparing to leave. Unlike the others, though, he didn't seem to want to draw attention to himself. He was practically on the coattails of the man in front of him, as if he wanted to melt into the confusion.

It took Rosie only a moment to figure out what Chris would do. She gathered up her things and prepared to exit.

"Where are you going?" whispered her mother.

"Bathroom. I'll meet you in the lobby." She grabbed her coat and squeezed out of the row. She turned around in time to see her mother trying to prevent her father from getting up and leaving too.

Rosie had no plan in mind at all. She knew only that this was her big chance to pursue Dr. Kamm.

When she reached the lobby, Kamm was there, pulling on a greatcoat that was much too heavy for the weather. They faced one another awkwardly. Rosie gulped. "Uh, sir, do you know when the service is supposed to be over?" What a stupid thing to say!

"No. But as you can see, I'm leaving."

"Are you . . . are you (oh, this was awful—her legs were shaking) by any chance Dr. Kamm?"

For a second he seemed to be looking through her. "I am."

Rosie forced her legs to calm down. "Well, uh, I just wanted to say that I sympathize with you. You must miss Mrs. Morrison."

Kamm peered over the top of her head, as if he were looking for someone. He buttoned up the greatcoat and glared down at her from under his mountainous brows. "We all miss Delia Morrison. She was quite a lady."

He turned to leave.

Rosie was feeling mildly desperate. "My, uh, friend works on our school newspaper. She couldn't be here tonight, but I know that she'd like to do an article on Mrs. Morrison. Would you let her interview you?"

His brows rose to astonishing heights, as if reaching for the grey cloud of his hair. "Why in the world, my child, would your friend want to interview *me*?"

"Well, Mrs. Morrison was your patient and all."

With pursed lips he emitted a dry chuckle. "My dear young lady, don't you realize that if she was my patient—and I'm not saying she was—any information I might possess would be strictly confidential? I advise your friend to confine his reporting to school events. Or, if he insists on spreading his wings," he said, his voice losing any semblance of mellowness, "why don't you tell him to write up this evening's pathetic little *soirée musicale*?"

◆　◆　◆

The receiving line had formed and was moving at a snail's pace. Rosie waited until she saw her parents approach before she ducked into the girls' bathroom so that she could make her lie believable by walking out to join them on the line. Good timing: her ruse worked. Her mother pressed Joan's hand wordlessly, and Rosie imitated her. Her father opted for a more formal handshake. Mrs. Sylvester was polite.

The lobby was much too small for the crowd of several hundred. Juice and cookies were available in the corridors (courtesy of the paper's advertisers), which did not help the traffic flow. In the crush Rosie again spotted Wylie Maxwell, who at the same time was looking in their direction. He was in front of the nearest table of refreshments, juice glass in hand. With the other hand he was waving to Mrs. Gooding, who had preceded Rosie's parents on the receiving line.

Mrs. Gooding greeted him warmly; her mother nodded, and Rosie did nothing.

"Have you heard from Frank?" Mrs. Gooding inquired.

"Sure. I try to see him as often as possible these days. I've never seen someone so . . . *defeated*. And, confidentially—just between us, all right?— I think that he's been overdoing it on the drinking. He's excited, though, about the start of your rehearsals. You'll probably see him dropping in every now and then."

"I certainly hope so," said Mrs. Gooding.

Wylie Maxwell turned to Rosie's mother and smiled boyishly. "Mrs. . . . uh . . . Madame Carrière, I'm hopeful that one day you'll change your mind and let me write about your work."

Her father had pointedly moved on.

"I'm glad you could be here," Mrs. Gooding said to Maxwell.

"Such a great loss," he murmured.

"And now with Delia, a double loss," Chris's mother added. "It's just so sad."

Maxwell looked at his shoes. "I didn't really know Delia. But I know that she was indispensable to the newspaper. Joan loved her very much."

"You seem," Mrs. Gooding said, "to have been as friendly with Corey and Joan as you are with Jack."

"They were like second parents to me when I was at Yale. My own parents were in Michigan, so I didn't get to see them as often as I did the Sylvesters."

Swallowing her hesitation, Rosie piped up, "Was it because of Mr. Sylvester that you went into journalism?"

Maxwell smiled at her. "I guess you could say he was an influence. But I got interested through my work on a Yale literary magazine."

"I thought that maybe you and Mr. Sylvester had business interests in common."

Maxwell looked at her keenly. "Business interests? What do you mean?"

"Oh, I don't know. Don't journalists exchange information?"

Rosie's mother put an arm around her daughter. "Please excuse Rosie. Her best friend is a budding journalist, and I think some of it may have rubbed off on her."

Wylie gave Rosie another look. "Well, good luck to you," he said.

"I didn't know that you were so friendly with Mr. Maxwell," her mother said to Mrs. Gooding once Maxwell was out of earshot.

Mrs. Gooding stiffened. "I've seen him here and there in New York. Once or twice when I lunched with Frank, Wylie came by."

"Oh, so they're good friends?"

"I don't know how good. But they're both arts writers, and they seem to have a lot of connections in common."

Rosie considered Mrs. Gooding's remarks for a moment. So Maxwell, Ewing, and Corey Sylvester were all friends. Well, maybe not friends, but they knew one another and had some kind of writing connection.

"Is Frank Ewing here?" her mother asked Mrs. Gooding.

"No." Chris's mother said, seeming embarrassed. "I think he felt it would be awkward to come if Hugh Morrison were here."

"Is Mr. Morrison here?" Rosie asked.

"I don't know, chérie," her mother answered.

"Come to think of it, I haven't seen him," said Mrs. Gooding.

Most of the people had now gone through the receiving line and were crowding into the lobby. Movement was blocked by volunteers setting up refreshment tables. Many of the men removed their jackets.

Eager for air, Rosie made her way to an exit. When she got to the threshold of the front entrance, she went rigid. Was that a figure stirring in the shadows? She peered ahead. No more motion, but under the branches of the old stand of trees that graced the north side of the lawn was Dr. Kamm, traced in outline against the street light. He was advancing straight toward her, his too-large greatcoat flapping around him like the wings of a gigantic crow. He looked creepy. She wasn't sure he recognized her, but she wasn't going to take any chances. She backed away and fled inside.

CHAPTER SEVENTEEN

Rosie took shelter in the girls' bathroom once more in order to compose her face. She was shivering and shedding a few nervous tears. When she came back out the door, she lowered her head in order to hide her crying. Someone said, "Oh, excuse me," and as she looked up she realized that she had nearly bumped into Caleb Lennard, the son of the Croton Players' director. He had just transferred from The Putney School in Vermont to the Croton-Harmon High School.

She excused herself in turn and tried to avert her face.

"I know you," Caleb said. "You're a friend of Andrea Lewis, aren't you? And you play in the school orchestra, don't you?" His face was all rough-hewn, as if carved out of rock like those presidents on the mountain, and he looked older than his years. He was sixteen, two grades ahead of Rosie in school. His large, deep brown eyes matched his thick mane of hair. If only he didn't have that funny crooked mouth he might even be considered good-looking.

She remembered meeting him in the cafeteria. His parents and Andrea's were friends. "Yes, I do. Violin. Do you play an instrument?"

"Once I tried the guitar. And I play the piano a little—badly. I'm really good at listening, though."

They had been edging through the crowd, past the refreshments area. By tacit consent they sat down on a couple of chairs in a corner.

"What kind of music do you listen to?" Rosie asked him.

"Oh, the usual. Bach, baroque, Mozart, Beethoven, and a few of the romantics."

The usual! It wasn't usual among Croton kids. Caleb was actually a music lover!

"I'm working on Shostakovich's second piano trio for my next recital," Rosie said. "It's very hard—I'm pretty nervous about it."

Caleb hunched his shoulders and dug into a pocket, producing a crushed Graham cracker. He offered to share it with her, but she declined. "Why waste your time on twentieth-century music? Composers like Shostakovich with all their crashing around just annoy me. If you're going to listen to sturm und drang, Verdi's "Requiem" is much better. And then the twelve-tone crowd, Schoenberg and company—what a bore! Jazz and folk are the only good twentieth-century music."

Rosie didn't know anything about jazz and only a little more about folk music. She wasn't going to ask Caleb what "sturm und drang" meant. She decided to get him off the subject of music. "I think it was disrespectful of people to walk out of the memorial."

Caleb made a face. "What do you mean, disrespectful? Worthington was the one who was disrespectful, as the guy said. Making innuendoes, Red-baiting. . . ."

Someone accidentally spilled a drop or two of apple juice onto Rosie's arm. Startled, she turned her head. "But it wasn't a political rally. People shouldn't have walked out."

Caleb moved his chair closer to the wall, and Rosie followed suit.

"Worthington turned it into a political rally," Caleb said. "Besides which, Rosie, don't you know that politics isn't fenced off? It's everywhere. It's why I have to go to this crummy school in Croton instead of a decent place."

"Why is that political?"

Caleb's voice sounded tired. "Because. Because my father is on the Hollywood blacklist, that's why. Because when he couldn't get any more movie work we moved back to New York, but then he couldn't get any stage work either, so we had to move here, and I had to stop going to Putney be-cause we couldn't afford it anymore."

So his father was in trouble, too—just like hers, only at least for now her father had a job. "That's terrible, Caleb," she said.

He sat up straight. "So why were you so upset that you nearly crashed into me?"

Rosie stiffened. "What do you mean, upset?"

"Oh, come on, Rosie. You were hiding your face, as if you had been crying."

Rosie fiddled with the tiny violin on the charm bracelet her parents had given her for her fourteenth birthday. How much should she say? There was something about Caleb, though, that made her feel she could confide in him.

"There's this peculiar doctor who lives here, Dr. Kamm. Have you heard of him?"

"Yeah, sure, the cult shrink. My parents are friends with some people in his group. What about him?"

"I was talking to him in the lobby, and then when I went to get some air I saw him on the lawn, in the shadows."

"So what? Didn't he have to go home, just like everyone else?"

"That's not the point, Caleb. I was talking to him inside when he was putting on his coat to leave. Then, about ten minutes later, when I wanted to go outside to get some air, I'm sure I saw him hiding in the shadows, where the trees are."

"Maybe he was just on his way home."

"No. I don't think he was going home. Why didn't he go around back, to the parking lot? And when I appeared he started coming straight toward me." She hesitated, and then lowered her voice. "I'm worried that maybe he was waiting for me."

Caleb didn't seem impressed. "You? What would he want with you? Is your family part of his group?"

"No, of course not. But I was asking him about my friend Chris. I don't think you know her, because she's been sick, and she hasn't been in school practically since the beginning of the year. Anyhow, she's a reporter for the "Tiger Rag," and I was asking Dr. Kamm if she could interview him. He didn't like that at all. Or me either."

Caleb finished munching on the Graham cracker. "So you ask him about your friend, and he gets annoyed. Then he lies in wait for you on the lawn? Doesn't sound logical. He may be weird, but he's probably not that weird."

Rosie's voice was down to a whisper. "He's pretty weird. I've heard some very scary things about him. That's why I told my parents I wouldn't go to a shrink."

"Your parents want you to go to a shrink?"

"Uh-oh, I didn't mean to say that. Uh . . . listen I haven't told anyone about this. You won't tell?"

Caleb put on a face of roguish solemnity. "Cross my heart and hope to die."

"You see. . . uh . . . I did just start going to one. But not in Croton. In the city. The only good part is that I get to stay and go to a concert afterward if I want to."

One side of Caleb's mouth twisted downward. "I used to see a shrink, too—in New York—but I quit. I couldn't take it anymore. He was such a pompous ass. And he was always taking notes, just like a secretary. Half the time he probably wasn't even paying attention to what I was saying. Or who knows? He could just have been doodling—or maybe writing a letter to someone." He pulled another Graham cracker from his pocket and extended it to Rosie, who shook her head no. "What have you heard about Kamm?"

"I know a girl whose parents left Dr. Kamm's group when she was little— maybe six. She remembers horrible things." She stopped, not sure how much she should say.

"Like what?"

"She was punished a lot. Kamm told her parents to hit her with a strap. She always choked on peanut butter and didn't want to eat it. But every time they had peanut butter and jelly sandwiches at Dr. Kamm's summer day camp and she didn't want to eat them, he would threaten her if she didn't. He said allergies were all in the mind. My friend said that Dr. Kamm sometimes punished her by locking her inside dark closets."

Caleb brushed some graham cracker crumbs from his chin. "My parents' friends, the Lewises, were in that group. But recently they . . . uh . . . quit."

"You mean Andrea's parents?"

"Yes. Hey . . I just thought, they've invited me and my parents over for coffee after the memorial. Why don't you come with us?"

It sounded like an interesting idea. She'd been to Andrea's once or twice and had been fascinated by the Lewises' collection of modern art. "I'll have to ask my parents." Out of the corner of her eye she could see that Mrs. Muller was talking to her mother, and her father was standing a bit on the sidelines. "One second—I'll go ask them."

"Mama," she said, as Mrs. Muller turned toward the refreshments, "Caleb Lennard just asked if I could go over to the Lewises' for coffee with him and his parents after the memorial. Can I? It's still early."

Her parents exchanged one of their inscrutable looks.

"Ask the Lennards to get you home by 11," her mother said.

◆　　◆　　◆

Rosie had never been to Andrea's home at night. The Lewises lived on Franklin Avenue, in a woodsy, poorly lit part of Harmon. The house was set back from the road, and Rosie could barely see it as the four of them piled out of the Lennards' car. Parked a few feet in front of them was a police car. No one seemed to notice it but Rosie, so she didn't say anything.

For a minute Rosie feared that no one was at home, but she had seen Mr. and Mrs. Lewis leave the high school quite a while ago. When the house came into view, it was blazing with lights.

Andrea opened the door, blinking at them as if she had just woken up. Her eyes were puffy. She blew her nose into a crumpled handkerchief. "Oh …uh, that's right. You were supposed to come over, weren't you? My parents are… upstairs with the police." They all moved uncertainly into the living room. Magazines lay helter-skelter on the floor. "My parents should come downstairs soon."

"Maybe we'd better leave," Mrs. Lennard said to her husband.

Andrea choked back a sob. "No, please sit with me until they come."

They distributed themselves on a small sofa and comfortable armchairs, all of which were set around a table graced with a bronze sculpture by Jean Arp. On the walls were a drawing by Ben Shahn and two oil paintings, one by Philip Guston, the other by Alice Neel. Rosie would have liked to view them up close, but the atmosphere was too strained.

A minute or two of silence, and then they heard voices and a clumping down the stairs. Into the living room trooped Police Chief Mangone and Chuck Riley, followed by Andrea's parents.

"We'll keep a patrol car in the area," Mangone said. "And you call us right away if you hear or see anything suspicious."

"We'll walk you out," said Mr. Lewis. They disappeared through the front door, talking in hushed tones.

Andrea turned to her guests. "See," she said, "I was babysitting down the street for the Hamiltons—they went to the memorial too. And when I came home—my parents hadn't returned yet—the police were all over the place. Mr. Tarnow next door had seen something funny going on here and called the police. Seems there were burglars here."

Mrs. Lennard arched her eyebrows. "Burglars?" It was practically unheard of in Croton. People didn't even lock their doors when they went out.

"It seems so," said Andrea. "But we can't figure out what they wanted. They didn't take anything from our art collection. They probably didn't take anything much at all. Look, come with me." She led them into her father's study. The old roll top desk was a mess—drawers pulled out, papers scattered everywhere. The bookcases had been ransacked. "But we can't see what they took. I right away ran up to my room to check on my gold locket, but it was there. All my mother's jewelry was there too."

Voices came from the living room, and Mrs. Lewis called out, "Andrea?"

Rosie felt like an intruder.

They practically tiptoed back into the living room.

Mrs. Lewis looked stricken.

Mr. Lewis stared at them. "Oh, God," he said. "I'm sorry. We completely forgot that you were coming over." No one seemed to notice Rosie.

"*We're* sorry," said Mrs. Lennard. She had a nice way about her, Rosie thought. She was small, around Rosie's size, with sparkling dark eyes. "We better leave you."

"We hope they didn't take anything of value." Mr. Lennard said.

Mrs. Lewis sat down on the sofa and put her head in her hands. "We don't think so. We've been over practically the whole house."

"It must be such a shock," murmured Caleb's mother. She sat down next to Mrs. Lewis and put an arm around her shoulder.

Andrea said to Caleb and Rosie, "There's one thing, though. I think they took my camp scrapbook. It was on the table in the family room. I know, because I was just looking at it the other day."

"Nonsense, Andrea," her father said, "What would they want with that? You probably just misplaced it."

There was a light rap at the front door, and Mangone reappeared, Riley behind him. "Left my cap," Mangone said, plucking it from a table in the foyer. "We'll be back tomorrow," he announced. He addressed Mr. Lewis.

"I want you to keep looking. It's not likely that whoever was here would turn everything inside out and then walk away with nothing at all. You say all the valuable stuff is here. So maybe it wasn't money or valuables they were after." Mangone turned to the younger policeman. "Those guys clearly wanted something, and I'm willing to bet that they got it."

CHAPTER EIGHTEEN

"Apparently you made a good impression on my mother," Caleb told Rosie a few days after the memorial. "She asked if I'd bring you over to visit the shop. We can give you a ride home after she closes up." Caleb's mother's little gift shop, which she had opened about a year ago, was located several miles from the school, near the Harmon Station. Rosie had never been there.

"You'll like it," Caleb said to her.

Normally Rosie would have wanted to rush home and practice. But almost without thinking she agreed to go.

"So why don't you like Croton High?" Rosie asked Caleb as they set out.

Caleb was walking at such a clip that Rosie, with her slight frame and short legs, had to trot to keep up with him.

"It's a wretched place," Caleb said. "One of these days I'm going to ask to give a talk in the auditorium about what a serious school like Putney is all about."

Rosie didn't know anything about Putney, and she hadn't thought much about her own school. She liked playing in the orchestra, and she was interested in English. "What do you mean?"

Caleb shot a withering glance into the air. "Well, at Putney classes were *interesting*. We had lots of good discussions. By my grade you'd be reading Jane Austen and *good* George Eliot in English class—not *Silas Marner*. And if you were the teacher you wouldn't have to deal with kids whistling, cracking gum, passing notes, giggling and generally making a nuisance of themselves."

Guilty as charged. She and Chris always passed notes. They had to do something to counter the boredom. Boredom, she assumed, was just something you had to put up with in school.

"Also," said Caleb, "we used to put on plays. Shakespeare, for example. Come to think of it, you'd make a good Juliet. Too bad they don't put on Shakespeare here."

Was Caleb hinting that he wanted to play Romeo to her Juliet? He went right on talking, though, and she decided that it was just an off-the-cuff remark.

Honey Lennard's shop took up one half of a bright yellow, wood-framed cottage on a hill overlooking the Harmon Station. When Caleb opened the brick-red door beneath a sign bearing the image of a hand and the legend "Sleights of Hand," a bell tinkled softly, and Caleb's mother greeted them with a broad smile. "Hello, weary travelers! How about some milk and cookies?"

In the display room a few comfortable armchairs were grouped around a little table, all set in the midst of brightly colored silk jackets and batik shirts for women, knit ties for men, and elegant glass counters filled with hand-crafted silver jewelry. Strains of music could be heard softly playing in the background.

"Chocolate milk," said Caleb. "Oh, you've put on that new Sarah Vaughan record I got for you." He turned to Rosie. "Isn't she great?

Sarah Vaughan? She had heard of her vaguely—a jazz singer.

Only when Mrs. Lennard disappeared into a small kitchen at the rear of the shop did Rosie realize that they weren't alone. Bella Lewis was sitting quietly in a wicker chair by the window, a coffee mug in hand. She was wearing a charcoal gray dress, which accentuated her pallor. She greeted them with a small smile.

Honey Lennard bustled out with a tray containing two glasses of chocolate milk and a plate of cookies. She asked Mrs. Lewis if she could refill her cup of coffee.

"Oh, no, thanks, Honey," she replied. "I've chewed your ear off enough. I really should be going. If you're both already here," she said, managing another smile at Caleb and Rosie, "it must be just about time for Andrea to come home."

The two women hugged.

"I'm terribly sorry about what's happened," Mrs. Lennard said. "You'll let me know if there's anything I can do?"

"Thanks, Honey," returned Mrs. Lewis. "It's good just to be able to talk."

"Any time," called Mrs. Lennard, as Bella Lewis trundled out.

Caleb bit into a home-made lemon cookie. "Anything more about the robbers?" he asked his mother, nodding toward the closed door.

"No. Bella is just a wreck."

"A wreck!" Caleb's lopsided mouth hooked upward in a sardonic grin. "Big deal—what's so tragic about a burglary? They didn't lose any of their precious art collection, did they? All these capitalist Commies in Croton make me laugh."

His mother was rearranging a display of jewelry. "Just because you're a big-city sophisticate from New York and L.A. doesn't mean you can't try to understand. Even left-wing people can get upset about such things in a place like Croton."

"Did anyone find out what they took?" Rosie asked.

Mrs. Lennard joined them at the table and reached for a cookie. "Bella says they've learned nothing more since the robbery."

"So why's she so upset?" Caleb demanded.

"You're just lucky," Mrs. Lennard said to her son, "that you've never had the experience of being robbed. It's like a violation. You feel that your personal integrity has been shattered."

The sardonic grin widened. "You mean that I'm my property? Steal my property and rob me of my identity? Bullshit. Remember Proudhon: 'Property is theft.'"

Mrs. Lennard wagged a playful finger at her son. "Oh, you and your Karl Marx. Not everything is political, you know."

"No, on the contrary, *everything* is political."

Rosie wasn't used to such conversation between parents and children. Almost as if they were equals. But then she always tuned out of politics. She left it to Chris to talk about that with her mother and the other grown-ups.

"Anyway," Mrs. Lennard continued, "it was a good thing Andrea got home before Harold and Bella so she could cushion the shock."

"She was pretty rattled too," Caleb said.

"Poor Bella!" sighed Caleb's mother. "As if she didn't have enough trouble."

Caleb was on his second cookie. "You mean with Kamm?"

"Yes. They had only just broken with him, and Bella seemed very worried about it."

"They were dumb to get mixed up with that guy in the first place," said Caleb.

Caleb could be very hard-hearted, Rosie thought.

Evidently his mother shared Rosie's opinion. "It doesn't have anything to do with intelligence, Mr. Wise-Guy. Some people are more vulnerable than others. In a moment of weakness they can easily fall into the clutches of a Dr. Kamm. Then he's got them hooked."

Mrs. Lennard was something! Funny and warm-hearted. Rosie was getting drawn into the conversation. "What do you mean," she asked, "they broke with Kamm? They quit being his patients?"

Mrs. Lennard sipped coffee from a large mug with a brightly colored patchwork design. "Yes. But it's more than that—I imagine it's like the break-up of a marriage. When you leave Kamm you leave a whole community and a whole way of life. And Kamm never makes it easy for people who leave."

"What do you mean, he robs their houses?"

Caleb snickered, and his mother laughed.

"I don't think that Kamm would bother to take such petty revenge," Mrs. Lennard said. "He goes in for bigger things. No, I think it was just a sad coincidence."

Rosie's mind was racing back to her fright at the memorial service. Maybe Kamm *was* waiting for someone, perhaps a confederate. But he wouldn't have had enough time to rob the Lewises before they came home, would he? Besides which, the robbers didn't take anything! It was a puzzle. Why was Kamm hiding on the high school lawn after the memorial? All Rosie could think was that he was up to no good.

♦　　♦　　♦

The stronger Chris got the more restless and irritable she became. She couldn't wait to get back to school, but Dr. Carroll was still grounding her. By late October she was permitted to go out on short walks when the weather was good. She had to admit, though, that her walks, which were getting longer and longer, still tired her. But staying inside and doing homework was boring. Whatever she did, it was lonely spending all that time by herself.

For the pleasure of doing something she wasn't supposed to do, she reverted to her old habit of listening in on the party line. She would pick up on a whim several times a day, hoping to get something good. One afternoon she got her wish.

It was two women whose voices let her identify them almost immediately—Rosie's mother and Maria Muller. She was about to hang up when she heard Mrs. Novac mention *Encounter.* Wasn't that the magazine Rosie's parents were always fighting about? And the one that Frank Ewing and Wylie Maxwell were all mixed up with?

Maria Muller: Well, of course you'd be upset, dear. Maxwell skewered you and Sandor. But, you know, he never wanted to publish in "Encounter" in the first place. He had set his sights on "The New Yorker." Hendrik heard about it at the Sylvesters' open house.

Lili Novac: So how do we get from "The New Yorker" to "Encounter?"

MM: Well, apparently—I don't know if I should be telling you this, but it might make you feel better—Corey wanted the essay for "Encounter." So badly that—at least according to Maxwell—he went and told someone on the "New Yorker" staff to cancel out on Maxwell's piece. Maxwell was furious. Accused Corey of trying to ruin his career for political reasons.

LN: Political reasons? You mean because "Encounter" is more political than "The New Yorker?"

MM: Yes, but of course it's all meaningless, since Wiley pretty much shares Corey's political views. The problem is that Corey, who had connections all over the place, was very close to the "Encounter" crowd, and had a real stake in the magazine. He did some work for the Congress for Cultural Freedom, I believe.

LN: So Maxwell must have felt betrayed by Corey.

MM: Exactly. And also, don't you know about Maxwell? Stardom. That's all he ever thinks about. "The New Yorker" would have been a much bigger feather in his cap than "Encounter." Anyway, yes, he felt betrayed by Corey, who was like a second father to him and who got him his job at "Time" in the first place.

The front door clicked shut. Oh, no, her parents! In her haste, she nearly dropped the receiver.

She was completely disoriented. She got it that Maxwell was ambitious and felt thwarted by Mr. Sylvester. But what did the Congress for Cultural Freedom have to do with anything?

It looked bad for her. Her parents came in and saw her standing by the phone—not leafing through magazines, not setting the table, or doing anything plausible.

Her father gave her a hard look. "Chris, have you been up to your old tricks again?"

She couldn't help herself. "Daddy, could you explain to me about that magazine *Encounter* and the Congress for Cultural Freedom?"

Her mother set her books down on the kitchen table. "Chris, really. Must you start in right away?"

"O.K., Missy," her father said, as he prepared the cocktails. "What is this all about? What did you overhear?"

Outsmarted again. Chris sat down and tried to reconstruct the conversation.

When she finished, her mother picked up her martini and turned away from Chris. "Gil, did you know anything about all this?"

"Not really. I heard rumors about a breach between Maxwell and Corey at around the time of the Sylvesters' open house. And of course we do know about Corey's ties to *Encounter* and the Congress for Cultural Freedom. I don't know how much Maxwell knew about those ties. Sylvester made it his business to make friends in the right places. He made sure that he got in with the Congress for Cultural Freedom crowd; they even sent him to Paris once for one of their events—you remember when he went over there last winter? It certainly wouldn't do any harm to the cause of the *Croton-Harmon News* to be in with a prominent group of intellectuals."

Her mother got up and began to peel potatoes for boiling. "Could Maxwell have been angry enough at Corey to . . .? Was he even on the train after the Union Square rally?" She tossed potatoes into a pot of water.

"I don't know. But come to think of it," her father said, "Corey said something about Maxwell to me at the open house. Said Maxwell had been behaving oddly recently—flying off the handle at the slightest thing. He thought maybe Maxwell's work wasn't going well."

Her father extracted the jar of martini olives from the refrigerator and popped one into his glass. He always ate the olives and then kept replacing them. "In any case, it's pretty clear that Maxwell felt he was robbed of a golden opportunity when Sylvester more or less forced him into giving his article to *Encounter.*"

CHAPTER NINETEEN

Rosie kept her word to Chris about cooking for her. Plenty of other people brought over food. Kids from school brought casseroles made by their mothers; Gail, Andrea, and some of the other girls also brought in a pizza from Emil's. But only Rosie came over three times a week to help out with meals at Chris's house.

She had just begun her preparations for the *sole bonne femme* when Chris surprised her by coming downstairs and bursting into the large kitchen-dining-living area.

"Rosie!" she said, her eyes gleaming in the old way. "I have so much to tell you. First, there was this phone conversation I overheard!"

"You mean you listened in to," Rosie said.

"It doesn't matter." She summarized the conversation between Rosie's mother and Mrs. Muller. "So Maxwell wrote this article for *The New Yorker*," Chris concluded, "but then Mr. Sylvester said he wanted it for *Encounter*. Maxwell didn't want to give it to him. It would have been a very big deal for him to get it published in *The New Yorker*. But Mr. Sylvester wanted it so badly for *Encounter* that he got *The New Yorker* to go back on the deal. Maxwell was furious at Mr. Sylvester."

Rosie stood with her mixing spoon suspended in mid-air. "His article— that must be the one my parents have been fighting about."

"Rosie, don't you understand about the telephone conversation? Maxwell was furious that Mr. Sylvester ruined his chance to be in *The New Yorker*—don't you see? He could be a suspect."

Rosie put the spoon back into a bowl. "Okay, maybe. But we don't even know if Mr. Maxwell was on the train home on June 19th. So my father is still right up there, probably number one."

"Yeah, but there's more. Listen to what I found out last night! I overheard Daddy tell my mother that he brought home important documents he got from Chief Mangone—evidence in the Sylvester case. You have to help me find them!"

"You know you're not supposed to go anywhere near the investigations."

"This is too important. We have to find those papers!"

There was no doubt about it. Chris was definitely feeling better.

Rosie stood arms akimbo, facing Chris, who had sat down on the couch. "Chris, your parents will be furious with me if they find out I've been helping you out with this."

"C'mon. Being a co-conspirator is fun. So where do you think they are? The documents, I mean. I figure Daddy would probably want to keep them private, so he'd probably put them in his study."

"What do you want me to do?" asked Rosie. "It's already 4 o'clock. Your parents should home in an hour."

"Yeah. Why don't you stand guard and let me know when someone's coming?"

It was no use fighting Chris. Rosie returned to her preparations, and Chris went upstairs.

Fifteen minutes later Chris shouted down, "Rosie! I've got it! Come up to my room—I've got it!"

Rosie was mixing ingredients for a sauce. Oh well . . . she just wouldn't stay too long with Chris.

Chris had spread out papers on one of her twin beds. "I've been trying to read these, but my eye is still too blurry. Will you read them to me?"

Rosie looked doubtfully at the papers on the bed. If she didn't get back to the fish soon, it wouldn't be ready on time.

"Here's what I figured out," Chris went on. "I think these are letters to Wylie Maxwell that the F.B.I. must have gotten—or stolen. Probably it was that F.B.I. guy Pike who did it."

Rosie twirled a strand of her hair around a finger. "I don't know. I don't think we're supposed to be looking at this stuff."

"Neither is my father. So … so what? Here it is in front of us! We can't miss the opportunity!"

What made Chris so hard to resist? More and more, Rosie was getting pulled onto Chris's trail. At this rate, she'd soon be Chris's assistant P.I.

Rosie sat on the other bed, while Chris gathered up the papers. "I've tried to put them in chronological order. I think they mostly have dates." She passed the pile to Rosie and sat down on the now cleared bed.

"O.K., "said Rosie. "Here's the first. It's dated June 5, 1953, and it's from Mr. Sylvester to Wiley Maxwell." She read:

I'd just like to add a personal note to Joan's reply to your letter. We were very happy to see you at our open house.

Now, about that piece of yours on Croton artists: I am sorry that things didn't work out with "The New Yorker." Will you give it to "Encounter?" It will be perfect for the journal. You were undoubtedly as dismayed as I was to learn that the Congress for Cultural Freedom has been planning to include photos of architectural work by Sandor Novac in its forthcoming international exhibit of American art and architecture. Including Novac in the exhibit will send absolutely the wrong message to our confreres in Europe. You also talk about his wife's work in your piece, as I recall. You've produced a fine critique of left-wing art. An interview with Novac and his wife will enliven it even further. I'm sorry that I didn't think of it before our party, but at the next opportunity I will plan to introduce you to Sandor and his wife.

Yours, etc.

Chris was smiling. "You see, Rosie? Mr. Sylvester was a real rat to Mr. Maxwell."

Rosie put down the letter with a sigh. "Okay, but what's this about my father? Do you understand what Mr. Sylvester was talking about? What's the Congress for Cultural Freedom?"

Chris wore her owlish look. "I asked Daddy about it." She rubbed her forehead. "Here's more or less what I've learned. The Congress for Cultural Freedom is this American organization with lots of branches—they call them committees—in different countries. It's an America-booster—it wants to show people overseas that we're a civilized country here. You know, the idea is to beat out the Soviets, to show the world that here in the good old U.S.A. we're as smart and talented as anyone else."

"Why? People think we're stupid?"

"I guess people don't think Americans are very intellectual. And Europeans can be snobs. So we have to prove to them that our anti-Communist politics are really very intelligent. The Congress is set up mainly in Europe. Some people think the C.I.A. has something to do with it, because they're international and the Congress is international, and they're both anti-Communist."

Chris plumped up some pillows and lay down on her bed. Was she getting tired out? It was going to be Rosie's fault for helping her snoop.

"Do you want me to read more?" Rosie asked. "Or should I let you sleep?"

"No," said Chris, "Please read. We may not get a chance like this again."

"O.K., here's the next. Dated June 16th, from Mr. Sylvester to Mr. Maxwell."

I look forward to seeing you in New York on the 19th. Will try to get you over to Leon Trask, who can serve you as an excellent informant on your Croton piece.

Yours, etc.

Rosie looked over to Chris, who was rubbing her forehead again. "Should I read more?"

"Go on, go on!"

"O.K., I've got two more. They're really just notes. The first is dated June 17th, to Mr. Maxwell from Leon Trask. Who's Leon Trask?"

"Don't know." Chris's voice was getting faint.

Rosie read: *I look forward to meeting you on Friday. Corey will introduce us. Please confirm with him that you will be there.*

Sincerely, etc.

The next—well, it doesn't have a date—is to Mr. Maxwell from Frank Ewing. *Glad to learn that you'll be at the rally, old boy. It will give us another opportunity to chat. Frank*

A car door slammed. Rosie ran to the window. "Your parents!"

Chris sprang up, gathered the sheets of paper, and hobbled over to her father's study with them. "I'm leaving the last one," she whispered to Rosie. "You still haven't read it to me."

"Rosie? Chris?" Mrs. Gooding called.

"Upstairs," Rosie called back. "I'm with Chris. I'll be down in a few minutes." She shut the door to Chris's room and looked at the last note. Like the others, it was to Wylie Maxwell, this time from . . . her father!

Please be advised that I'm aware of your cozy little relationship with the late Corey Sylvester. I'm not falling for any of your overtures. And I'd thank you to stay away from my wife.

◆   ◆   ◆

As Rosie put the finishing touches on her fish, Mr. and Mrs. Gooding settled into armchairs with their cocktails. Although they were just across from her in the large, open-plan room, she had to work quietly in order to hear them.

"So this agent, Trask" said Mr. Gooding, "may not have stolen Chris's notebook and camera at the Rosenberg rally or taken her book bag in Croton. But maybe he was in on the theft at the Lewises'. Maybe even Pike helped in that burglary. But when Mangone suggested it to Pike, he denied it. 'Not me. Listen, I'm straight with you guys. We're in this together. We're all on the same side.'"

Mrs. Gooding looked overwhelmed. "What is it with the F.B.I.? Pike, Trask—it seems like the right hand doesn't know what the left is doing."

"Apparently Trask is new on the job—came back from hunting Reds in Hollywood only recently. So this is what I make of it for now: Wylie Maxwell, Frank Ewing, and Leon Trask were all at the Union Square event on June 19th. Probably Trask made contact with Maxwell there. Maxwell can be helpful to the F.B.I. with his Croton connections. It still doesn't add up to a murder, though, especially not the murder of Corey Sylvester."

Mrs. Gooding stared hard out the window. "Gil . . . we know that Wylie Maxwell got very angry at Corey shortly before he died. Do you think that Maxwell may be mixed up in all of this?"

"I don't know. Look at all that's gone on. Delia dies a violent death, like Corey before her. Why? And how does Chris's thief fit in, if at all? And finally, a mysterious burglary that maybe wasn't really a burglary." He leaned back in his chair and stretched out his arms. "These incidents could be entirely separate, or . . ."

"They could be linked," Mrs. Gooding finished for him.

Chris's father straightened up. "Oh, wait a minute," he mumbled. "I nearly forgot." He pulled an envelope from a rear pants pocket, opened it, and dropped a black and white snapshot on the table. "Mangone gave me this today. It's supposed to be Trask."

Mrs. Gooding came over to examine it. Rosie tiptoed her way to where she could look over her shoulder.

"What a funny-looking man," Mrs. Gooding said. "He has such big ears."

CHAPTER TWENTY

Uncaged! Finally she was allowed to go back to school. No after-school activities for the time being. Mrs. Novac chauffeured her. Rosie was her monitor, rarely letting Chris out of her sight. She even took her to lunch and made sure that they sat together in the cafeteria.

On Chris's first day back, the cafeteria loomed huge and crowded. Things were indistinct. Although she would never admit it, she was happy to have Rosie guide her. At a neighboring table sat Andrea Lewis, all by herself. Andrea nodded to Chris but made no move to come over. Ever since the burglary, Rosie said, Andrea had been keeping to herself. At lunch time, she always sat alone, refusing invitations from friends to join them.

Chris made a face at Rosie, motioning her to sit still, and got up. In a minute she was at Andrea's table. "Please come sit with us," she said, "I haven't seen you in so long."

With a little coaxing Andrea opened up. There were no usable fingerprints from the burglary, she said. She and her family had gone over their house with a fine-tooth comb. The only thing missing was her scrapbook from day camp, Andrea said. Why anyone would want it was beyond them, but it was the *only* item taken.

Rosie had filled Chris in about the burglary, in a sketchy way. Andrea's day camp, Chris knew, was run by that Dr. Kamm, and it was for members of his group only.

"How do you know he didn't take something else that your parents didn't tell you about?" Chris asked. Andrea was emphatic that they *would* have told her if anything else was missing.

That evening Chris reported to her parents on the lunchtime conversation.

"Harold and Bella are hiding something," her father said.

"Why?"

"Maybe they know that Kamm is worried about some information in Andrea's scrapbook. All his secrets are getting out. Maybe he's afraid of blackmail or whistleblowers. Maybe the group members are afraid."

"So you think Dr. Kamm broke in?" Chris asked.

Her mother intervened, "That Kamm is so strange. What kind of a doctor is he anyhow?"

"A crackpot doctor," her father said. "Someone should check his credentials."

♦ ♦ ♦

It was like a see-saw. One day Chris felt better. The next day she had to force herself to get out of bed. Just when she thought the headaches had gone they came back. Her face was still purple and green, although the colors were fading. Her vision was still blurry, but less so than when she was in the hospital several weeks ago.

Dr. Carroll said she had to be very careful to rest as soon as she got home from school. In two weeks, her mother was supposed to return to teaching from her leave. When Chris's mother was not in New York, she was learning her lines. Sometimes she asked Chris or her father to help her. Her mother's unpaid leave made Chris feel terrible. All because of her they might have even less money. Now her mother was out on one of her periodic grocery runs. Especially at times like this, when no one was home but Willie, a bone-chilling loneliness set in. By the time her friends were free to chat on the phone, it was evening, and she had to follow orders and go to bed early.

On one of those solitary afternoons, she welcomed the unexpected ring of the doorbell. It was a bright day, and she was sitting in front of a downstairs window, soaking up the sun and leafing through the cartoons in back issues of *The New Yorker*.

Willie jumped up, barking, and sped to the door. He was even more excited than Chris. She loped behind him and admitted . . . Chuck Riley! What was he doing here? "My parents aren't home, Officer Riley." she said. She looked down at her dog-bitten slippers and the raggedy cuffs of her faded dungarees. If only she had worn a skirt today!

Riley grinned. "I didn't come to see your parents. I'm on my way to a call from West Mt. Airy, so I thought I'd stop to see how you're doing."

She invited him to sit down for some tea, but he said he really didn't have the time to stay. Willie retreated to his usual spot under the kitchen table.

"You look much better than the last time I saw you," he said.

"Me? Oh, yeah, that was in the hospital. I was pretty smashed up. Do you have any news?"

"News? You mean about your book bag?"

"Well, yes, and about the Sylvester and Morrison cases." She thought she sounded very professional.

"No, not much. But I didn't come to talk shop."

She waited.

"My little cousin Luke tells me that you're a terrific chess player."

Luke Riley? He was a sophomore, and he had recently joined her chess club. She didn't know that he was Officer Riley's cousin. There were a lot of Rileys in town.

"So Luke asked me . . . er, he wanted to know if you'd like him to come over for a game."

Chris made an effort to smile. Why couldn't Chuck Riley have asked her to play chess with *him*? Maybe he didn't know how. Even if he did, he clearly wasn't thinking of asking her. Luke was a kind of skinny runt. But he was taller than Chris. And he didn't have acne. He was a very quiet boy.

"Sure," she said. "If my parents say it's okay. I'm supposed to rest after school. But I guess chess is restful. You want to see our chess set?"

Riley looked at his watch. "Just for a minute. I have to answer that call."

Chris got up to take the set out of the living room cabinet, which protected it from Willie. But almost as soon as she stood she sat back down again. "I'm sorry," she said. "Just a little dizzy spell."

Chuck looked at her with concern. "Will you be all right alone here? Should I call your parents?"

"No, thanks," Chris said. "I'll be fine. It happens sometimes."

"I'll ask Luke to call you," Chuck said on his way out. "You take care of yourself."

♦ ♦ ♦

It was going to be Rosie's first Village Board meeting. Chris went with Mr. Gooding sometimes, but Rosie never wanted to go along. Now the Board had a whole bunch of interesting issues to deal with: two deaths, one unsolved burglary, and—still—the matter of the "red letters," which had appeared all over the Hill. Rumors were flying that the motorcycle crowd of high school juniors and seniors was responsible for them. For the time being the letters had ceased arriving, but the matter of rowdy teens still needed to be addressed.

Mr. Gooding had called this extra meeting because the local V.F.W. had lodged a complaint that Miss Kellner, the municipal librarian, was a bad influence on the kids. She was said to promote subversive books. Among her reading selections, posted faithfully on the library's bulletin board every month, were Theodore Dreiser's *An American Tragedy*, and—even worse—*Spartacus*, by Howard Fast.

A group of parents was in attendance. One father stated that Miss Kellner had held the position for thirty-five years, a period of time that would put her around retirement age. But no one knew for sure how old she was. This man wanted the Board to retire or fire her. Another man, purple with rage, said, "Listen, my brother works for the United States Information Agency in Germany. Over there they're removing some of the same books from their libraries that we object to here. If these books aren't good enough for foreigners, they're not good enough for us Americans."

Rosie could just hear her mother saying: "Book-burning! Just like the Nazis."

In addition to the parents, a number of high school students came to testify. Other than Rosie and Andrea Lewis, the group was made up mainly of high school juniors and seniors. The small meeting room was so packed that someone opened windows for air.

Andrea was one of the strongest advocates for the librarian. Rosie scribbled notes. She had promised Chris that she would bring home material for a "Tiger Rag" article, maybe write it with Chris.

The most eloquent witness, Rosie thought, was Caleb. "English classes here are a farce," he said. "The library is our only alternative. Miss Kellner recommends all kinds of books to us that we would never read for school—*Portrait of the Artist as a Young Man*, Gertrude Stein's poetry, *The Invisible Man* . . . I could go on and on. The high-school library, of course, has nothing."

Rosie forced herself to say a few words. She felt comfortable in playing her violin for an audience, but public speaking made her stammer and want to hide. "Miss Kellner has always helped me a lot," she said. "She gives me suggestions on what to read if I need to write an essay. And she's the one who led me to Jane Austen. I love Jane Austen." She sat down mortified.

Why did she have to say that she loved Jane Austen? Maybe she said so to impress Caleb. The thought made her even more embarrassed.

One of the Board members, Vincent Trevini, addressed the entire group of students. "What's wrong with what they assign you in school?"

Andrea answered. "Some of the books are boring and some are just too childish, like *Johnny Tremain*. Besides, I want to read *more*, not just a book or two a term."

The students tittered.

Another Board member pointed a finger at Caleb. "*The Invisible Man?* So Miss Kellner recommends Negro writers?" Rosie stole a look at Bruce Jamison, the oldest son in one of the few Negro families in town.

Caleb opened his mouth, but Andrea beat him to it. She threw the Board member a scornful look. "Sure," she said. "And she also recommended *Uncle Tom's Cabin*. Isn't that shocking?"

Mr. Gooding tapped his pencil on the table.

Several other students spoke up, but the meeting was now running late. Chief Mangone had business and did not want to be kept waiting, Mr. Gooding reminded the Board members. He asked the students to conclude their presentation and thanked them for coming.

Mr. Gooding caught up with Rosie as the kids were leaving. "I'll give Chris a good report on your performance tonight. You're taking over very nicely for her."

Before she had a chance to reply, Mangone approached. "Hello there, Rosie. Chris's dad tells me you've been taking good care of your friend." He turned to Mr. Gooding. "Did you show Chris that snapshot of Trask I gave you? I'd like to know if she recognizes him."

Mr. Gooding stepped back. "Not yet, Charlie. She needs to rest."

He was right, Rosie thought. They should leave Chris alone until she got better.

♦   ♦   ♦

The next morning Rosie came down to breakfast to find her mother waving a magazine in her father's face and shouting, "*Encounter*, of all vile rags! Maxwell never told me about this. I thought that the piece was maybe for *The New Yorker* or for *Time*. But *Encounter!* It's such a propaganda sheet—sounds just like the Congress for Cultural Freedom. They're out to prove that American anti-Communists are intellectually and culturally superior to European leftists. And that the United States was right to kill the Rosenbergs. If I had known what Wiley Maxwell had up his sleeve . . ."

"Well, you should have known, my darling. You *know* what Maxwell's politics are."

"And now I appear in this reactionary journal! You too, chéri. See what he says?" She held out the open magazine. "He's talking about your new building and about the drawings for the Tarrytown Arts Center. Look! He just lifts the words from Corey Sylvester—the great art critic! 'Leninism in glass and steel,' 'a monster glass bat.' And Maxwell has the gall to question *my* originality!"

"It's your own fault, for God's sake, Lili," her father shouted back. "I told you not to have anything to do with Maxwell. But no—you wanted the publicity."

"Told me so, told me so." Her mother flung the magazine across the room. "Can't you be more understanding?"

In the car to pick up Chris, Rosie made a decision. Fed up with hearing her parents argue about *Encounter* over and over again and understanding next to nothing, she resolved to stop at the public library on her way home from school and see if they had a copy of the issue.   Looking at the magazine would be better than getting into the midst of quarrels she couldn't even follow.

But what would she say to Miss Kellner? "My mother is in the latest issue of *Encounter*. Do you have it?" No, that was stupid. Why wouldn't she have read it at home?

The library always calmed Rosie down. No noise, comfy chairs and tables, and the kindly librarian, who was always ready to help. When she entered the large, cheerful room, Miss Kellner was sitting at her desk reading. She was a tall, slim woman with a crown of thick white hair swept up in an old-fashioned pompadour. She was so absorbed that she didn't hear Rosie come in. Rosie stood at the desk until Miss Kellner lifted her head, pushing her gold-rimmed spectacles back up onto the bridge of her nose.

"Oh, Rosie, what a coincidence! I was just reading about your mother." She showed Rosie the cover of the journal that she was reading. *Encounter*! "It's a bit of free publicity for Croton."

Rosie forced herself to ask, "Do you think I could look at it?"

"Of course, dear. I should have thought you would have seen it by now. Look at the article on page 18. That's the one about your parents—and about other Croton artists too."

Rosie wound a strand of her hair around a finger. "But you haven't finished reading it yet."

"I'll have plenty of time to look at it when you're done."

Opposite Miss Kellner's desk was a small round wooden table littered with the most recent issues of a variety of magazines. Rosie sat on one of the wooden chairs covered with thick cushions made by patrons. On page 18 she found "Beyond Politics: The Abstract Expression of Pure Art," by Wylie Maxwell. She began at the beginning and heaved a sigh. By the time she waded through the first paragraph her eyes began to close.

The nineteenth-century impressionists had it right. It was not simply that they rejected the Old Masters' representational style; it was that the very notion of art had changed. Once upon a time, "art" meant the kind of craft that in the Old Masters made you marvel at the immediacy of the textures that they painted. In the large ateliers of olden times, apprentices learned the craft of transposing "reality" to narratives on canvas. The art of the impressionists, on the other hand, consisted in evoking an impression of things. You look at their brush strokes, and you say, "With paint and brush Monet created the divine light of the cathedral at Rouen. What art!" His cathedral tells no story of saints or sinners. It has no message.

Rosie folded her arms on the table and rested her head on them. What was all this jabber? She would never understand what her parents were fighting about.

In a second Miss Kellner was at her side. "Rosie, are you ill? May I help you?"

Rosie lifted her head. "No, Miss Kellner, I'm fine. But I can't understand a word Mr. Maxwell is saying."

Miss Kellner chuckled. "Let me see where you are."

Rosie pointed to the first paragraph.

Miss Kellner laughed outright. "Yes, he does like to take the long way around an idea, doesn't he? What he's trying to say here is that several centuries ago, the dominant style of painting was realistic. Painters tried to give their viewers the illusion that they were looking at things as they really were. And their images often told a story—like the nativity, for example. But then, later on, painters became more interested in forms of painting than in telling stories or making an object look real. By the nineteenth century the Impressionists . . . do you know who they were?"

Rosie nodded her head.

". . . the Impressionists wanted to give their viewers only an *impression* of light and forms—not a faithful representation of reality. Now, do you want to try to go on reading on your own?"

"Oh, Miss Kellner, thank you!" said Rosie. "Will you rescue me, though, if I have more trouble?"

"With pleasure," said Miss Kellner, and returned to her desk.

Artists in more recent times have turned the Old Masters' narrative paint-ing into sloganeering. What matters to Alice Neel, or Ben Shahn, or George Grosz is not the miraculous luminousness of "art," but rather the message. It is in this sense that they approach the "socialist realism" of the Iron Curtain countries. Diego Rivera paints a panorama of oppression by the ruling class. Alice Neel's grotesqueries, or Grosz's caricatures are meant to make me rage at the inequities of modern capitalism. Art has become propaganda.

Devotees of this kind of art, or what I may call vulgar representation, ac-cuse art that does not broadcast a message—such as abstract art—of being incomprehensible or pretentious. The work of Arshile Gorky, Jackson Pollock, Robert Motherwell, and other Abstract Expressionists is dismissed as so much visual gobbledy-gook. And yet what the Abstract Expressionists are pointing us to is perhaps the purest of pure art. They take us to a realm beyond nar-rative and beyond politics, where the perfection of form—light, shadow, color, line, texture—is our sole and sublime gratification. To vary a well-known phrase, art is long and politics brief. But the socialist realists and their follow-ers are doomed to the transience of the merely and basely political.

Rosie had to reread these paragraphs in order to get something out of them. Finally she decided that the gist was that Maxwell did not like politi-cal art. But that's what her mother did—political art. *Come on, get to my parents.*

Just to make sure, she brought the journal up to Miss Kellner. "I think I get it," she said to the librarian. "Mr. Maxwell thinks that political art is like the Old Masters, because it tells a kind of story and looks kind of real. And the Abstract Expressionists are more like the Impressionists, because they are more interested in form."

"What an interesting way of putting it, Rosie," Miss Kellner said. "Yes, I suppose you could say that."

Back at the magazine table, Rosie planted her feet on the lower bar of the chair and hunched over the magazine. She riffled through the pages until she came to what she was looking for.

In architecture, perhaps no one as much as Sandor Novac exemplifies the combination of heavy-handed Soviet style and the politicization of modern visual art. In Manhattan, his new Cronin Center and Grayson Building are nothing more than Leninism in glass and steel. His proposed Tarrytown Arts Center, figured as a dove of peace, will surely overwhelm the site like a monster glass bat. His structures are inseparable from their message: the sleek functionalism of the machine age in the New York City buildings, art as peacemaker in the Tarrytown design.

The work of Novac's wife, painter Liliane Carrière, is another matter. Carrière nods to Courbet and to the socialist realists in her depiction of humble, ordinary folk at their tasks. In her barge series, it is the muscular bargeman's struggle with the elements and, implicitly, with his poverty, that she evokes in all its bathos. In other work, she denounces the power of money or glorifies Communists like Paul Robeson. Carrière's signature themes are her sympathy for the common man and his self-proclaimed champions and her condemnation of bourgeois life. So eager is she to emulate her socialist realist models that whatever "art" she may possess is obscured by the banality of her message.

"The banality of her message?" No wonder her mother had a fit.

And here was something about Chris's father!

Caricatures and cartoons have always been a dubious art form, and perhaps should not be considered art at all. Daumier led the way in caring more about the point of his image than about the image itself. But the form has sunk to new lows with practitioners such as Boardman Robinson, William Gropper, Robert Minor, and Gilbert Gooding. Gooding is only the latest in a long line of acerbic visual commentators from Croton-on-Hudson's vociferous left wing. His publishers have finally had the good taste to discontinue the scurrilous "Kookie Kutt" series. Gooding has produced more respectable work in his illustrations for children's books.

So her father was right! This Wylie Maxwell was a snake in the grass. And what did 'acerbic' mean anyway?

CHAPTER TWENTY-ONE

Early on, Rosie had dreaded her visits to the Goodings'. It was lonely making dinner downstairs while Chris was upstairs sleeping. But now that Chris was back in school, Rosie could report to her on anything she may have missed in after-school activities. The visits were getting easier, even pleasant. Besides, with the constant fighting between her parents at home, she was eager to escape as much as possible.

As she turned onto North Highland Place, she was alarmed to see a police cruiser parked in front of the Goodings' house. A few moments later Chuck Riley and someone who looked like a high school boy went out the front door and drove away.

Rosie ran inside without knocking. "Has something bad happened?" she asked Chris, who was sitting at the kitchen table, chin in hand.

Chris looked quite normal now. Her bruises had cleared up, and she was dressed in her uniform of dungarees and an old shirt of her father's, with the tails hanging out. "What do you mean? No, of course not."

"What was Officer Riley doing here?"

"He came to pick up Luke."

"Who's Luke?"

"He's a sophomore in the chess club. He's Chuck Riley's cousin. He came over to play chess with me."

"But . . . I thought you were supposed to rest after school."

Was that Chris looking sheepish—self-possessed Chris? "My parents said it was okay, because I've been getting a little bored here. Anyhow, he's good, and I'm improving my game."

Lately Chris had been champing at the bit to resume all her activities. But the doctor's orders were for Chris to continue to rest as much as possible for a while yet. Her central nervous system had suffered a shock, and she would never regain her strength if she overdid it. And now Mr. Gooding had passed on to Rosie the photo that Mangone had mentioned the night of the Village Board meeting. Mr. Gooding seemed to think that Chris would talk more easily with her than with him, her own father. Everyone had been trying to steer clear of the investigations in talking with Chris. Little did they know that she had already dragged Rosie into her snooping.

Chris nestled in an armchair in the kitchen-living area while Rosie fed Willie. Even though it was a relatively mild afternoon, Chris had a light blanket wrapped around her legs. She had been trying to keep up with homework in her classes. "What do you think, Rosie? I've been trying to write a human-interest story for the 'Tiger Rag.' I'm going to call it 'Doing Homework with a Concussion.' Think they'll accept it?"

Rosie handed her a mug of chamomile tea. She smiled at her friend. "I think it's a great idea, Chris. Everyone misses your articles."

Chris sipped the steaming liquid and eyed her friend closely. "Rosie, how come you never visit on Saturdays? What do you do? I thought you mentioned something to my mother about concerts in the city."

Here it is. Chris was bound to ask someday. Maybe I can brush her off. "Well, now that I'm allowed to go to the city by myself, I try to get in the interesting afternoon concerts."

"Every Saturday?"

"Well, not every Saturday. But most Saturdays."

"You've been sounding so mysterious. I'm sure there's stuff you're not telling me."

Rosie got up and started to put her groceries away in the refrigerator.

"Anyhow, Rosie, is that all you do in New York—go to concerts?"

Chris could be so pushy when she wanted something. You couldn't get away from her. Rosie drew in her breath. "Okay, I go to a shrink on Saturdays. Now are you satisfied?"

Chris set her mug on the floor and looked up at Rosie. "A shrink? Why?"

Rosie couldn't think. Chris would produce an answer in a split second. In a pinch she'd make up something.

Chris continued to stare at her friend.

Rosie stared back, but she always lost in these staring contests. It doesn't look like she has to worry about brain damage, does it? "Well, maybe you remember . . . my parents were fighting a lot. They still are, but . . . . I got pretty upset. I think I must have said something about killing myself, like, 'If you don't stop, I'll kill myself.' My mother got scared, and they both started talking about how I had to see a shrink."

To Rosie's utter dismay, Chris burst into tears. She had never seen Chris cry, except maybe once, when they were about ten and little Mitchell Roberts nearly drowned when the ice broke on the Duck Pond. Chris was supposed to be the strong one, the one who always protected *her*.

"Oh Rosie, how could you?" said Chris, between sobs. "How could you? What would I ever do without you?"

Rosie rushed to hug her friend. Did Chris remember the days when Rosie wouldn't talk to her? Ever since Chris's hospitalization she had wanted to apologize, but somehow it never came out. "I'll never do it, Chris, I promise. You know I'm a big coward."

Chris's tears subsided slowly, over several minutes. "Rosie, what's it like, seeing a shrink? Is he helping you?"

"She," Rosie said. "It's a woman. She's okay, I guess. She said she thinks my parents are a handful. That's funny, because it was Mama who found her for me." Chris wanted to know more, but Rosie put her off. There was this photo. Not a good time to ask Chris about it, but she had promised Mr. Gooding. "Chris," she said, "I have to show you a snapshot that your father got from Inspector Mangone. Will you look at it?"

Rosie thought she detected another flash of the old Chris, poised to spring for any tidbit of information.

Chris stretched out a hand. "Sure. They wanted *me* to look at it?"

Her reaction was instantaneous. "The man in the brown suit!"

◆　◆　◆

Dr. Sternfelt leaned back in her leather chair, hands folded upward in a prayer position. She wore dark red nail polish that matched her lipstick. "So you began violin lessons when you were five. What made you start? Did you want to play?"

"Oh yes. We have lots of records at home, and I really liked Beethoven's violin concerto. I would go around the house humming it and tapping it out on tables. Then I started pestering my parents to let me take violin lessons."

"And then . . . ."

"And then they got me a teacher from the Bennett Conservatory. But . . . um . . . it took them a while to do it. My mother kept worrying that it was a waste of money."

"Your *mother*," said Dr. Sternfelt, leaning forward and letting her hands fall to the desk.

Oh, there it was again—Dr. Sternfelt harping on her mother. She wanted to get Rosie to admit that she was in competition with her mother for her father's affections. It was getting very annoying.

Rosie fingered a strand of her hair and glanced at the low-lying teak bookcase containing volumes with odd titles: *Fight Against Fears*, *The*

Future of an Illusion. "Why," she asked, "do you keep asking me about this 'triangle?'"

"It's like music, Rosie. You know how some themes keep repeating and coming back. We want to listen for those themes."

Rosie didn't buy it. Her troubles with her parents didn't seem musical at all. "Well, anyway, they both finally agreed, and I got to have lessons once a week."

"And did your parents follow your progress? Did you play for them?"

"They came to my recitals."

"But you didn't play for them at home?"

"No."

"Why not?"

"They never asked me."

"Would you have liked to play for them?"

Rosie squeezed her eyes shut and thought. There was that time, when she was about seven, that she had come downstairs after a particularly good practice session of the violin part in a Mozart piano and violin sonata. She had brought down her violin, and she started to play in the living room. It was true—she was hoping that her mother would come out of her studio and applaud. Instead her mother shut her studio door.

"We have to stop now," Dr. Sternfelt said.

♦　　♦　　♦

Rosie didn't have a concert that afternoon. It was a sunny day, so she decided to walk—quickly—from the office on West 12th Street to Grand Central. She made it in plenty of time to catch the 1:50 express and even to find a window seat on the river side. As she was opening her paperback volume of *A Tale of Two Cities*, she became aware of a man struggling to pile some packages onto the window seat across the aisle from her. He had several cardboard boxes taped up and tied with heavy-duty string. The train was chugging out of the tunnel, when the man finally sat down on the aisle seat next to his packages, and she recognized him as Andrea's father.

"Oh, hello, Mr. Lewis," she said leaning across the empty seat next to her.

He turned to her with a blank look. His eyes were very red.

"It's me," she said, "Rosie Novac."

"Oh, hello, Rosie. What are *you* doing here?"

Think fast, Rosie. Like Chris.

"Mama let me come in to do some shopping. Didn't find anything though."

"Well, that's nice."

Mr. Lewis sounded funny, like he was tongue-tied. Or maybe his speech was slurred?

"Think they have a club car on this train?" he asked Rosie. Definitely slurred.

"Maybe." She knew there were club cars on the commuter trains, but this was Saturday. They might have a dining car for lunch. "Did you come in to work today?"

"Work?" He threw back his head and snorted. "What's that, work? Yeah, in the old days I came in to work on Saturdays. Now I'm out of a job, little lady. Out of a job! What will your parents have to say to that?"

What? Did he really lose his job? What would happen to Andrea's family? How would they manage without Mr. Lewis's salary?

"So I didn't come in to *work*," Mr. Lewis went on. "I came in to clear out my office. Have to be out by Monday, they told me. Nice, huh?"

Rosie tried to think of a polite way to get back to her book. Mr. Lewis sounded belligerent. She recoiled as he reached over and tugged at a sleeve of her jacket.

"You just tell your father to watch out, little lady. If it happened to me, it could happen to anyone. See, my firm must have gotten something on me. Did I say 'gotten?' Someone *gave* them something on me. Great gift. I've been screwed. Put on the blacklist."

He let go of her sleeve. "Who has something on you?" she asked.

"The firm. You know, my law firm, my buddies, the ones who just made me partner. But they got tipped off by someone. Someone you should never trust." He pulled out a handkerchief and wiped his eyes. "Nothing's been going right since Corey Sylvester died. Then Delia, then the robbery. God, how I need a drink. They were clever, those robbers. They sank me. They got exactly what they wanted."

♦   ♦   ♦

Mrs. Lewis was there at the Harmon Station to pick up her husband. She offered Rosie a ride, but Rosie decided to walk. She needed to think through a few things. How come Mr. Lewis got fired? She didn't like that man, especially when he was sloshed. But people said he was a very good lawyer. And what did his getting fired have to do with the burglary at his house?

Poor Andrea! She couldn't be too happy at home these days. But then Rosie thought about her own home and all the quarreling over the issue of *Encounter*. She still didn't feel that she understood the whole thing, even though Miss Kellner had helped her a lot. She needed to talk to Chris. Badly. On an impulse she continued up the hill to the Goodings' house and knocked on the door.

Chris broke into a big grin when she opened the door.

"Rosie! What a great surprise! I was just wishing I could talk to you!"

Her parents weren't home, so Chris led Rosie into the kitchen where she fished around for some snacks and came up with potato chips and peanuts to go with Coke.

"Listen to what happened on the train home from New York. Andrea's father sat down across the aisle from me . . ."

"On a Saturday?" Chris interrupted.

"Yes. Just listen. He's been fired from his job! He'd been clearing out his office, and he had all these packages with him. And you know what? He seemed drunk."

"Oh, yeah? Well, I guess I would be too if I had just lost my job. I thought he was supposed to be this terrific lawyer."

"Well, yes, that's the point. And I think he just got some kind of promotion, too."

Chris leaned forward, cupping her cheek in her hand. "Did he say why they fired him?"

Rosie swigged her Coke. "I thought he said that it had something to do with the robbery at his house. Said he had been blacklisted."

"H-m-m-m." Chris crunched a few peanuts. "What could the robbery have to do with getting fired?"

CHAPTER TWENTY-TWO

Rosie grinned to herself when she thought about Chris these days. Chris was becoming the It Girl. It all started when her piece on "Doing Homework with a Concussion" appeared in the "Tiger Rag." Kids from the "fast" crowd, like Connie Waldo and Don Rizzo, now wanted to sit with her at lunch.

The published version of the article came out somewhat more sedate than the original, which had circulated underground. Rosie preferred the uncensored copy: *I was writing excuses all over the place. I would type them up and give them to my mother to sign. But even that task was sometimes too much for me. "Dear Mr. Ratpole (Trapelo to you)," I wrote, "Please excuse Chris from workhome. She has a bad ache in the head." My mother refused to sign anything. So I was stuck with "Julius Caesar." But it was hard to read. "The fault, dear Brute, lies not in me but in my mother?" No, that couldn't be right.*

And to top it all off, Chris included a few line drawings as illustrations: herself at the typewriter, nonsense streaming from the machine; her mother frowning at one of the notes that Chris waves in her face.

Rosie was at Chris's when Connie came over one afternoon with an invitation to one of her parties. Her parties were famous. They went on very late into the night, and Connie's parents, if they were at home, kept to themselves. In Connie's crowd, girls and boys had been dating for about a year now. The girls wore eye shadow and mascara. Connie didn't seem to notice Rosie's presence until after she had issued the invitation to Chris.

Then, in an apparent afterthought, she added, "Oh, you too, Rosie. Please come along."

When Chris's mother, who had returned to teaching after her leave, walked in with an armful of books, Connie stood up. "Gotta go—I have an algebra test tomorrow. See you both this Saturday, okay?"

Chris's mother dropped her books on the kitchen table. "What was that all about?"

Chris's eyes had brightened. "Connie just invited me—I mean *us*—to a party at her house. Can I go?"

Her mother smiled. "Of course not, darling. You know your activities are still very restricted."

"Yeah, but . . . I could just stay a little while."

Her mother's smile faded. "Chris dear, even if you were completely fine now, I doubt that your father would let you go. You know how wild those parties are. The Waldos, well, they raise their daughters very differently from the way we're raising you. Your father thinks they're completely irresponsible."

Could Chris's brain be affected after all? Rosie wondered. "What do you want to go *there* for anyhow?"

"I just want to see what it's like. We've heard so much about those parties." She paused to stare at Rosie. "I know. *You* go. Then you can tell me all about it."

"Me? You know I can't stand those kids. And Connie just invited me because of you."

"So what? You got an invitation, didn't you? Please, Rosie—for me?"

There it was again. You can't fight City Hall; you can't fight Chris. Especially now. "I'll ask my mother. But I don't think they'll let me go either."

◆ ◆ ◆

To her surprise, when Rosie dutifully put the issue to her parents, her mother beamed. Her father was uncertain. He explained to Rosie that a scandal had erupted when Dr. Waldo, a psychiatrist, had quit the New York Psychoanalytic Society. Waldo called himself a "post-Freudian," and he was a firm believer in Wilhelm Reich's orgone box. Rosie wasn't sure what an orgone box was, and neither one of her parents made a move to enlighten her. Her mother had a nodding acquaintance with Mrs. Waldo, who occasionally did substitute teaching at the elementary school.

"I know," Rosie said on an impulse. "I'll ask Caleb to go with me. Would that be okay?"

"Better, I guess," her father said.

Rosie got Caleb to agree by telling him about the Waldos' collection of Mexican crafts, which they had picked up on their two trips there. Caleb was very interested in Mexico. The Lennards lived not far from the Novacs, on East Mt. Airy, and Mrs. Lennard would drive them to the Waldos' at 8:30. Rosie's mother would come get them promptly at 9:45.

Rosie wasn't sure that she liked the compromise. "If you're letting me go, you might as well let me stay longer. Everybody stays out late at Connie's parties, and the seniors have cars, so I could get home. I'll look like a baby."

But it was better than nothing. When the appointed Saturday arrived, Rosie was unsure what to wear. Her recital dresses seemed stiff for that crowd. Caleb would wear his old jeans, she was sure, because he never appeared in anything else. She decided on a pair of plaid slacks and a matching green sweater.

The Waldos lived on Finney Farm, which had once been a flourishing artists' colony. A sharp turn to the right on Old Post Road North, just past the block of large, gracious stone houses built by the Stevenson family architects, led up a steep incline to the hilly, woodsy Finney Farm, which offered splendid views of the Hudson. This part of Croton, Mrs. Lennard said, dated back to the seventeenth century, when it was a real, working farm. Every fall Rosie went with a group of friends to pick apples there. She rarely got to see Finney Farm at night.

Caleb rang the bell of the Waldos' oversized, brown shingled house separated from its neighbors by thick stands of spruces and elms. No one answered after several tries, so they let themselves in. From a radio or phonograph Rosemary Clooney was belting out "C'mon a My House." Caleb threw Rosie a scornful look. "I have to do this for Chris," she whispered to him. They entered an enormous living room with a cathedral wood-beamed ceiling and an oversized stone fireplace. A loft jutted out from the rear wall, beneath the ceiling's high arch.

Snooks Morante got up from an ungainly, long sofa piled high with cushions and covered in multi-colored Mexican fabrics, where at least six other people were lounging. Some of the cushions had spilled onto the floor. Reclining on them was Andrea Lewis, in Bermuda shorts and a yellow Shetland sweater with matching knee socks. She waved at them. "Slumming, Caleb?" she called. Everyone was casually dressed, except Mary Beasley who stood out like a sore thumb in an ice-blue taffeta dress. "She gets invited," Andrea whispered to Rosie, "because she sneaks beer for us from her father's liquor store."

Snooks, wearing a school sweatshirt and tan chinos, greeted them with a grin. "Hi, Rosie, Caleb! You can get a beer in the kitchen." Snooks (a.k.a. Roland) got his name from his voice, which before it changed had sounded like Baby Snooks's, on the radio. Now he was a high school senior with a reasonable baritone, but the name stuck. He shepherded Caleb to the kitchen.

Rosie surveyed the scene. Some rugs were rolled up, and a few of the kids were dancing. About twenty or twenty-five guests were in the room, but they seemed lost in the large space. A couple of enormous, unframed abstract oil paintings filled two of the walls. Two masks and a big Mexican serape were hanging on the wall below the loft. The cigarette smoke was making her eyes smart.

Andrea blew smoke circles into the air, which smelled of spilt beer and hot buttered popcorn. "Hey, Rosie, how's Chris?"

Rosie had to hand it to Andrea. Her house had been burglarized; her father had lost his job. And through it all she began to hang out with Connie's crowd. Here she was, having a good time, as if nothing had happened. In her place, Rosie would be home in bed, weeping.

A senior whose name Rosie couldn't remember crashed through the swinging door to the kitchen, carrying a large bowl of popcorn. Rosie slipped through the door on its downswing in search of a soda. The kitchen wasn't all that much smaller than the living room. Above the restaurant-style gas stove hung a ceiling rack dangling copper-bottomed pots and pans. In the center of the room was a round table in gleaming dark wood, which looked like it could seat ten people. Caleb was sitting there, drinking beer from a glass. Everyone else drank from the bottles.

She was heading for the refrigerator when she was intercepted by Jimmie Halperin, a junior who looked like Frank Sinatra and was the current school heartthrob. He didn't sing, but he played trombone in the school band. "Hi, Rosie! Can I get you a beer?"

So far, everyone was unexpectedly friendly. Probably Chris's reflected glory.

Rosie remembered trying beer once and not liking it very much. She hesitated. "I don't think I like it."

Jimmie laughed. His whole face seemed to sparkle. "You don't *think* you do? Here, try some of mine." He held out his bottle to her.

To be polite, Rosie took a sip. "Ugh," she said before she could catch herself. It was like champagne gone vinegary. "Is there any Coke?"

Jimmie laughed again. "Sure. There's all kinds of stuff in the refrigerator."

Scattered on top of the round table were bowls of chips and popcorn along with a box from Emil's Pizza. A few of the slices in the box had been taken, so Rosie helped herself to one and sat down. She offered the box to Caleb, who took a slice. She still hadn't seen either their hostess or the parents. "Where's Connie?" she asked. She wasn't going to ask about Dr. and Mrs. Waldo. Connie's older sister Sylvia, if she was there, hadn't shown her face.

Andrea Lewis waltzed through the swinging door in time to catch the question. She looked at another girl, and they both giggled.

"Why don't you look downstairs in the pool room?" one of the boys said. "Or maybe in the rumpus room." He winked at her, and Andrea and the other girl giggled again. Rumpus room? Pool room? Did the Waldos have an indoor swimming pool?

"Yeah," said another boy. "Wanna go shoot some pool?"

At that everyone got up and left the table. Everyone, that is, except Rosie and Caleb.

Caleb pulled a small paperback from a pocket—Dashiell Hammett's *The Thin Man*. His father probably knew Hammett. Caleb's father knew all kinds of interesting people. Caleb made a show of looking at his watch and then mouthed at her "8:45."

"Did you see the serape and stuff?" she asked.

"Too many people," Caleb said. "I can't get a good view." He held up his beer bottle and made a face. "Think they have any wine in this place?"

Rosie went over to the refrigerator and rummaged around. Way in the back of a shelf she found an open bottle of Frascati and pulled it out. But Caleb only made another face. Maybe she shouldn't have dragged him here. Loud noises were coming from the living room.

She returned to find a few boys packed into the small loft. One by one they climbed over the railing onto the narrow ledge in front of it. From there it was an eight-foot jump onto the sofa. Evidently they were practiced at the exercise, because no one missed. Each time a body landed on the sofa with thuds of varying intensity, squeals of delight went up from the audience of girls below. That sofa must be made of rubber, thought Rosie. She watched the spectacle for a while, and then, more bored than ever, went back to the kitchen.

The kitchen was deserted now, except for Caleb and another person at the table. Mrs. Waldo! At least, that's who Rosie assumed it was. She had subbed for one of her teachers long ago. The slim brunette was drinking coffee from a chipped purple mug and reading a book. Caleb was deep into *The Thin Man*. Mrs. Waldo's hair was pulled back in an unruly French knot. No make-up hid the premature crinkles of age around her eyes and mouth. She wore a long skirt of coarse blue cotton with a baggy black sweater over it. She didn't seem aware of Caleb's or Rosie's presence.

Rosie tugged at the bottom rib of her sweater, which always curled up. It seemed only right to make introductions. She sat down. "Excuse me. I'm Rosie Novac." These days she was embarrassed by her name. *Daughter of the murder suspect.* "And this is Caleb Lennard."

Mrs. Waldo looked up from her book and acknowledged them. "Yes. Your mother is a fine artist, Rosie." Then why didn't they have any of her paintings?

"I've met your parents, Caleb," Mrs. Waldo said.

Rosie helped herself to another slice of pizza. There were no plates or napkins visible, so she held it in her hand. Mrs. Waldo had gone back to her book. But Rosie didn't want to pass up an opportunity. She bit into her pizza, which was cold. "It was nice of you and Connie to invite us over."

Mrs. Waldo sighed, put her book face down on the table to mark her place—it was Irving Stone's novel about Van Gogh, *Lust for Life*—and turned to Rosie. "I'm afraid I didn't even know you were coming. Connie's invitations are her own business." Her voice was dry and raspy. "Pass me that pack of cigarettes, Caleb, would you?"

There were two Camels left in the pack that Caleb sent her way. Rosie was looking for a place to deposit her unfinished slice of cold pizza, but none was visible. For want of better, she placed it on the table. "I saw you and Dr. Waldo at the memorial service for Mr. Sylvester."

Mrs. Waldo took a deep drag on her cigarette. She reached for a full ash-tray. "Oh yes, nice service. They could have done more for Delia Morrison, though."

Maybe there was a trash can under the sink, but Rosie didn't want to get up yet.

Andrea Lewis sauntered in. Oh, darn, just when she was about to pry Mrs. Waldo for information. Andrea sat down at the table and reached for the pizza box.

Mrs. Waldo smiled at Andrea. "I hear that your family is about to defect."

"Oh, you mean about leaving Kamm? Yes, I think so."

"Well, it's about time," Mrs. Waldo said, taking another drag on her cigarette and blowing out the smoke through her nostrils. "That charlatan."

"What's a charlatan?" Rosie asked.

For a moment she thought she wasn't going to get an answer. But Caleb put down *The Thin Man*. "A phony," he said, "like nine-tenths of our politicians."

"Or a doctor who only pretends to be a doctor," said Andrea.

Dr. Sternfelt's walls flashed through Rosie's mind. They were plastered with her diplomas. "Where did he go to medical school?" she asked.

Andrea and Mrs. Waldo exchanged a brief look.

Mrs. Waldo stubbed out her cigarette, squishing it around in the ashtray. "A lot of people would like to know that."

"Doesn't he have his diplomas on his office wall?" Rosie's question was directed at Andrea.

"No," she answered. "He has all these photos of Silver Lake and the Croton River and the Croton Dam. Taken by one of his patients."

A huge collective shout came from the living room, and a few guests burst through the swinging door and clustered around the refrigerator.

"He's a louse," said Mrs. Waldo. I can say it, now, Andrea. Now that your parents are leaving."

"It's okay, Molly," said Andrea. "He's never been one of my favorite people. But I did like going to his summer camp."

Mrs. Waldo sat up straight and adjusted her chair to face Andrea.

"Andrea, we told your parents. Told them long ago not to trust him, not to get mixed up with all his hocus-pocus. Then there was no good way out. And now look what's happened." She lit another cigarette.

"You mean the burglary?" Rosie asked.

A stifled cough came from the mudroom off the kitchen. Rosie could barely hear the sound of a door closing.

Mrs. Waldo sniffed. "Burglary. Sure. And Delia's dead. Your parents should have known that Kamm wouldn't just sit back and let them leave, Andrea. Oh no, he'd have to flex his muscles."

Jimmie Halperin reappeared and said to Rosie, "Dr. Kamm, huh? You want to hear about him? I can tell you all about Dr. Kamm."

Mrs. Waldo got up and faced Rosie and Andrea, who had also gotten up. "I'll tell you what about Dr. Kamm, Rosie. Andrea knows. Let sleeping dogs lie. Otherwise they can wake up and bite you." She gathered up her book and mug and left the room.

♦   ♦   ♦

Jimmie was dribbling beer from his bottle. Caleb returned to his book.

"C'mon, Rosie baby, lemme tell you about Kamm." He took her by the hand and dragged her into the living room, following Andrea.

People laughed when they came in.

"Hey, Rosie," called one of the older boys. "Watch out for him. Don't let him get you into the rumpus room!"

What was wrong with the rumpus room? She wrenched her hand away and whispered her question to Andrea.

Andrea giggled in amusement. A girl nearby patted Rosie on the back. "You'll find out soon enough, honey. Just don't let Jimmie get you into it. He's dead drunk."

"They keep it dark, so you can make out in there," Andrea whispered back to Rosie, who had just figured it out.

Someone began to bang out "Chopsticks" on the Waldos' old upright. Until then, Rosie hadn't even noticed the piano. She went over, mildly interested, and watched the pianist, a sophomore she knew vaguely. But the pianist got pulled away to dance, and, for want of anything better to do, Rosie took her place. She had taken piano lessons for a short time a few years ago, but she had decided it was too great a diversion from the violin. She liked playing the piano, though, and she especially liked picking out tunes. Caleb had been teaching her about jazz, playing his records for her. She decided that she really liked the blues. It was the big, brassy sounds, like Cab Calloway or Dizzy Gillespie, which put her off. She strummed the keys idly, playing snatches of Ella Fitzgerald and Billie Holliday songs. But it was hard to hear herself above the rock n' roll music and the laughter of dancing couples. When she started singing "Strange Fruit," Caleb came in from the kitchen, and other people began to drift her way. Soon she found herself surrounded by a little crowd singing along with her. The rock n' roll music had been turned down, and more dancers deserted the floor.

When she finished the song, everyone applauded. Jimmie Halperin caught her hand and tried to pull her up from the piano bench. Rosie shook free and started improvising a bluesy tune. The Red Hill Blues, Rosie said to herself. *How 'bout a round of the Red Hill Blues? How 'bout a round of the Red Hill Blues?* She let her mind drift as her fingers wandered over the keyboard. What did Mrs. Waldo know about Dr. Kamm? Rosie thought back to the memorial service and her encounter with Kamm outside the high school. Maybe he really was a partner in the burglary. What would he do it for? It couldn't have been just retaliation. He must have wanted something in the Lewises' house. That scrapbook? Out of the question to press Andrea. She seemed eager to put the whole thing behind her.

Jimmie Halperin was not giving up. He caught her hand once more. "Come dance with me, cutie-pie. C'mon." Rosie didn't know how to dance. Then a few more boys approached. "No, she's going to dance with *me*," one of them said, grabbing her hand away from Jimmie. This one was a six-foot hulk with greased black hair. He got her up from the piano bench and wrapped both arms around her tightly. "See? She's all mine, aren't you, Rosie?"

Caleb lumbered over and shoved the hulk away from Rosie. "Get lost," he said to the greaseball. And to Rosie, "Come on. It's time to leave." He took her by the hand and led her out the front door, stopping only to give her a chance to pick up her coat.

They were a little early for her mother, but it was better to wait outside than in there. Caleb and Rosie sat down on the front steps of the Waldos' house. The October harvest moon tinted the evergreens pale silver. A loon let out a plaintive cry. Across the road, pine trees shivered like shadowy spirits. In the center of the pine grove Rosie and Caleb could glimpse the outlines of an old concrete foundation. By day it was overgrown with weeds, but you couldn't see them now.

"Do you know about Isadora's barn?" Caleb asked Rosie.

"A bit. My father once told me about it. Something about a dancer, but I don't remember much."

"Once," Caleb said, "it was a big barn. Listen to this: The barn burned down on the 4th of July. In 1786. See? 1776-1786—seems a bit too coincidental, doesn't it? Anyhow, then in the 1930s, the brother of Isadora Duncan— she was the famous modern dancer—turned the ruined barn into a theater. At night Isadora and the other performers danced to light from buckets of oil. Lots of other celebrities came to Finney Farm, too. Um-m-m—John Reed and Mabel Dodge, Horace Greeley, Henry Ward Beecher. . . ."

Rosie didn't know all these names. She was picturing Isadora Duncan in her flowing gowns (it was all coming back to her now) gliding around in the moonlight. If only Rosie had been alive then! She would have played the violin for Isadora.

Voices drifted from the house, far from the world of Isadora Duncan. Behind them the creak of the front door broke the spell. Jimmie Halperin emerged, in a halo of beer.

"Hey, R-rosie," Jimmie stuttered. "Thought you had left. He sat down next to her, obliging Caleb to squeeze in on her other side so that they could all fit in on the stoop.

Jimmie threw an arm around Rosie. "So let me tell you about Kamm, Rosie baby." He threw a glazed look at Caleb. "You wanna hear too?"

Jimmie, Rosie realized, was harmless in his stupor. Maybe he did have something to say. It was very dark out here, anyway, so it was probably better that there were two boys with her. "What do you want to tell us?" she asked Jimmie.

"About Dr. Kamm? Oh, yeah, Dr. Kamm. Well, you see, he . . . uh . . . he lives right near me, on Nordica Drive. My house is on Morningside Drive. So, see . . . uh, . . . well, we're neighbors. So I know all about the crazy shrink. When I was little, I used to spy on Kamm. I'd hide in the trees around his house to see who went in and out. Every once in a while I'd hear kids crying, or maybe even screaming. One day I saw a mother carry out her kid, who was maybe three. The kid was kicking and screaming something awful."

Caleb stood up and looked down at Jimmie. "Do you know who they were?"

"N-no idea," said Jimmie. "Never saw them again either. But here's something else. Starting last year. . . ." He stopped himself in mid-sentence. Rosie thought he seemed embarrassed. Last year? So he was still spying?

"Yes?" Rosie prodded. "Last year? What happened last year?"

Jimmie hesitated. Rosie put a hand on his arm. "Last year, Jimmie?"

"Uh, starting last year I would see a black car pull up in front of Kamm's house. Black, with U.S. government license plates. Two funny-looking guys would get out. One was very short, with spiky hair. Don't think they were patients. I waited around to see what would happen, but they just stayed and stayed. I could never wait long enough."

Was Jimmie just saying whatever came into his drunken head? Maybe, though—what was that expression they learned in Latin class?—maybe *in vino veritas*.

CHAPTER TWENTY-THREE

Rosie's world was getting complicated to the point of oppressiveness. She longed for those faraway, simpler times, when she and her father used to take Saturday walks into the village together. Her father always said that the walk cleared his mind and refreshed his being. He needed only the flimsiest of pretexts: buying the paper, picking up a box of sugar for her mother.

But ever since her father had discovered his tail he had been acting wary and nervous. Sometimes, he said, the tail was there, sometimes not, and sometimes he wasn't sure. He called it a constant shackle on his freedom.

On a sunny, late October Saturday, Rosie finally dared to ask him if he would walk with her. What a surprise when he said, "Oh what the hell? I can't go on hiding forever."

The autumn leaves were luminescent. Tears stung Rosie's eyes as she peered at the maples' brilliant yellow and scarlet crowns through the sunlight. Heavy with age, the evergreens seemed to bow ever so slightly to the superior coloring of their neighbors.

As her father strode beside her in his Irish fisherman's sweater, looking almost like his old self again, he said, "I saw Lou yesterday." Lou—that was Lou Jacobsen, her father's lawyer. "He was very reassuring. Told me I had his full support, and that he was sure he could rub me off the suspect list."

Rosie lifted her eyes to the unclouded sky and took in a sharp breath of pure air, lightly spiced with the scent of nearby pines. It was that rare moment, suspended between summer and winter, when the compound of sun, color, and mild temperatures goes to your head.

Traffic was sparse enough so that Rosie could hear a car braking gently behind them. As it rumbled past, she recognized the driver as a neighbor who in former times would have stopped to offer them a ride. Her father said nothing.

Rosie loved the crunch-crunch of fallen leaves under her shoes, the occasional breeze that set them aflutter along their path. She loved the sound of branches and leaves crackling in the stronger gusts, the moments of stillness between sounds. It was a never-failing surprise to round the corner from Mt. Airy onto Grand Street and to find herself plunged into civilization. First Konco's Garage on the left, and then the street lined with shops stretching even beyond the traffic light at the intersection with Old Post Road a few yards ahead. Stepping onto Grand Street was an entry from rural serenity into the peaceable commerce of a small village.

Only it no longer felt so peaceable.

As they passed the grocery store on their right, Rosie could feel her father tense up. It was as if a shadow had fallen over him, as if a mechanic under one of the cars at Konco's had silently and stealthily as a ghost sprung up in the form of a gumshoe. Whatever it was, real or imagined, her father's mood shifted. "Rosie," he said in an undertone, "cross the street and keep to that side."

She understood. It was the tail again. On the other side of the street, deprived of her father's company, she didn't know exactly what to do. She looked at him from the corner of her eye. Did he want to pretend he didn't know her? He probably wanted to protect her. He was walking along at his former pace, so she kept up with him.

Not too far from the traffic light, he sprinted to the doorway of the Parkway Delicatessen and halted. Rosie hung back and watched him. Was that a man lurking behind him, just under the awning of Otto Krauss's tailor shop? Her father veered around and started walking casually down Grand Street in the opposite direction, back toward Konco's and Mt. Airy.

With no warning, her father whirled around again, just in time for Rosie to see the man duck into an alleyway. This time her father was too fast for him. He leapt past some garbage cans, which clattered to the ground, and grasped the man by his jacket collar. Not for nothing had he grown up in one of Brooklyn's toughest neighborhoods, Rosie thought. She held her breath and crossed to her father's side of the street, taking shelter in the entrance to the cooperative grocery store at the intersection of Mt. Airy and Grand.

"Hey you," she could hear her father snarling. He dragged the stranger to the curb of the sidewalk. "Why are you on my tail?" By this time the stranger was struggling to keep both feet on the sidewalk. Her father let go. They stood face to face, and her father shouted, "Huh? What do you want with me?"

Shivering, Rosie kept watching. It was like one of those silent horror movies, except that she could hear the two men tussling and arguing.

Her father's persecutor was a sturdy man. He was adjusting his plaid woolen jacket, along with his sunglasses and navy wool cap, which her father had thrown askew. "What the hell, Mister," the man shouted. "I'm just on my way to Konco's."

Her father leaned in toward the man. "Oh yeah? Then why did you run away from me?"

"You would have run, too," the man replied, doffing his cap, pulling out an immaculate white handkerchief and mopping his brow, "if someone was threatening you the way you were after me."

Without his woolen cap the stranger, probably not yet out of his twenties, was strikingly handsome. She had seen him somewhere before. That strong cleft chin and thick, wavy blond hair were very familiar. Kirk Douglas! He was a ringer for the actor Kirk Douglas!

Her father paused for a minute, and the two men glared at one another. Then the stranger seemed to become aware of her presence.

"And you, young lady, you just stay out of the way. You're a busybody and a meddler, and you're going to get yourself in big trouble."

Rosie stepped back in alarm and nearly fell off the curb. To make it worse, she realized that she wasn't the only witness to the scene. Bella Lewis, just coming out of the tailor's shop with a bunch of parcels, loaded them into her station wagon and watched.

Her father was yelling. "I don't care who you are. I know you've been on my tail, and I won't stand for it. And don't you dare threaten my daughter! Now that I've caught you, if you don't get out of my life I'll report you to the proper authorities."

The stranger just grinned.

"So you think it's funny, do you? And you have nothing to say to me?"

A few people had joined Mrs. Lewis and were gaping at the spectacle.

"I have to say," announced the handsome man in a loud, rich bass, "that if you don't quit harassing me, I'll have you charged with disturbing the peace. A citizen should be able to go about his affairs unmolested. It's a free country."

"Yeah, disturbing the peace all right," Rosie's father shouted. He raised an arm. "So just don't disturb mine anymore, okay? Or I'll . . . ." He dropped his arm, and his voice trailed off. The blond demigod, with a toss of his mane at the small audience he had attracted, sauntered away.

Rosie was wishing for a rabbit hole to swallow her up.

The little knot of spectators dispersed, but Mrs. Lewis remained rooted to the ground. Was she a spy too? As Kirk Douglas continued on his way, Mrs. Lewis trotted behind him. What was going on here? Was the whole town going crazy?

CHAPTER TWENTY-FOUR

It all came out in Nick Salvucci's report for *The Croton-Harmon News*—her father's run-in with the blond stranger, even her father telling the stranger to quit disturbing his peace and raising his arm in a threatening gesture. Rosie—Rosie, who never used to read the papers!—got to the issue first and was deep into the article when her parents came in to breakfast. Her father tore the paper from her hands.

"What is the matter with that woman?" he shouted. "She went to the police, Lili, the *police*, for God's sake. Is there no one we can trust?"

"Oh, Sandor, calm down. Nick leaves out something important that Bella told the police, doesn't he? That the blond man on Grand Street was the same one she had seen following Delia when she left Dr. Kamm's party. So you see, there's a new piece of evidence, and it's not one about you."

Her father spilled a few drops of coffee on his trousers. "Damn! But if Nick didn't see fit to mention it. . . ."

"Because perhaps he didn't know."

"For whatever reason, I'm still the Bad Guy. And day by day everyone respects me just a little less."

Rosie left the house as quickly as possible. She spent the whole walk to school dreading the kids' reactions, but to her surprise, they treated her with a certain amount of awe. In the cafeteria Carmine Nardone followed her as she carried her tray of macaroni and cheese to a table. "Wow, your father rates a tail!" he said. "Does he have a direct line to Moscow, or what?"

And then a boy from her math class caught up with her. "So your father's a hero, huh?" he huffed eagerly. The boy weighed about two hundred pounds, and it had cost him to run after her. "Could have K.O.'d the guy, I bet."

Rosie couldn't tell if he was kidding or serious.

After school she was dreading returning home as much as she had dreaded school in the morning.

It was as if her mother was lying in wait for her. Usually when Rosie got home the door to her mother's studio was closed. Today her mother popped out to greet her as soon as she walked in. "Your father was summoned to the police station again," she said.

Did her mother have to pounce on her before she could even take off her jacket? In a surge of anger, Rosie burst out, "Why don't they just send him to Sing-Sing and be done with it?" She ran up to her room and slammed the door shut. She pulled her violin from its case and went to her music stand, where the Shostakovich trio was open to the last movement. As she began to practice it, she noticed that she couldn't see the music through her tears.

Her father came home in time for cocktails. When she heard the front door close, Rosie ventured into the living room.

"What did they want from you?" her mother asked, before her father could even get to the liquor cabinet.

At first he didn't say anything. He mixed the drinks. Rosie's mother sat down on the couch, and Rosie stood in the doorway.

Her father sat down on an armchair and stirred his Manhattan with a swizzle stick. "The railroad workers found a pen the other day when they were repairing the tracks where we were stalled on June 19."

Rosie knew what he meant. Where Mr. Sylvester's body had been found.

Rosie's mother raised her eyebrows. "So?"

"The pen was quite badly damaged, but apparently they could make out an "S" engraved on it. They're trying to decipher more initials."

Rosie's mother sipped her martini. "So what? You think they thought it was your anniversary pen?"

On their tenth anniversary her parents had exchanged silver pens engraved with their respective initials.

"They don't know about our anniversary pens, of course," her father said, "but I think they suspected that the pen was mine."

"So just bring them your anniversary pen and tell them it's the only engraved one you own."

"That's just it. I can't." He thrust his head back and took a large swallow from his drink.

"Why not?"

"I . . . I lost it."

"You lost it? When? Why didn't you tell me?"

"I don't know when—maybe a few weeks, or even months, ago. I couldn't bring myself to tell you when I realized it."

Why? Because he might hurt her mother's feelings? Or because he was hiding something? Rosie's throat tightened.

"So what did you tell them?"

"What did I tell them? What are you, the Grand Inquisitor?"

Her mother's voice was shrill. "Just tell me what you said."

"I said, go ahead, charge me; put me in jail." He pounded his fist on the cocktail table. "I'm ready."

Her mother downed the contents of her martini glass.

"What do you think I said, for God's sake? I told them that the pen couldn't be mine."

Rosie turned away from them. She was still stuck on a passage in the finale of the Shostakovich trio, but it would be useless to try to practice tonight.

"I'm going over to Chris's," she called over her shoulder.

♦　　♦　　♦

Chris's mother invited Rosie to share their dinner, and as soon after dessert as they could get away, Chris and Rosie escaped to Chris's room. Rosie phoned her parents and got permission to stay overnight.

"I just don't want to go back there," she said to Chris. "They'll probably be up all night arguing. The police asked Daddy about a silver pen the railroad workers found when they were repairing the tracks near where Mr. Sylvester . . . uh . . . fell. Chris, it could have been Daddy's pen, the pen my mother gave him for their tenth anniversary."

"Yeah," said Chris, "but it could be anyone's, couldn't it?"

"No. Mama and Daddy gave each other silver pens engraved with their initials. My father's said 'SLN.' The one the railroad workers found was badly damaged, so all they could read was the 'S.'"

"Maybe for 'Sylvester,'" suggested Chris.

"No. They asked Mrs. Sylvester. He didn't have a pen like that."

Something struck a chord with Chris. What was it? If only she could think fast, the way she used to before her concussion. That pen . . . it meant something.

♦　　♦　　♦

After school the following Tuesday Rosie walked over to Honey Lennard's shop with Caleb. She was getting into the habit of going there with him every Tuesday.

Under his arm, with his stack of books, Caleb had a copy of the latest *Croton-Harmon News*. "Have you seen this?" he asked Rosie, pointing to the paper.

She hadn't, although recently she had been following the news in the village paper with obsessive anxiety.

"Remember that letter to the editor from last week?" Caleb asked Rosie. "You know, the one by that creep Horace Howard?"

Rosie didn't know Horace Howard, and she didn't recall seeing the letter. The front-page news about her father had absorbed all her attention.

Mr. Howard, Caleb said, had blasted the law-enforcers for their alleged indifference to the nests of Reds in Croton. "I can almost quote him verbatim, Rosie: *Maybe you catch more flies with honey, but what are you doing with those flies? Letting them go, letting them spread their poisonous propaganda wherever they wish.*"

"But just look at this." They were at the Duck Pond. Caleb stopped, opened the paper, and pointed to another letter. Rosie had to put her books on the ground in order to read it.

"This letter," Caleb said, "is from no less than Clarence Renfrew—you know him; he's a big deal Quaker, and he has that large estate on West Mt. Airy. Old Croton brickyard money—an upstanding citizen with a lot of credibility."

Mr. Clarence Renfrew's letter: *Some people say that our village is infested with subversives. These subversives, however, do not seem to have accomplished very much. No one has blown up our railroad tracks or bombed the Croton Dam. Of what are we accusing these people? Talking? Reading books? Writing articles or painting pictures? It's time that we sat up and noticed that the problem is not an infestation of subversives, but of spies. People are being wiretapped, followed, and hounded. It is this constant peeping, prying, and harassment that will destroy our peace, not the activities of a few political oddballs. The other day one of our distinguished neighbors, architect Sandor Novac, was driven to the verge of fisticuffs with an interloper who had apparently been following him for days, if not weeks. There is no rhyme or reason to this massive invasion of privacy. Nothing corrodes like suspicion. Yes, the*

*law is sitting idly by, but not in indifference to Reds. It is tolerating nothing
less than the destruction of our democratic way of life.*

Rosie looked up at Caleb. "So finally my parents are getting some *good*
publicity."

♦   ♦   ♦

Mrs. Lennard wasn't at the door of the shop when they arrived, but
Rosie could hear voices coming from the back.

"I need a nice piece of jewelry—maybe a medallion necklace—
something a teen-aged girl would like."

"Mrs. Sedgwick," called Rosie, "Hello!"

Mrs. Sedgwick flashed her a warm smile. "Hello, Rosie. Maybe you can
help me—I need to get a gift for my niece's sixteenth birthday."

They poked around the jewelry counter together for a while until Rosie
held up a charm bracelet. "It's exactly the right thing," Mrs. Sedgwick said.
And to Mrs. Lennard, "May I get two more charms for it, for a total of sixteen?"

Mrs. Lennard nodded and invited them all to sit and have coffee and
cookies with her. Caleb and Rosie got their customary chocolate milk.

"Did you see Clarence Renfrew's letter in the paper?" Mrs. Sedgwick
asked. "It makes me proud to be a Quaker."

Mrs. Lennard had not yet seen it. Caleb passed his copy to her.

"Isn't it nice to know we have friends?" Mrs. Lennard said after reading
it. Then she laughed. "No pun intended. But you Quakers really *are* friends."

"Something rather disturbing happened, though," Mrs. Sedgwick said.
"I got a phone call from that Wylie Maxwell. Apparently he wants to do an
article on the Quakers and politics for *Time*. Wanted to know if he could
interview me. I said no."

"I don't really know him," said Mrs. Lennard. "But Leland doesn't think much of his art criticism."

"After Maxwell's phone call I remembered something I don't think I told the police," Mrs. Sedgwick said. "On that awful day when we were boarding the train back from the Rosenberg rally, Wylie Maxwell got into a tussle with a man over a seat. The man had just come back from somewhere to claim his seat. Said he had deliberately left his jacket on the seat to show that it was occupied. I saw the jacket plain as day. Mr. Maxwell dug in his heels for a while, but eventually he gave in and moved to the coach behind. It was most unpleasant."

"Wylie Maxwell was on that train?" Rosie asked.

"Yes, dear. Why?"

◆　◆　◆

"Mate," said Luke Riley. They were about an hour into the game, which had been close.

Hey, how did that happen? Chris was used to winning at chess.

"How long have you been playing, Chris?" Luke asked.

"Oh, since I was five," she said. "My mother bought my father this chess set. I loved the carved glass pieces, and I was always picking them up. It made my father nervous, so he taught me how to play. I guess he wanted me to learn the value of a chess piece." She hesitated. "How long have you?"

Luke picked up a bishop. "It's a really beautiful set." He turned the bishop over a few times and set it down on the board carefully. "I've been playing around four years now," he said.

Four years! And he was already so good. He was worth playing with again.

♦   ♦   ♦

That night, Chris had a dream.

She is in a large, echoing courtroom, packed with spectators. Its floor looks like a chess board. The judge looks like Dr. Kamm. He pounds his gavel and booms, "Next witness!"

The next witness is Chris. She drags herself to the witness stand.

A young man approaches her and fixes her with his bright blue eyes. She recognizes him as the rookie patrolman who works with Chuck Riley. She understands that he will be questioning her. "Miss Gooding. Will you please tell the court all you know about Wiley Maxwell?"

"Nothing. I've only met him once or twice."

The rookie moves closer to her. "Are you sure that you know nothing about Wiley Maxwell? You know that he's a family friend of the Sylvesters. Haven't you picked up any information about him at the Croton newspaper?"

Before she can answer, Chuck Riley approaches her from the other side, pointing a finger at her.

"Chris, what do you know about Sandor Novac?"

"He's my friend's father."

"Come on, Chris, we know you have more information on Novac."

"And on Maxwell," the rookie joins in.

The courtroom is now empty, the echoes much louder.

"Novac," says Chuck, pulling her by one arm.

"Maxwell," insists the rookie, pulling her by the other.

"Maxwell . . . Novac . . . Maxwell . . . Novac" The syllables resound through the courtroom.

"Checkmate," says the judge.

The courtroom dissolves to Mt. Airy Road. The road looks like the chess board in the courtroom. Chris is walking uphill, and Rosie is pulling her by one arm in the opposite direction.

"It's not my father, not my father, not my father . . . ," Rosie repeats, turning up the volume each time.

♦   ♦   ♦

The following day Chris awoke feeling groggy and cranky. It was just going through motions: letting out the dog, letting him back in, letting her mother drive her to school, leaving her things in her locker, going up and down stairs and hallways echoing with the strange sounds of schoolmates, attending class after class. Images of the dream kept coming back to her.

Especially in history class she couldn't keep her mind on the subject at hand.

"Now who can tell us about Manifest Destiny?" Mr. Yarrow was asking.

"Chris?" He had a sixth sense for wandering minds.

"Don't know," she mumbled. "Don't know him."

The class burst into laughter, and she straightened up.

"No, wait a minute. Hey!"

But Mr. Yarrow had already moved on to Marty Kruger.

At the end of class she let everyone leave before her and then put her head down on her desk. Mr. Yarrow came over to her side. "Chris, it's time to leave. The next class will be coming in a minute." He shook her gently.

Finally she let him help her up, but she was wobbly on her feet. Somehow she made it to the end of the day. Through half-closed eyes on the ride home Chris noticed that the heavy rainfall from the night before had left shiny little puddles in the middle of Mt. Airy Road and lots of mud stuck with brown leaves along the shoulders. Once home, she drowsed on the living room couch. An image of the courtroom in her dream appeared to her. The judge was asking for evidence to rule out either Maxwell or Mr. Novac. Chris's mind, somewhere between sleep and waking, wandered to the evidence concealed in her closet. She hadn't examined it in a while, although she did periodically check to make sure that it was there. Sleepily she did a mental inventory: Maxwell's note to Sylvester about June 19th, the copy of Kamm's letter to Delia—oh, no, that was stolen—and Mr. Novac's threatening letter to Mr. Sylvester. Just before leaden weights began to press down on her eyelids, Chris realized that her mind was made up. She would never give the police that note from Mr. Novac to Corey Sylvester. Come what may, pen or no pen, she had to help Rosie's father.

CHAPTER TWENTY-FIVE

Chris, lying on her bed with another one of her headaches, was more than ever wishing that she could call Rosie and have a long, confidential chat. She really should take her evidence to Officer Riley. Still, she held back. She felt a twinge of guilt about her decision not to release Mr. Novac's letter. What if . . . what if? No, it was unthinkable. So giving over the letter could just get him into trouble for nothing. And wreck Rosie. But what about Maxwell's note? Maybe that alone? Yet wouldn't that be trying to prejudice the case, to throw the police off Mr. Novac's trail? If only she could hang on a little longer, maybe she'd be able to solve the whole puzzle herself and scoop everyone.

Oh well, when could she do anything anyhow? Now that she needed more medical testing, her parents were tightening the reins on her. She tried to imagine herself putting her stash into a sealed envelope and mailing it. But she knew she wouldn't include Mr. Novac's letter to Mr. Sylvester. Perhaps she would destroy it. She fell asleep with the image of paper curling in smoky embers.

When the telephone woke her up, she was so groggy that it took her a few minutes to recognize Luke Riley's voice. He was saying something strange. Something about a tournament.

"Chris, I asked if you've ever played in a tournament."

"Huh? You know that our club plays with other high school chess clubs, don't you?"

"No," Luke said. "I mean a real, county-wide tournament, like the annual one they have in White Plains."

"No," Chris said, rubbing her eyes, "I never heard about that."

"Well, this year's one is coming up in December. I thought I'd put in my name. You have to qualify to get in. I was thinking . . . you should try too. You're really good."

"Yeah, so good that you beat me twice."

"The games were close. I mean it. I think you're an excellent player. If I can qualify, I bet you could too. Why don't you try it? Then we could both go to White Plains."

♦   ♦   ♦

After she hung up, Chris heard a familiar voice downstairs. Someone was there with her mother and father. She reached for her alarm clock: 6 p.m.—almost time for dinner. Who could it be at this hour? She forced herself to get up. From the landing just outside her parents' bedroom she could see through the set of several open steps to the living area, where her parents and Mrs. Lewis were having cocktails. She sat down on the landing, her favorite place for observing unobserved. No one so much as turned toward her.

Mrs. Lewis was looking good. She had gotten herself a chic haircut along with a new dye job. She had lost weight. She was wearing a very flattering navy blue, light wool dress, probably brand new.

"You've always been good friends to us," Mrs. Lewis was saying.

Well, not exactly. But Daddy's the Village Manager, isn't he? People think he can pull strings.

"I've come to see you," she began, looking around her like a caged bird, "because there's something we didn't tell anyone about the burglary at our house."

She cradled her drink in one hand and swirled it around a bit. Or maybe her hand was shaking?

Finally Chris's father asked, "Does Harold know that you're here?"

"Oh yes. We decided together." There was a hint of pride in her voice as she emphasized the word "together." She fidgeted with the embroidered buttons on her dress. "It's like this," she resumed, "Harold and I are pretty sure that we know what the burglar was looking for."

The scrapbook story did sound kind of fishy. Maybe they had a cache of stolen art in their basement.

Mrs. Lewis put down her martini and lit up a Pall Mall. Chris's mother hastened to bring her an ashtray. Her parents didn't smoke, and her mother brought out the ashtrays only when they were expecting company.

Mrs. Lewis blew a smoke ring. "I need advice. I assume I can trust you."

Her mother reached for Mrs. Lewis's hand. Her father leaned forward.

"You see . . . ," She paused. "It's very embarrassing. Because of us and Dr. Kamm, I mean. I don't believe that we've ever discussed all this with you."

"I don't think so," her father said. He was trying to sound encouraging; Chris could tell.

"We didn't like outsiders to know that we were part of his group. Of course, people did know; people get to learn such things around here. But we were . . . ashamed . . . yes, that's it, ashamed. And it was hard to leave. We couldn't talk about it with anyone except the Mullers. You know what happened with us and the Mullers. Everyone does. So it wasn't easy to talk with them. But it was on account of what happened with the four of us that we all decided to leave. All Kamm ever did for us was to approve anything

ERICA HARTH

we did and mistreat our kids. So we just wanted out, and we didn't think about certain things." She stopped to take a sip of her martini. The glass was nearly empty.

Her mother got up. "Would you like a refill?" she asked.

For a split second Bella Lewis hesitated. "Oh no, no," she said. "I'm fine, thank you." She took a compact out of her bag, thought the better of it, and put it back. "Then Delia—she was such a love—Delia came to me and told me that she was planning to leave. She didn't say why. You know, people have been saying that Dr. Kamm was making passes at her. Everyone knows what went on with the Mullers and us, so I didn't mind telling her that we were probably going to leave too. She said she figured we would, and that was why she came to see me."

Pause for a drag on the Pall Mall. Mrs. Lewis dropped some ash on her lap. Maybe her hand *was* shaking a bit. "Delia was afraid to let Kamm keep her file. She didn't want certain information about her to get out. You see, he had files on all of us. Of course, psychiatrists take notes and keep records; everyone knows that. But Dr. Kamm's files were *very* detailed."

If only Chris could take notes right now! She would have trouble remembering all of this.

"I got that idea," her father said.

Mrs. Lewis sat back, as if she was all out of words.

Her father's voice dropped. "But you want to say more, don't you, Bella? You would like to tell us why Harold took your files from Kamm, wouldn't you?"

Her father really had a way with people. That was probably why he got to be Village Manager.

"Yes," she said. "You see, it doesn't matter now that . . . well, you know that Harold has lost his job. And our file—it's all there—the informal consulting Harold did for Leland Lennard and other HUAC victims, our political connections—*everything*."

"So after the burglary someone may have turned in the file to your husband's law partners."

"Exactly."

"Did Dr. Kamm help burgle your house?" Chris burst in.

Heads swiveled toward the landing.

"Chris . . . ," her father said in his serious warning tone.

"No, it's all right," said Mrs. Lewis. "Chris is a big girl."

Her father scratched an ear. "The scrapbook—Kamm was serious about not letting anything having to do with his practice out of his hands, wasn't he?"

Mrs. Lewis downed the last drop of her martini. "Yes. But the scrapbook seemed such a harmless thing."

"A question of control? He wanted control over all of you?"

"Yes—he wanted complete control over all of us, over all our files, our lives—everything. And maybe he thought that in the scrapbook—that silly scrapbook—he'd find more information on the kids' activities. You know . . . maybe they were making fun of him behind his back." Her mouth twitched in a weak grin.

"What about Delia? She took her file at the party, didn't she?"

"Well . . . um, when she told us that she wanted to leave, we told her about taking our files. We should never have told her. It's because of us . . . ." Her voice broke, but she managed to stammer, "We don't know how much she was planning before the party. But I guess when the fire started she figured it was a golden opportunity. Everyone's attention would be elsewhere."

Oh, so that's what Delia was carrying when she rushed out of Kamm's place.

They all sat silent until her father, like a pussycat on tiptoe, stage whispered, "You think Delia may have paid with her life for removing her file?"

Mrs. Lewis burst into uncontrollable sobs.

Her mother got up and put her arms around Mrs. Lewis. "You have to go to the police, Bella," she said. "That's our advice."

Her father nodded.

CHAPTER TWENTY-SIX

Ever since Connie Waldo's party, Rosie couldn't rid herself of the thought that Dr. Kamm might be a "charlatan." And if he was, then what? He'd have to go to prison, wouldn't he? Maybe for more than one crime. Wasn't a charlatan more likely to be a partner in the burglary at the Lewises' house than a real doctor? She had to get Chris's advice. That evening she called Chris.

"That Kamm is a real rat," Chris said. "Maybe you can find out more about him from your shrink. Ask her, maybe, how would you know if a shrink is a fake? Anyhow, listen to what I just found out . . . ."

Click.

This time both Chris and Rosie were prepared.

"Gotta see a man about a dog," said Chris, and hung up.

Rosie was getting fed up with the spies. She resolved to do whatever she could to find out more about Kamm.

On the train to New York for her next session with Dr. Sternfelt, Rosie tried to do some math homework, but it was no good. All she could think about was Kamm and the burglary at the Lewises. She was so distracted that when the train stopped at Grand Central she forgot to take her jacket from the empty seat next to her. She turned back to the coach. Coming down from her coach to the platform was a familiar figure. Kirk Douglas! Without a doubt it was the blond stranger. She shuddered and looked around for a place to hide. Nowhere. She scurried past K.D. toward the coach behind the one where she—and probably he—had been sitting. As she mounted the steps to the coach, she turned her head to see if he had followed her. He was sauntering toward the station. Maybe he had seen her returning to the coach or maybe he hadn't.

She had been planning to walk to the office on West 12th Street, but now she stopped to reconsider. It might be safer to take a bus. In the cathedral-like Grand Central Station she kept an eye out for K.D. Nothing doing. There were plenty of places for him to hide. She walked over to Fifth and waited at the downtown bus stop. No sign of K.D.. But once she was seated, there he was, depositing his fare. She slunk down into her seat. He walked past her without appearing to notice her.

Her teeth chattering as she got off the bus, Rosie tried to plan her strategy with Dr. Sternfelt. Toward the end of the hour, she asked, "Are doctors listed somewhere? How would I find out where a doctor went to medical school?"

Dr. Sternfelt smiled at her. "You're free to examine the diplomas on my wall," she said.

"Oh, no, I didn't mean *you*," Rosie said. "But what if there aren't any diplomas on the wall?"

"Are you concerned about someone's credentials?"

Rosie hesitated. Chris, help me! "I guess so," she answered. "I . . . I have a friend who needs to see a doctor, but she wants to check out his . . . credentials."

"H-m-m, I see," Dr. Sternfelt said. "That's a very good idea. You don't want to go to just anyone."

Oh no. She probably thinks my "friend" is looking for an abortionist.

"You can start," said Dr. Sternfelt, "with the New York State Medical Licensing Board. In order to practice in the state of New York, you have to be registered, and you can't be registered if you're not licensed."

"So," Rosie asked, "How do I find the Licensing Board?"

Dr. Sternfelt was looking over Rosie's head at a clock that hung on the back wall. "We have to stop now," she said. "Try the New York Public Library."

Rosie stepped out onto West 12th Street in a muddle. She looked west and east, but no one was in sight. Her parents had gotten her a ticket for the Toscanini concert at Carnegie Hall this afternoon, but Carnegie Hall had become less important than the New York Public Library. Should she really skip out on the concert to go to the library? She had been planning to take the Sixth Avenue bus to 57th Street. She could always get off at 42nd Street instead. She would make up her mind on the bus.

By the time the bus reached Bryant Park she had decided. Those stone lions on Fifth Avenue were calling to her. K.D. didn't appear to be on the bus, but she had put on a scarf and kept her head down so he wouldn't see her.

Rosie climbed the steps between the lions. Inside, there was the big climb up the grand marble staircase to the huge reading room with the long tables and desk lamps. They'd have to have a librarian there. She was directed to the reference desk, where she waited in line to speak to a reference librarian. The librarian said he would bring several directories and published records to her. In about ten minutes, she found her view totally blocked by a stack of volumes that someone set down on the table in front of her. She stopped her heart from sinking by the thought of *Encounter*. Nothing could be as difficult as plowing through that issue in the Croton Municipal Library.

After a half-hour she found what she was looking for:

Kamm, Leopold S. Not registered in New York State.

Not registered! She felt like getting up and doing a dance. He was a charlatan after all! He was practicing medicine without a license!

She hopped down the front steps of the library and sprang along in a trance to Grand Central. What would Chris say? The big clock on Fifth Avenue brought her back to earth. She had totally lost track of the time. Now she saw that she could easily make the 5:14, which was the train she had planned to take in the first place. When she got to the gate, it wasn't even open yet. She was still aglow with her discovery, but the sight of

K.D. walking toward her nearly stopped her breath. She thought of running away, but there were people around, and anyhow K.D. seemed smart enough to catch up with her.

"Hello, Rosie," he said to her, as if she were a casual acquaintance. Her blood chilled. "You seemed to be doing interesting research at the library." He lowered his voice. "If I were you, though, I'd keep my information under my hat. You see, we can make things very difficult for your father."

The gate slid back, and a conductor behind her announced the train. K.D. turned and walked off toward the 42nd Street exit of Grand Central.

♦   ♦   ♦

As soon as she got home Rosie telephoned Chris and in a rush of words spilled her story.

"Rosie, this is great!" Chris cried. "You did a fabulous job!"

Rosie half expected her to say, "I couldn't have done better myself." That was unfair—Chris didn't talk that way.

Then Rosie told Chris about K.D. "So, now what do we do?" she asked Chris.

Chris didn't hesitate. "We tell Andrea, and we get Andrea to tell her father. After all, he's a lawyer, and he's certainly mad at Kamm. He can find out if Kamm even went to medical school."

"Chris, I can't do that. I'm scared. Remember what K.D. said about my father."

"What can he do to your father? Land him in jail? We'll get him out."

"Or maybe they'll just kill him," Rosie said.

Chris was silent for a minute.

"Look, Chris, I can't, that's all. Please don't tell anyone. First we have to figure out how to protect my father."

"Rosie," said Chris, "Did you ever think about how Dr. Kamm—I mean, Kamm—got all the money that he's supposed to have if he's not even a doctor?"

"I was wondering about that."

Chris laughed. "You see, that's the idea. You don't have to be a doctor to charge people a fee as long as they think you are one."

Only Chris could make her feel dumb in that way. "Yes," Rosie said, "but would he have enough to be able to send some of his patients through college? I've heard he's thrown a huge lot of money around."

Chris didn't have an answer, which gave Rosie some small satisfaction.

♦   ♦   ♦

After her musical début at Connie's party, Rosie's star had risen with the "fast crowd." At lunchtime they would wave her and Chris over to their table. Shortly after Rosie's visit to the New York Public Library, Andrea Lewis sat down with a radiant expression. "Guess what?" she said to the three or four people who were there. "You'll never guess!" she said. "It's about Dr. Kamm."

Rosie looked over at Chris, but Chris was studiously avoiding her glance.

Everyone was still trying to digest the news from yesterday. Over the weekend, the police had had to quell a fight at Emil's Pizza at about eleven o'clock at night. Emil was trying to close up. But a crowd of boys, some of them certainly under-age, had been swilling beer, and they were getting rowdier and rowdier. There was talk of sending out more "red letters." The boys didn't want to leave, and they started shoving Emil around. Two of them sprang to the middle-aged proprietor's defense, and a classic barroom brawl erupted. Someone pulled a knife, and one of the defenders suffered a gash on his right arm.

Not one to prolong suspense, Andrea burst out, "Kamm's a fraud! He isn't even a doctor!"

The group was noisy with questions. "When did you find out?" "How do you know?" "Will he go to jail?" "What will happen to his patients?" Rosie and Chris were silent.

It was like this, Andrea explained, her fork suspended in midair. Her father had started nosing around, lawyer-like. He went to the New York State Medical Licensing Board and asked for the records on Kamm. It took him a while, but he finally learned that Kamm's status in New York State was "not registered," and so he was not allowed to practice there. Rosie caught Chris's eye with a triumphant smile that said, "See? I can talk about it now."

Mr. Lewis had poked around more and found out that no degree date was listed for Kamm at the University of Oklahoma's College of Medicine, where he had enrolled as a first-year student in 1919. Andrea's father had gotten copies of several general documents on the processes for licensing and registration and had closely followed Kamm's paper trail. He wanted to know if Kamm ever been professionally disciplined or criminally prosecuted, but he couldn't learn anything more from the New York licensing office.

It was like a detective story. Andrea's audience was enthralled.

Andrea glanced down at her untouched plate of spaghetti. Her father, she said, decided to check up on the records in Norman, Oklahoma. He got in touch with the Westchester County District Attorney, Cobb Stewart, who helped him out. It took some doing, but they got a grumpy clerk to agree to hunt up the files from decades ago. After a long wait, the D.A. received a mailed copy of the report from the clerk.

Andrea sat back in her chair, basking in her father's victory. "So," she said, "Kamm never even went beyond his second year at the University of Oklahoma Medical School! He's a complete phony!"

"Wow!" said one of the boys, "How'd he ever get away with it?"

"Wouldn't we all like to know!" said Andrea. "But look, everyone fell for it. I never liked him much, but I never figured him for a fake."

"Maybe," Connie said, "he was the one who killed Delia because she was onto his secret?"

Andrea arched her eyebrows. "Well-l-l, he's a louse, but I don't know if he's all that much of a louse. I can't picture him going out and killing Delia in cold blood."

"Maybe," Rosie ventured, ignoring Chris's warning cough, "he hired someone. He has lots of money, doesn't he?"

Her suggestion was taken up with enthusiasm.

Someone asked, "How'd he get all that money in the first place? Just from his . . .um . . . practice? I heard he gave a lot away to his patients."

"Yeah," said Andrea, "I always thought he was loaded, but maybe you can't make that much from shrink's fees."

Chris caught at Rosie's sleeve as they were leaving the cafeteria.

"Wait a minute," she whispered. "I have to talk to you."

They lagged behind, and Chris wagged a finger at Rosie. "Don't you say a *thing* about Kamm now. Let everyone think it's Mr. Lewis who's going to get him in trouble. Remember what that spy said to you in Grand Central."

◆　◆　◆

On some days Chris felt as if she had returned to where she was a month or two ago—headache, queasy stomach, unsteady legs. When she was feeling bad, she was assigned only one domestic task—the dog. Willie, poor thing, was so happy to have her company that whenever she let him in from the back yard he leapt up to her in joyful greeting, licking her face, his eyes ablaze with gratitude. But on this November afternoon, Chris was feeling more cheerful than she had been in the past several days. She had returned to working on a report for the "Tiger Rag," on the need for more and better books in the high school library's collection. She was going to try to draw up a list of essential books that the school library did not own.

Secretly, she had entered her name for the county chess tournament and was accepted, along with Luke Riley. He said that his cousin Chuck would be happy to drive them there. Now the problem was asking her parents if she could go with Luke and Officer Riley. She decided to spring for it today. Her father was coming home early, which meant a leisurely cocktail hour. She placed a little bowl of mixed nuts for them on the cocktail table.

After her parents had exchanged news of the day, her father turned to her. "So, missy, to what do we owe the honor of your company today? What would you like?"

Rats! And she thought she was being subtle.

"I . . . uh . . . I wanted to tell you that I've been accepted for the chess tournament in White Plains next month."

Full stop. Should she go on?

"You mean the all-county?" her father asked.

No one congratulated her, she noticed. But she didn't really expect a round of applause from this audience.

"Whatever made you do that?" asked her mother. "Aren't you busy enough with the chess club?"

"Yes, Chris," her father said. "We had no inkling that you were about to try for the Big Time."

They needed an explanation. Uh-oh.

"Well, you see . . . you know, I've been playing chess with Luke Riley. . . ."

She saw her parents exchange one of those dreaded What-To-Do-About-the-Chris-Problem looks.

". . . and he suggested that I enter. He's very good, you know. And he thinks I am too."

They were waiting. They knew more was to come. Oh, they were too smart, those two.

"He's going to play too. So he said Officer Riley would take us both."

A very long minute of silence.

"Well, Chris . . . ," her parents began simultaneously, and then laughed at themselves.

Her mother deferred to her father. "Do you think you'll be up to it? Wouldn't it make more sense to wait until next year?"

But her mother could hardly wait until her father had finished. "Chris, I really haven't liked these chess games at all. I put up with them, because they seem to be important to you. But I think they tire you out, and I don't like your being home alone with Luke Riley, unsupervised."

Despite the biological evidence, her mother still hadn't caught on to the fact that Chris wasn't a little girl anymore.

"Mother, you've met him. You even said you liked him because he's so quiet and polite. He isn't about to try anything with me."

"He's an adolescent male. You never know."

"Look, what can be so terrible? Luke's only offered to give me a ride to White Plains with his cousin."

"It's a bit inappropriate, Chris," her father said, "for you to go with Luke and Chuck. If you really want to play in this tournament, why don't you let us take you there?"

No! It would spoil everything! No parents!

Chris got up, folded her arms, and faced her parents. "Chuck Riley is a *policeman*. Won't he be a good enough chaperone? If I go at all, I'm going with him and Luke. If I'm old enough for the Rosenberg rally, I'm old enough for this. In three more years, I'll be in college." She went to her room.

◆　◆　◆

Nothing further was said about the chess tournament. If her parents weren't going to bring up the subject, Chris certainly wasn't. She would just go ahead and make her plans. So what if her mother was frosty to Luke when he came over? At least she hadn't kicked him out of the house or forbidden the visits.

Chris was still having trouble with her right eye. Dr. Carroll suggested that her parents might want to take her to an eye doctor. Maybe corrective lenses would help.

"Glasses!" she said to her mother. "No way. I'd rather have a blurry eye." *Men don't make passes at girls who wear glasses.* She had always kind of liked the look of eyeglasses—reporters and writers wore them—but now the saying had meaning for her. She didn't want to appear at the chess tournament wearing glasses.

In the meantime, her domestic chores were gradually expanded. On an unseasonably warm afternoon, as she was preparing a salad, she started thinking about Delia and Dr. Kamm again. Then her mind drifted back to Mr. Sylvester. An idea was rising above the mist in her head. She needed to look at those two comic strips she thought were from the Sylvesters' spring open house. She hadn't seen them around recently. Her father periodically swept the debris from his worktable and filed away his drawings. She had never dared to open his antique wooden file cabinet. But why not? It was going to be a late evening. Her father was in New York, and her mother had the Drama Club after classes.

Unlike the visible surfaces in his studio, her father's files were very orderly. There were all sorts of business headings (publishing contracts, income tax returns, etc.), headings for his various illustrations, sorted by publisher, and for his comic strips—"Kookie Kutt," "Kultur Kop," "Candid Pen,"—and the like. Chris began to page through the comic strip files. Her head started to hurt, and her right eye impeded progress. The job was bigger than she had anticipated, but fortunately her father dated all his comic strips and filed them in chronological order. She could hear Willie barking loudly in the yard, but she ignored him.

In a few minutes she found the two she wanted.

#1

#2

Chris's knees were shaking, and her head was starting to throb. Why, she asked herself, did her father want to rework Number 1 as Number 2? Okay, he added the spy to Number 2. The reference to "little pitchers" even suggested Jughead. So there was a spy at the Sylvesters' open house. Big news. She compared Numbers 1 and 2 more closely, holding each one up in front of her in turn and inspecting them side by side on the worktable. After a minute or two, she saw it.

If you looked at Number 1 as a stand-alone, without comparing it to Number 2, you might ask: Who are these people? She massaged her forehead and closed her right eye. The man, whose features were very roughly sketched, could be Mr. Sylvester. But on closer inspection he could also be Mr. Lewis. It was hard to tell with rough pencil sketches. Now if the man was Mr. Lewis, the woman was probably Mrs. Muller. It fit. Only the woman didn't look too much like Mrs. Muller, except for her height. She looked more like . . . Delia Morrison. Mr. Sylvester and Delia?

Now, for Number 2: In Number 2 there is no mention of divorce. So it's probably not Mr. Lewis and Mrs. Muller. Besides, in Number 2 the woman really looks like Delia. As for the man, her father had added the detail of a watch fob. She hadn't seen Mr. Lewis wear a watch fob. But . . . Mr. Sylvester! He did! She never saw him without one. The watch fob was a giveaway so that people in the know could easily identify the two characters in comic strip #2.

So let's say comic strip #2 is about Mr. Sylvester and Delia. What about them? Were they supposed to be having an affair? But the Number 2 lady is concerned about her reputation, as Chris knew that Delia was, and the Number 1 lady isn't cooperating either.

Something heaved in Chris's stomach. If she was going to throw up, she'd better get to the bathroom. She leaned back in her father's desk chair and breathed in deeply until the nausea subsided.

Her father had probably witnessed this scene between Delia and Mr. Sylvester at the open house—or overheard their conversation from his perch in the gazebo. The two victims. Were they killed by the same person? Why? And why the spy? Why would the man in the brown suit care about anything going on between Delia and Mr. Sylvester?

Maybe he wouldn't. Maybe her father hadn't figured out who *would* care. An image of Delia at the condolence call to Mrs. Sylvester flashed through her mind. Delia looking up at Wylie Maxwell, Japanese maple leaves spattered over her straw hat. And then, weirdly, another image—an image of a silver pen engraved with the initials "FSS."

CHAPTER TWENTY-SEVEN

"Chief Mangone wants to see you tomorrow, Chris," her father announced over cocktails. "There's going to be an important meeting at the police station."

"Me?" Chris tried to dampen down her excitement. "And what do you mean important?" Chris asked. "Who's going to be there?"

Her father stared into his martini glass and rolled off names: "Rosie's father—with his lawyer Lou Jacobsen, Dr. Kamm, a few federal agents, and the Westchester D.A., Cobb Stewart. Oh yes, Chuck Riley and some other men from the local force will be there, of course."

Chris went over to her father's chair. "Is Rosie going?"

"No. Mangone invited her, but she declined."

Her mother coughed over her martini olive. "Gil, why does Chris have to go? Is it such a good idea for her at this stage of her recovery?"

"Mangone thinks she's an important witness. She was on the train when Mr. Sylvester was killed. She was at Dr. Kamm's party when Delia disappeared."

Chris gloated inwardly. *If they only knew what evidence I'm going to bring to the meeting.*

Her mother frowned.

At 9 o'clock the next morning, she waited with her father and Rosie's father to be called in to Chief Mangone's office. The officials were closeted inside. When Mangone finally opened the door to let them in, he hardly looked at them. He was deep in conversation with the F. B. I. man, Alfred

Pike. He motioned for them to take seats at the long rectangular table. Mangone and Pike remained standing, facing one another.

"Well, I'm sorry Trask is late," Pike squeaked, "but he'll be coming. He said he would. I'm sure of it. You know, we had a helluva time getting him to come back to New York from Hollywood. There he is in L.A., sunning himself on movie sets with the stars, shooting the breeze and swilling white wine. Who would want to come home? Trask says Hollywood breeds subversives faster than rabbits."

"Trask? A spy?" Chris whispered to her father.

"Just wait," he whispered back. "I think you'll know him."

Pike was going on, even though it was obvious that Mangone wanted to shut him up. "So he doesn't want to come back to dull old New York. Of course he doesn't. But we were short of personnel here, see. So I went to my boss and told him in plain English that we need Trask here. So Trask says, okay, I'll go on the next Twentieth-Century Limited. Train, my ass! Who does he think he is, a movie star? He'll fly, we tell him, and he'll take the next plane out of L.A. for Idlewild. Twentieth-Century Limited! How do you like that?"

◆　◆　◆

When Mangone called the meeting to order, Chris noticed for the first time a man sitting at the far end of the table, a blond man.

Chris gave a cry. "You! I know you!" Out of the corner of her eye she saw her father stiffen. Mr. Novac could be heard muttering to himself. "Kirk Douglas! Finally!"

Mangone looked at Chris, deadpan, and said, "This is Curtis Winner."

Curtis Winner stared at her for a moment. Then, with a disarming smile, he spoke up. "I must apologize to you, young lady. I meant you no harm that day on Grand Street, and I really didn't know what happened to you. I left the scene immediately and wasn't even aware that you had fallen."

Chris hung her head. So this *Silver Screen* type was the one who snatched Kamm's letter to Delia from her! Who are you trying to kid, mister? You did too know I fell. "You didn't hear the crack of my head?" she said. "Before I was knocked out, I must at least have said 'ouch.'"

Before he was even called on, Mr. Novac shouted out, "That's the guy! The guy who was following me on Grand Street until I stopped him cold."

"Yeah, and nearly knocked him out cold, too," Mangone said.

Cobb Stewart shifted his gaze to Kamm. "Have you ever seen either one of these men before," he asked, gesturing toward Pike and Winner.

"In my profession," Kamm answered, biting off each word, "I see many people. I can't be expected to remember them all."

Stewart lit his pipe. "Dr. Kamm, we have witnesses who can affirm that both these men were present at your party in October, when your house caught fire."

"Me?" Pike squeaked.

Kamm was silent.

The D.A. nodded in Kamm's direction. "Mr. Winner, do you know this man?"

Winner shot a warning look at Pike before admitting that he did. Pike was silent.

Cobb Stewart's chair squeaked as he moved it closer to the table. "Dr. Kamm, when did you enter medical school at the University of Oklahoma?"

Kamm iced up. "I don't see what my professional history has to do with the matter at hand."

"It has everything to do with it," smiled Stewart.

Kamm's gaze was fixed on a point somewhere beyond the window panes. He sounded like a wind-up doll. "If you are going to interrogate me, I will refuse to answer until I have my lawyer with me."

Stewart took time to light up his pipe. "Dr. Kamm, as District Attorney for the county of Westchester, I advise you that it will be in your own interest to answer us now. You may want to settle this matter before it ever comes to trial."

In the momentary lull that followed, Kamm and Stewart could have been alone in the room. No one uttered a sound. "The year, Dr. Kamm, please."

"1919."

"And when did you graduate?"

A sliver of raw November air sent a chill through an ill-fitting window. A siren wound down as a squad car peeled into the parking lot below. Mangone got up and tried unsuccessfully to close the window.

"And when did you graduate?" Stewart repeated.

"It would have been 1923."

"Yes," agreed Stewart. "It *would* have been 1923 *if* you had graduated. I'll spare you the effort of telling us what happened, because, of course, you did not graduate."

Kamm was silent, but his enormous brows were knitted in a cold fury.

"So," pursued the D.A., "You are not listed in the New York State Licensing Board's records, which means that you have been practicing illegally."

Behind her, Chris heard the rookie whisper to Chuck Riley, "How come he didn't graduate?" "Because," Officer Riley whispered back, "he flunked out after his second year."

Kamm sat rigid as a stalagmite. "Is there a point to all this?"

"Yes, but perhaps now I can turn over the proceedings to Mr. Curtis Winner."

Winner addressed Stewart and Mangone, ignoring Kamm and Pike. "I made contact with Leopold Kamm in 1948. By that time, Dr. Kamm had been in Croton long enough to gather a growing crowd of devoted followers.

We got involved because a lot of his people are subversives, and we wanted to keep tabs on them. We had the perfect set-up with Kamm. He claims he's a psychiatrist, and so he has a confidential relationship with his patients. Even more so because his patients aren't about to talk to any of their comrades outside the group. Commies don't approve of psychotherapy—too individualist and bourgeois. And of course Kamm will keep their little secret. So Kamm's patients tell him things, and he takes notes. You can imagine how valuable his files are to us."

Mangone wheeled around in his chair to face Pike. "I get it, Pike. You double-crossed us. You lied to us. On our side, huh? That's a good one. You shifted the blame for the assault on Chris Gooding to the C.I.A. when you knew damn well it was one of your own. Winner is F.B.I., isn't he? And you were with Winner when he ransacked the Lewis house, following Kamm's directions. You could have guessed that Kamm could get Harold Lewis fired by leaking information from his confidential file to his firm. Pure revenge—that's Kamm for you. Worse, you knew all along that Winner was at Kamm's party. But because it was you who invited him, and . . . ."

Chris was reeling. What difference did it make if her attacker was C.I.A. or F.B.I.? The words began to rush past her like whitewater.

Pike was twirling his fedora. "I told you from the get-go that we don't share all our information with you."

"Not sharing," Mangone said, "isn't the same as lying."

Stewart let his pipe clatter onto the conference table, the edge of which he now grasped with both hands. "Hold it please, gentlemen. He turned to Pike and Winner. "And just why would Kamm agree to let you look at his files?"

"Why wouldn't he, is more the question," Winner answered. "We were on to him. We knew all about the good doctor's brief career at the University of Oklahoma. So it was a fair trade. He gives us information on his patients, we keep quiet about information we have on him."

The D.A. was shaking ash from his pipe. "Except that it wasn't exactly a fair trade, was it? Kamm's information came with a pretty expensive price tag attached to it."

"So we threw in some cash. It's standard practice."

Stewart leaned forward. "Yes, cash that came in handy when Kamm wanted to bankroll his patients so that they wouldn't walk out on him. People who threaten to leave get treated as charity cases—no fee, plus hardship money for a B.A. or even medical school. And Kamm gets points from his patients for his generosity. Quite a racket."

Kamm was still sitting at military-like attention, his spine ramrod straight and barely touching the back of his chair.

Stewart picked up his pipe. "And now we come to the interesting part. Is this part standard, too, fellas? Kamm can't bribe everyone, so people start to leave. They've had enough of his 'suggestions,' his hypnosis, his control over their lives, his punishment of their kids, his sexual advances. The impression this exodus makes on outsiders doesn't matter; people do leave their psychiatrists. It looks normal. But then people start to worry about leaving their files in the good doctor's hands. Meanwhile, Kamm gets wise: the Mullers, the Lewises, and who knows who else will probably try to leave with their files in hand—his bread and butter. The F.B.I. (he looked at Winner and Pike) doesn't want to lose these files any more than Kamm. So it will try anything to get them back—even burglary, intimidation, or what have you. Kamm and the agents have such a cozy little relationship that Kamm agrees to keep watch over the Lewises at the memorial service to make sure they don't get home early enough to surprise their unannounced visitors."

So Rosie was right. Kamm *was* involved in the burglary!

Stewart paused, and Pike picked up the thread. "Kamm sends Mrs. Morrison a letter. He makes it sound as if he just doesn't want her to leave, but it sounds threatening. She makes a bad decision. She decides to accept his invitation to go to his Labor Day party. Maybe she wanted to talk him into giving her her file."

The D.A. jumped back in. " . . . And at the party a fire starts in the kitchen of the new wing. If Mrs. Morrison is going to do something about her file, now's the time, when no one is in Kamm's office and everyone is otherwise occupied. Next thing you know, she rushes out of the house, file in hand. Winner goes after her. He may intend to use serious tactics, perhaps some form of bribery or blackmail—who knows?"

"Now hold on a minute, Stewart," Winner interrupted.

Stewart turned to him. "Winner. You were seen going after Mrs. Morrison." He turned back to his audience. "Winner follows as Mrs. Morrison heads toward the river bank. And that's the last we ever see of. . . ."

"Hey, Stewart, take it easy," Pike interrupted.

"You see," Stewart continued, "it was essential that Kamm protect his files. Kamm was onto the fact that a number of his patients were getting itchy, and he didn't want business to slip out of his hands. The agents are prepared for anything. If they don't get her file back, they'll spill her secrets, such as the fact that she was briefly in the C.P. She'll lose her job, which she desperately needs. All we know from forensics is that Winner and Delia Morrison struggled at the edge of the river bank, and that whatever happened next meant the end of Mrs. Morrison's life. I am *not* accusing you of major foul play, Winner. What I am saying is that Mrs. Morrison was harassed and threatened, perhaps to the point of distraction, or even suicide."

The room was completely quiet.

At that moment the door opened, and "Hold it boys," Mangone called. "We'll call you in a minute."

The door clicked shut.

Winner favored everyone with a movie-star smile. "Interesting hypotheses, Stewart, but completely unprovable."

"Let's just say it was an accident that didn't have to happen."

◆　◆　◆

Stewart asked Mangone to escort Winner and Kamm out of the room. Another policeman waited outside to receive them, and Mangone led in two men. The man in the brown suit! And Wylie Maxwell! That was Wylie Maxwell with Jughead! What were they doing together? So it really must have been Jughead in her father's comic strip #2!

Wylie Maxwell came in looking unhappy. "You've made me waste my Sunday," he said to Stewart.

Mangone waved a small piece of paper at Maxwell. "How do you explain this note?" he asked. *"I'd like to finish picking that bone with you? Was this going to be just a casual meeting of friends? Or was there a score to settle?"*

Chris rubbed her forehead. Unbelievable! They were actually using her "evidence!" As she looked at Wylie Maxwell, she could see a pen tucked into the breast pocket of his jacket. The pen! It was that fat silver pen with "FSS" engraved on it, she was certain. In a flash she pieced a few things together.

"I mentioned to Corey that I'd be attending the Rosenberg event," Maxwell said. "And yes, Corey did want to discuss what you call business with me. He had recommended me for certain writing assignments."

"Yeah, we know," said Stewart. "Mr. Sylvester had a lot of important connections: *Time Magazine,* the Congress for Cultural Freedom, *Encounter,* and plenty more. One of Mr. Sylvester's pet projects was to be an essay by you on Sandor Novac and his wife."

Mr. Novac's chair creaked as he moved it forward and leaned his elbows on the table.

"I don't know what this has to do with Corey Sylvester," Maxwell replied. "How do you happen to know so much about me anyway?"

"Never mind, Mr. Maxwell," snapped Stewart. "Corey Sylvester had promised to get you together with Mr. and Mrs. Novac to help you with your writing project. We have it on reliable testimony that you were seen with Mr. Sylvester at the rally and that you also got on the 8:56 to Croton."

"Yes, I was on that train. It's common knowledge that I was to visit the Sylvesters that weekend."

"But you didn't sit with Mr. Sylvester."

"No, I didn't. Because he said that Sandor Novac wanted to talk to him. So I found another seat."

Chris hadn't seen Maxwell on the train at all.

Leon Trask—Jughead to Chris—said, "You dragged me all the way across the country for this? I have better things to do with my time. You're interrupting my work just to turn me into another gumshoe?"

The D.A. pointed a finger at Trask. "Look, Trask, you were assigned to the Rosenberg rally—or have you forgotten? You happen to be needed on the East Coast right now."

"So, let me get this straight," Maxwell said, a note of fear creeping into his voice. "You are not exactly calling me a suspect. But you're intimating that I could be one. Your theory is that I was angry at Corey for quashing my deal with *The New Yorker*. Right. And for that reason I did in an old friend."

Mangone leaned back in his chair, lifting the two front legs of it off the floor. "Take it easy, Maxwell. This isn't all about you."

The D.A. stood up and walked around to where Maxwell was seated. "Maxwell, you, Ewing, and the late Corey Sylvester may have had noble motives in keeping company with the Congress for Cultural Freedom and *Encounter* crowd. But thanks to your efforts you've nearly derailed the careers of Sandor Novac and his wife Liliane Carrière, and you've turned people's lives upside down. You didn't count on the human factor, did you?"

Rosie's father was on his feet in a second, pointing a finger at the District Attorney. "I resent that, Stewart. You're intimating that I killed Sylvester out of revenge for all his red-baiting of me and my wife. On the basis of what? A pen? You've ruined my life just as much as these spies have."

"Hold on, Novac," Mangone thundered.

Mr. Novac' lawyer, Lou Jacobsen, put a hand on Mr. Novac's shoulder and talked to him in a voice that was inaudible to everyone else. Mr. Novac sat back down.

Chris started to raise her hand before she realized that she wasn't in school. "Chief Mangone," she called in as loud a voice as she could manage. "Chief Mangone, can I please say something?"

Separate conversations spun out of control in all directions until Mangone rapped his knuckles on the table. "Gentlemen. Let's hear what the young lady has to say."

Chris stood up and pulled two pieces of paper from her bag. She laid them on the table in front of her and said, "I brought in two of my father's comic strip drafts, because I think you should see them. My father probably did them at the Sylvesters' spring open house."

In the silence that followed, a growl of warning from Chris's father came through loudly.

Chris ignored him. "You can all look at them." Paper rustled as the comics were passed around the table.

"You can see in the one I've labeled #1 that it's hard to identify the man and woman. I had some ideas, but I guess it's not polite to say what they were. After I studied the one I've labeled #2, I decided it was a revision of #1. Why, though? Why would my father want to do over the first comic strip?"

Her father was muttering in annoyance.

"You see that he's added an important detail in #2, the man's watch fob, making it clear who the people are. Daddy? Who are the man and woman in #2?"

"Chris dear, I don't see what this has to do . . . ."

"Please answer your daughter, Mr. Gooding," Cobb Stewart said.

Her father cleared his throat. "Corey Sylvester and Delia Morrison."

The room broke out in murmurs and audible whispers.

"Quiet!" shouted Cobb Stewart.

Chris was still standing, and Cobb Stewart nodded a signal for her to continue.

"Thanks, Daddy. That's what I thought. So that means that maybe Mr. Sylvester was making passes at Mrs. Morrison. And maybe, if my father knew about it . . . maybe it was nothing new." She had decided to say nothing about the way Mr. Sylvester was flirting with Rosie's mother at the Rosenberg rally. "And maybe . . . ." Here she faltered. It wouldn't be right to accuse anyone. She wouldn't mention names. "Maybe other people knew too. And maybe they didn't like it one bit. Maybe they didn't like it enough to try to get back at Mr. Sylvester."

A hubbub erupted in the room, and the D.A. rapped loudly on the table. "Is that all, Chris?"

"No. I have something to say about a pen. It's a silver pen that some railroad repairmen came across at the site where Mr. Sylvester was found. It was engraved with initials, but all anyone could make out was an 'S.' So people thought Mr. Novac, because his first name is Sandor. They also asked Mrs. Sylvester if it could be Mr. Sylvester's, but she said no, he didn't have a pen like that. I think that if you ask Mr. Maxwell to show you his pen, you'll get another idea."

She stopped. The D.A. turned to Mangone. "Do we have the pen the railroad workers found?"

"Yes," Mangone said. "It's in my office. I'll go get it."

When he returned, the D.A. asked Wylie Maxwell to turn over his pen.

"What the hell is going on?" said Maxwell. "Is this legal?"

"And now," Cobb Stewart said to Mangone, "if you'll kindly place the other pen, the one found near the body, on the table." He set down Maxwell's pen next to it.

"Do you have more to say, Chris?" Stewart asked her.

"Yes. If you look at Mr. Maxwell's pen, you'll see that the initials on it are 'FSS.' I was bothered by this for a long time, because I remembered seeing that pen, but I didn't remember where. You know, my head hasn't been right for a while."

Nervous laughter bubbled up in the room.

"But today, when I noticed a pen in Mr. Maxwell's pocket, I remembered." She faltered once more. "It's a bit embarrassing. You see, a while ago, when Delia was still alive, I snooped around where I shouldn't have (more laughter), and I found myself in her apartment. She wasn't home, but Mr. Ewing and Mr. Maxwell were there. And on the kitchen table there was a kind of fat pen with 'FSS' on it. But that wasn't the first time I had seen it. I had seen it before at the Dardanelles Restaurant in New York when I barged in on a lunch my mother was having with Mr. Ewing. Mr. Ewing asked another man there if he could borrow his pen because he didn't seem to have his own with him. The other man, Mr. Raven, was also a critic or writer, or something. I noticed the pen he loaned Mr. Ewing because it was so fat, and the initials weren't the owner's. So then, in Mr. Ewing's apartment—follow me, everyone?—when I saw that same pen, I asked Mr. Maxwell what the initials stood for. He said 'From Stephen Spender.' And he reminded Mr. Ewing that at an anniversary party for some literary magazine Mr. Spender had handed a lot of them out to people as gifts. From what I could understand, Mr. Ewing was at that party, and he got one too. But he didn't have it with him when I was in Delia's apartment."

A polite cough sounded in the silence.

"So if Mr. Maxwell will let you keep his pen for a while, and if you compare it with the one on the railroad tracks, I think you'll find that . . . ."

"Okay, thank you, Chris," Mangone said, getting to his feet. "I think you've been a great help, but we can take it from here."

CHAPTER TWENTY-EIGHT

On an unnaturally mild early November afternoon, Rosie opened the door to Chris with an ear-to-ear grin. "Frank Ewing's confessed," Rosie shouted at the top of her lungs. "Hurray! He's confessed!"

Chris, whose parents had told her the news early that morning, hugged her friend tightly. Chris had tried to get details from her parents, but they were both rushing out of the house to work. Chris, reveling in Rosie's jubilation, would have skipped all the way down to school with her, if they weren't getting a ride with Rosie's mother. She and Rosie had helped to solve both the crimes! And the next evening they were going to Connie Waldo's Halloween party.

In the evening, when Chris and her parents assembled around the kitchen table, Chris nagged her father to tell the whole story, even before cocktails. He gave up trying to refuse.

Right after the meeting at the police station, her father, Mangone, and D.A. Cobb Stewart had put their heads together and gone to work.

"You did a great job, Chris," her father said, with the FSS pen."

She noticed that he said nothing about the comic strips.

"That was a crucial piece of evidence. But to go back to June 19: Frank Ewing was definitely on the 8:56 from New York, and he was sitting in the same coach as Corey Sylvester. You didn't see him, Chris, probably because he was sitting at the rear of that car. You were right in your guess about Corey Sylvester and Delia. For months, it seems, Delia had been complaining to Ewing about Sylvester's insistent and unwanted sexual advances.

Ewing confided all this to his friend Wylie Maxwell. Just before the June 19 event, Sylvester had Delia stay late to work on some pretext and launched an all-out assault. Delia managed to run out of the office. She came home in tears, and Ewing told her he would "punch out" Sylvester, according to Wylie Maxwell. But Delia wouldn't hear of it. She needed her job. She was under extreme stress."

"Poor Delia," Chris said. "And she couldn't complain to Mrs. Sylvester— or anyone."

"Frank Ewing said he didn't expect to see Corey Sylvester on the train," her father continued. "He was simply going home to Delia for the weekend. Frank knew that Wiley Maxwell was going to visit the Sylvesters that weekend, but the train was crowded, and he couldn't get a seat with Maxwell. Just before the power went out, he saw Corey get up. On impulse—so Frank says—he himself got up too. Finally he would tell Corey off. He gets to the front of the car just as Sylvester finds out that the lavatory is occupied."

Chris's father fixed himself a scotch and took a swig. "Ewing can just about make out the outlines of Corey's body. Stewart thinks it went like this: Ewing says, 'I need to have a word with you, Corey.' He gets him to go out on the platform between the two coaches, where the other passengers won't hear them. He raises his voice; he threatens Corey. Corey works up a self-righteous anger. How dare Ewing insult him in this way! Ewing is in a rage. He puts his hands around Corey's neck. But Corey is a big man, and he struggles free. In the process, he falls—or is pushed—to a gruesome death. The gates on the platform were closed, but of course the killer could have opened and closed a gate. In the fracas, Ewing's FSS pen went overboard too."

It looked like her mother was hearing all of this for this first time. She seemed just as stunned as Chris herself. The three of them sat still in a long silence.

Chris spoke up first, her voice quavering. "What about Mr. Novac's anniversary pen?"

Her father smiled. "Sandor really did lose it. But more important, Wiley Maxwell knew that Ewing was on the train. He himself is on the suspect list, so he's ready to cooperate with the police. Ewing's confession is no surprise. He's been a wreck ever since Delia's death, drinking like a fish—he's even said he has nothing to live for. He'll probably be charged with manslaughter and not murder. That's his only hope, if he still has any hope at all."

Another silence. This time it was Chris's mother who broke it. "What about poor Delia? Who's going to be charged with her death?"

"The problem is," her father said, "that it's pretty damn hard to haul the F.B.I. into court—as if we didn't know. No one can prove a thing about what happened at the edge of the cliff, and even if they could . . . . Pike is pretty steamed up. Kamm's information mill will be closed down—a big loss for Pike and company. This is probably how it'll play out: the F.B.I. will 'retire' Kamm with a generous settlement. Kamm will even be able to stay on in Croton, in the Playhouse, if he wants to, but his little community will be disbanded. He can claim age and ill health."

"And Delia?" Chris asked. "Didn't she take a pretty big risk during the fire?"

"She did," said her father. "But better dead than read."

♦ ♦ ♦

November was veering toward winter. On the next Saturday, under steady sleet, Chris trooped over to the newspaper office in her galoshes. She was surprised to find Mrs. Sylvester and her new assistant, Anita, amiably chatting over coffee. Usually Chris had the office pretty much to herself on Saturdays. The two women smiled at her as she hung up her rain jacket and removed her muddy galoshes.

"Chris, dear," said Mrs. Sylvester, "I was waiting for you. I have some good news. You have been such a help in this whole ghastly affair—serving as a witness, tracking down clues, giving me support. How would you like to work on some real stories?" She sounded choked up.

Chris balanced herself on one leg—she was able to revert to her old habit now!—and faced her.

"Since Frank Ewing is being held, we're ready to do a story on the follow-up to . . . uh, my husband's death on June 19th. As you know, we've had to be cautious about printing anything without full information. You, dear, have been invaluable to the police from the beginning."

Chris held her breath.

"So I've asked Nick Salvucci to let you work with him on the story. You'll both bring everything up to date . . . you know, up to Frank Ewing's arrest. Later, you can both cover the trial. And you'll have a byline, Chris. It will read 'By Nick Salvucci, with the assistance of Christabel Gooding.' Also, I'd like you to help Nick write up another story on the whole, ghastly business of poor Delia, which may take a while to complete, because you'll have to wait until the investigation ends."

It was as much as she could hope for. Chris grinned and tried to say something.

"Well, I . . . I, uh . . . thank you."

The clouds on Mrs. Sylvester's face cleared. "Chris, can you be speechless? You?"

Nick banged the door heavily against the driving sleet, and stamped slush from his boots on the floor mat.

"Hiya, kid!" he greeted Chris. "Joan tell you the news? Welcome to Grub Street!"

"Cat's got her tongue," said Anita. "She's been rendered speechless."

"Yeah, it's the big time for you, kid." Nick patted Chris on the shoulder. "We're going to have to get to work."

Anita looked up at Nick and across at Mrs. Sylvester. "What's the latest on Frank Ewing?"

Joan Sylvester, with her raincoat on and all set to go out, stood waiting.

"He's retained a lawyer. Some guy from the city. They're going to try for a manslaughter conviction." Nick glanced at Joan Sylvester, but she was wearing her usual unruffled look.

"See you on Monday," called Mrs. Sylvester, as she opened the door to the beating sleet.

"We'll have to go over all the evidence, won't we?" Chris asked.

"We'll see," said Nick. "We've got a big job ahead of us, kid."

◆　　◆　　◆

Rosie, Chris, and Caleb went together to Connie's Halloween party. Rosie wore a big Beethoven mask that her mother had made for her. Chris gave her parents a rundown of the party on the morning after. "You should have seen Rosie," she said. "She was fantastic.　When the kids started the jumping off the balcony routine, Rosie sat down at the piano and played her 'Red Hill Blues.' She's written it all up now, you know. Anyhow, everyone stopped and hung around the piano to listen. Then Caleb played—he's pretty good—and Rosie stood up and sang the lyrics. Wow! It was great. Everybody applauded and cheered."

The phone rang, and Chris picked up, fully expecting to hear Rosie's voice at the other end. But it was Luke Riley, wanting to know if he could come over for a chess game that afternoon.

"Sure!" Chris said. He really was very nice, this Luke Riley.

"And I have something to tell you," Luke said. "My cousin Chuck is getting rewarded for his work with Chief Mangone on the two big crimes. He's being promoted to sergeant! The chief called him in yesterday. He said someone needs to be in charge of the red letters and the trouble that's been going on at Emil's Pizza Place recently. So it'll be Chuck."

"Tell him congratulations!" said Chris, with a broad smile.

"What was that all about?" asked her mother, after Chris had hung up.

"Oh, nothing. It was Luke Riley. We're playing chess this afternoon." And with an offhand explanation of how she needed to get to her geometry homework, she went to her room.

◆ ◆ ◆

"My mother," announced Rosie to Chris on their next walk to school, wants to celebrate. She said it wasn't decorous to be happy about Mr. Ewing's indictment, but we're going to celebrate anyhow. Oh Chris, what a difference now that Daddy isn't a suspect anymore! There's some peace at home!"

Chris had seen the difference in Rosie's father lately. He was still pretty tense, but in recent days he had burst out with a good long laugh or two. She couldn't remember hearing Mr. Novac laugh like that in months. And Rosie said just the other day that she felt ready to cut back on her psychotherapy.

The two families always had a Thanksgiving dinner together. This year it was special. Mr. Novac started a fire in the fireplace. Mrs. Novac had added extra touches to the festive seasonal décor, with table settings of evergreens and candles in wooden holders that she had painted herself.

Rosie told Chris that it had taken her mother two days to prepare the first course of smoked trout mousse. After cocktails (for adults only), Rosie and Chris were offered the same beverages as their parents: champagne with the trout mousse, and a good red Burgundy wine with the main course of butterflied lamb.

At the first course, Chris's father lifted his flute of champagne. "A toast to our friend and neighbor, Sandor, who has weathered the storm."

"Hear, hear!" everyone chorused, as they all lifted their glasses and drank.

Mr. Novac stood up. "A toast to my wife for standing by me more than heroically." Rosie's mother smiled up at him, as they all drank.

"And," Chris's father signaled the others to raise their glasses once more, "to my good friends here, and . . . to my daughter, healthy, wiser, and not too wealthy."

Rosie stood to her full four feet nine inches tall and lifted her glass, "A toast to Chris, reporter and future Westchester chess champion!"

Yes, Chris's parents had finally caved in.

They drank again, and then Chris stood up. "A toast to Rosie!"

"To Rosie," echoed the four parents, uncertainly.

"Wait! Wait!" Chris called. "I can see that you don't know why."

Rosie was glowing.

"We have an announcement to make," said Chris. "We've saved it for this occasion. Rosie . . . you want to tell?"

"No, no—you."

"Caleb's father knows this jazz pianist, Larry Davis, who came over to their house the other day. Caleb played Rosie's 'Red Hill Blues' for him. Guess what! He loved it! He's going to play it at the Village Vanguard, with Betty Bainbridge singing. She's a fabulous vocalist—just ask Caleb and Rosie. So we're all going—aren't we? And then—here's the best part—Mr. Lennard's friend says maybe it'll be on Larry Davis's next record album!"

"Rosie!" her parents gasped in unison.

Rosie sprang to her feet and sang. Everyone joined in the refrain.

The Red Hill Blues

Refrain
How 'bout a round of the Red Hill Blues?
How 'bout a round of the Red Hill Blues
For us who'll wind up as front-page news?

And the news ain't good for us poor Reds
The news ain't good for us poor Reds
'Cause Uncle Sam he wants our heads.

Oh, Uncle Sam he says to us
Just sign this oath, and make no fuss,
While we're as lonesome as can be
Here in our home, the land of the free.

Refrain

You never saw us try to shirk,
But in a heartbeat we're out of work.
For this we thank old Mr. Hoover,
The fastest ever spy-remover.

Refrain

Don't let them drag you to the Committee
But if you go, just don't be witty.
All they're looking for from you
Is a nice, big cheer for the red, white, and blue.

Refrain

EPILOGUE

Kookie Kutt, Model Citizen
By Chris Gooding-Kado, November 2012

ACKNOWLEDGMENTS

In the abundant historical literature on anti-Communism in the 1950s, I have relied particularly on: Frances Stonor Saunders, *The Cultural Cold War: The CIA and the World of Arts and Letters* (New York: The New Press, 1999); and Ellen Schrecker: *Many are the Crimes: McCarthyism in America* (Boston: Little, Brown, 1998).

My husband David Gallant, to whom I owe infinite thanks, has been my most constantly supportive critic and editor, and my photographer of Croton. Mimi Nelson, my dear, longtime friend from the Croton days, provided me with major inspiration for this novel. I am also grateful to my writing group: Nancy Gardner, Joan Sawyer, and Paula Steffen, whose patience and careful readings of my novel have been invaluable. Many thanks to my other readers: Rosanna Alfaro, Karen W. Klein, Ellen Schrecker, and Alan Scribner. It has been a great pleasure and privilege to have Karen Klein as my illustrator. She got into the groove right away and made my narrative come to life. The Croton Historical Society has provided me with helpful and rich materials. Thanks to Shoshana Pakciarz for help with the front cover and for her loyal moral support over the years.

AUTHOR BIO.

Erica Harth grew up in Croton-on-Hudson during the period about which she writes. A professor emerita of Humanities and Women's Studies at Brandeis University, she has authored several scholarly books on early modern France. She also compiled and edited an original collection of essays, *Last Witnesses: Reflections on the Wartime Internment of Japanese Americans* (New York: Palgrave, 2001-2003), to which she contributed the Introduction and one essay. Others of her personal essays on this subject have appeared in various publications.

ILLUSTRATOR BIO.

Karen Klein is a visual artist, modern dancer, and poet. Her drawings have been published in periodicals in the United States and Canada and in books from Beacon Press, Shank Painter Publishing, Holly House Publications, McGraw-Hill, and the following university presses: Oxford, SUNY, Oklahoma.

Made in the USA
San Bernardino, CA
18 February 2014